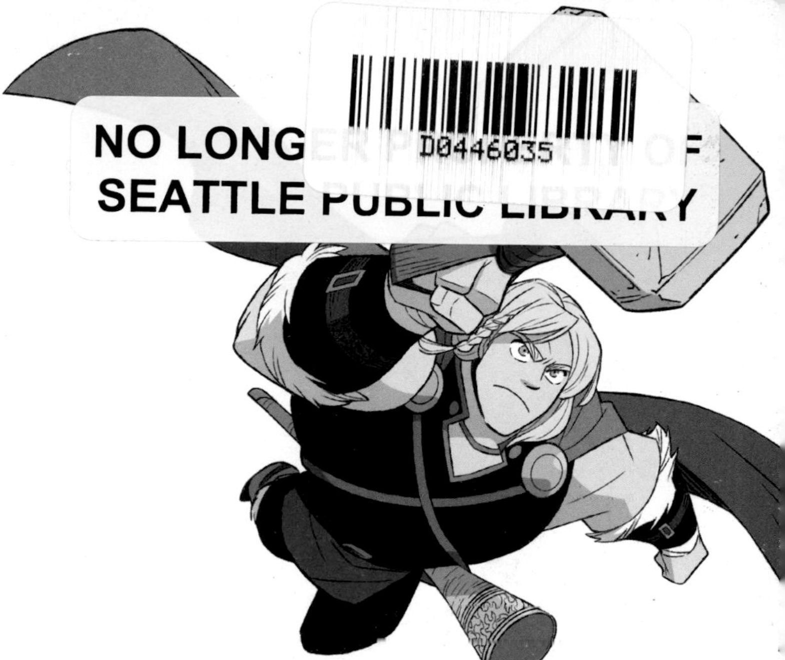

THOR & LOKI:
DOUBLE TROUBLE

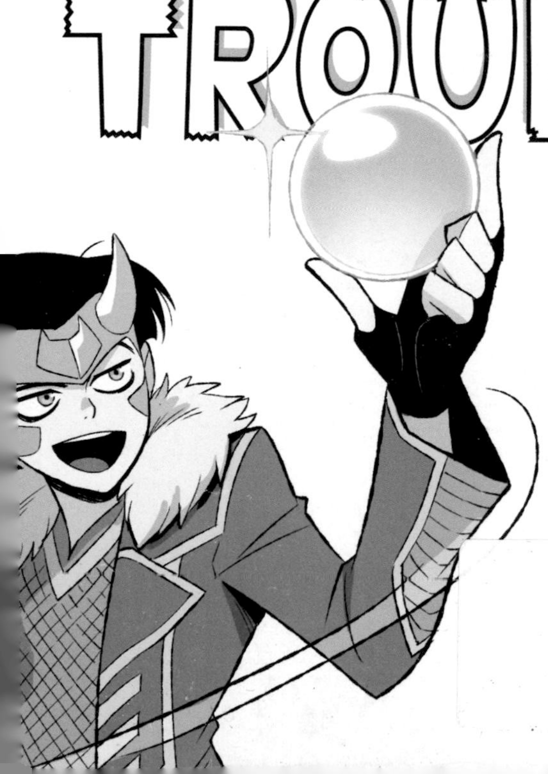

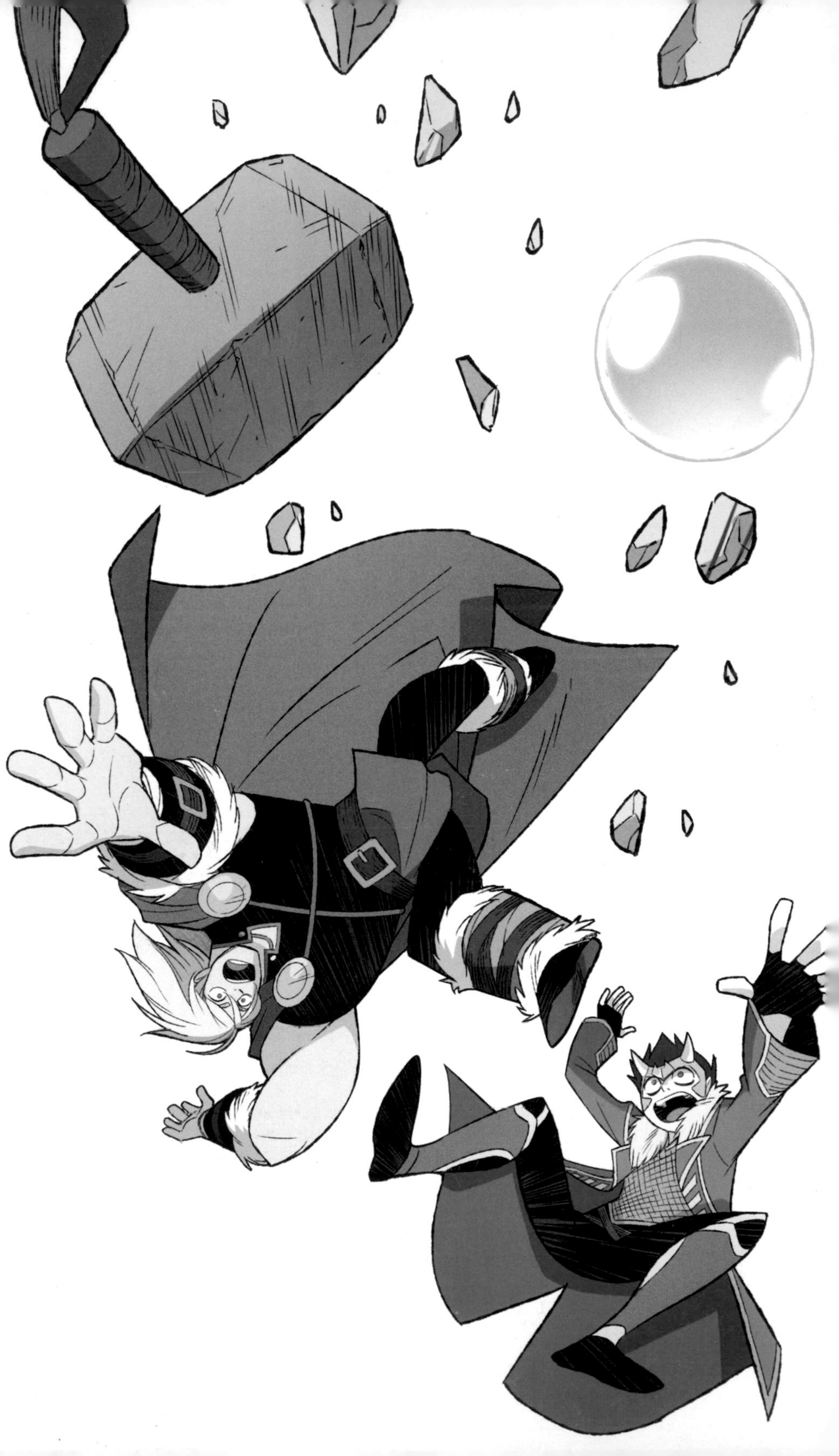

THOR & LOKI:

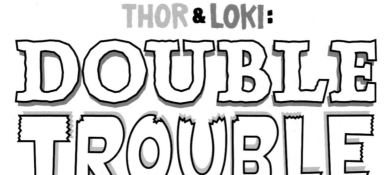

DOUBLE TROUBLE

MARIKO TAMAKI
WRITER

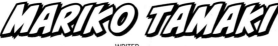

GURIHIRU
ARTIST

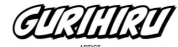

VC's ARIANA MAHER
LETTERER

GURIHIRU
COVER ART

ADAM DEL RE & STACIE ZUCKER
LOGO DESIGN

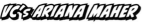

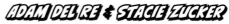

MARTIN BIRO
ASSISTANT EDITOR

ALANNA SMITH, SARAH BRUNSTAD, & WIL MOSS
EDITORS

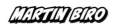

THOR & LOKI CREATED BY **STAN LEE, LARRY LIEBER** & **JACK KIRBY**

COLLECTION EDITOR: **DANIEL KIRCHHOFFER** ASSISTANT MANAGING EDITOR: **MAIA LOY**
ASSISTANT MANAGING EDITOR: **LISA MONTALBANO** SENIOR EDITOR, SPECIAL PROJECTS: **JENNIFER GRÜNWALD**
VP, PRODUCTION & SPECIAL PROJECTS: **JEFF YOUNGQUIST** BOOK DESIGNER: **STACIE ZUCKER**
SVP PRINT, SALES & MARKETING: **DAVID GABRIEL** EDITOR IN CHIEF: **C.B. CEBULSKI**

THOR & LOKI: DOUBLE TROUBLE (SDOS). Contains material originally published in magazine form as THOR & LOKI: DOUBLE TROUBLE (2021) #1-4. First printing 2021. ISBN 978-1-302-92625-0. Published by MARVEL WORLDWIDE, INC., a subsidiary of MARVEL ENTERTAINMENT, LLC. OFFICE OF PUBLICATION: 1290 Avenue of the Americas, New York, NY 10104. Printed in Canada. KEVIN FEIGE, Chief Creative Officer; DAN BUCKLEY, President, Marvel Entertainment; JOE QUESADA, EVP & Creative Director; DAVID BOGART, Associate Publisher & SVP of Talent Affairs; TOM BREVOORT, VP, Executive Editor; NICK LOWE, Executive Editor, VP of Content, Digital Publishing; DAVID GABRIEL, VP of Print & Digital Publishing; JEFF YOUNGQUIST, VP of Production & Special Projects; ALEX MORALES, Director of Publishing Operations; DAN EDINGTON, Managing Editor; RICKEY PURDIN, Director of Talent Relations; JENNIFER GRÜNWALD, Senior Editor, Special Projects; SUSAN CRESPI, Production Manager; STAN LEE, Chairman Emeritus. For information regarding advertising in Marvel Comics or on Marvel.com, please contact Vit DeBellis, Custom Solutions & Integrated Advertising Manager, at vdebellis@marvel.com. For Marvel subscription inquiries, please call 888-511-5480. **Manufactured between 7/9/2021 and 8/10/2021 by SOLISCO PRINTERS, SCOTT, QC, CANADA.**

10 9 8 7 6 5 4 3 2 1

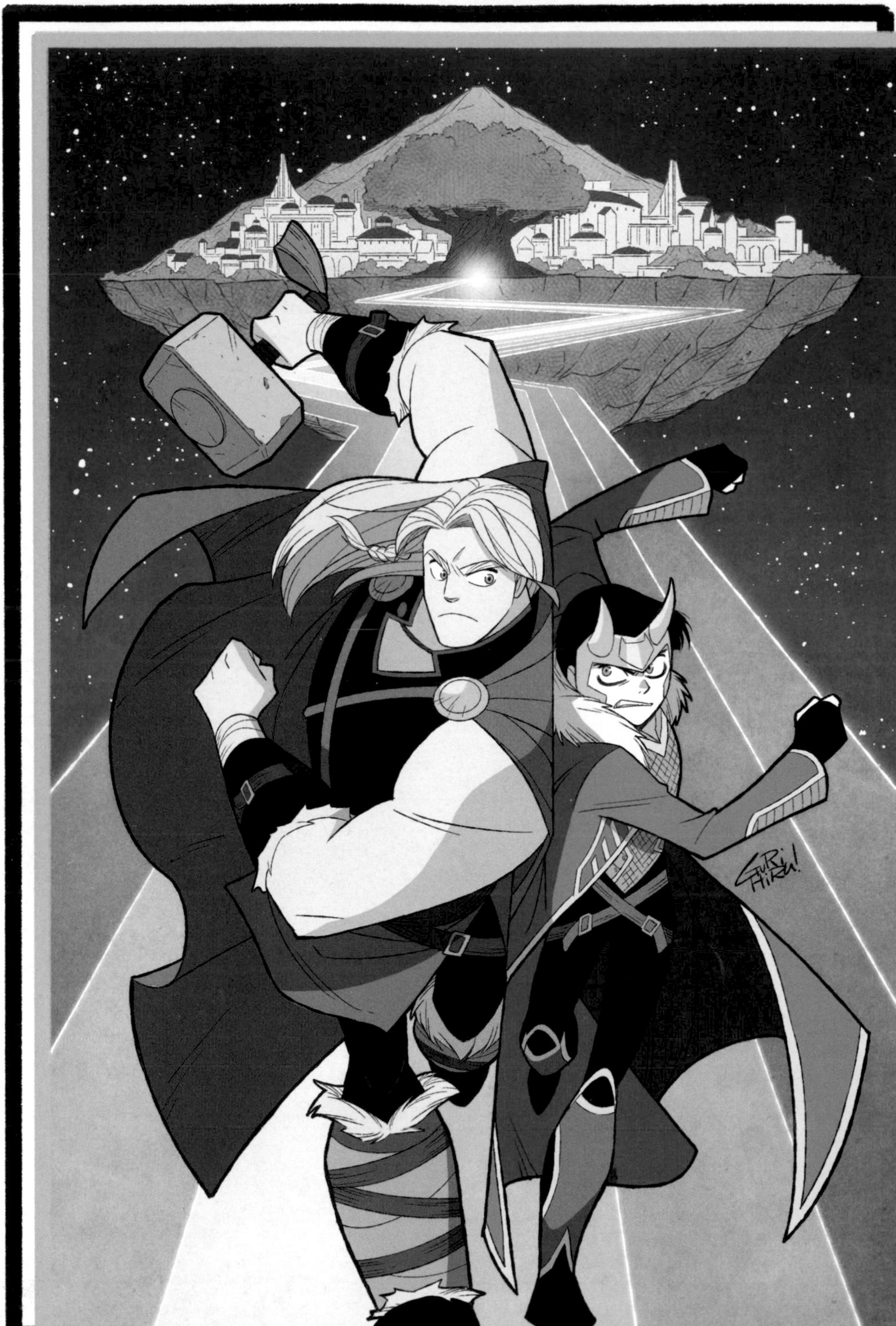
GURIHIRU!

1

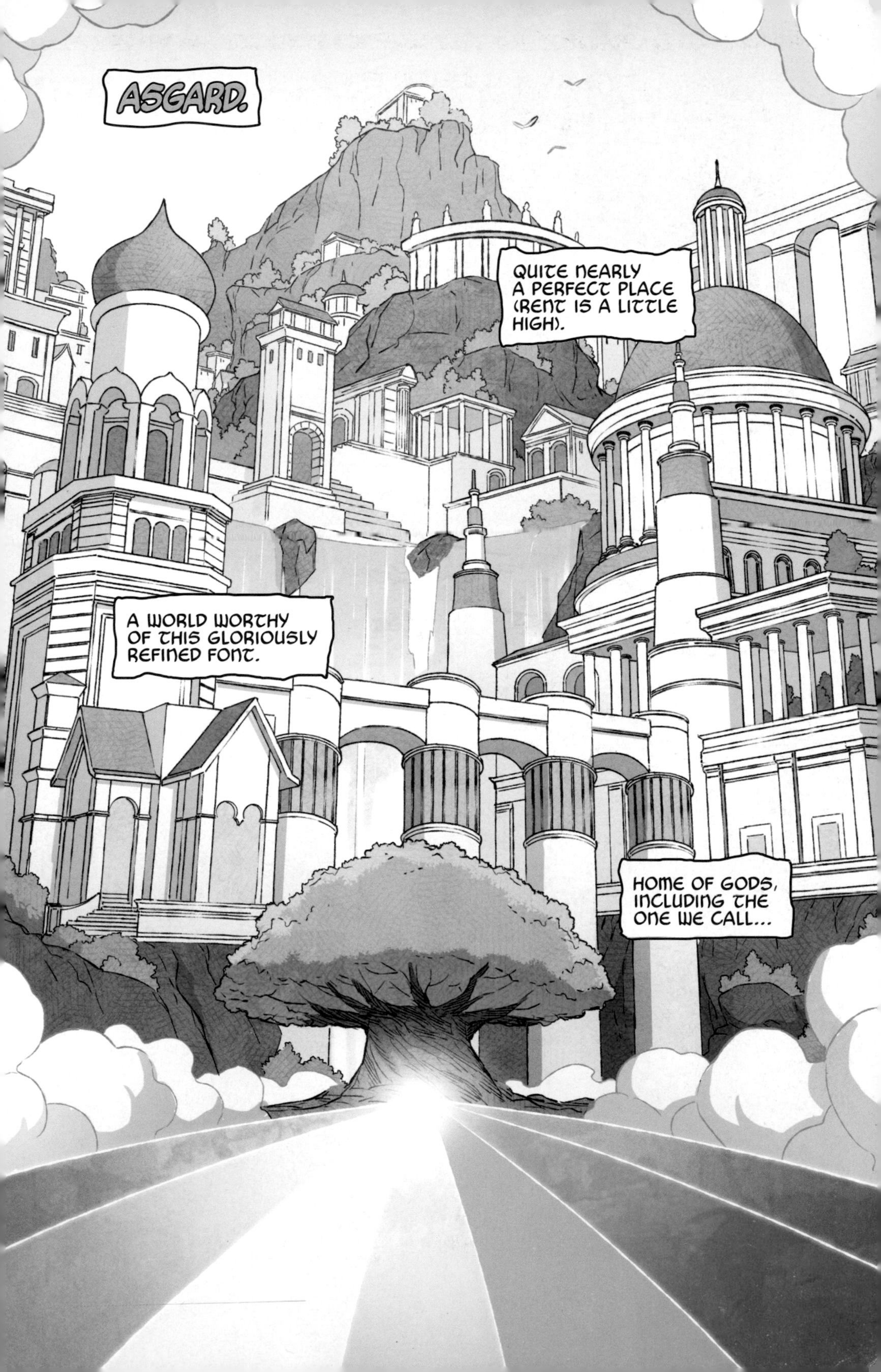
ASGARD.
QUITE NEARLY A PERFECT PLACE (RENT IS A LITTLE HIGH).
A WORLD WORTHY OF THIS GLORIOUSLY REFINED FONT.
HOME OF GODS, INCLUDING THE ONE WE CALL...

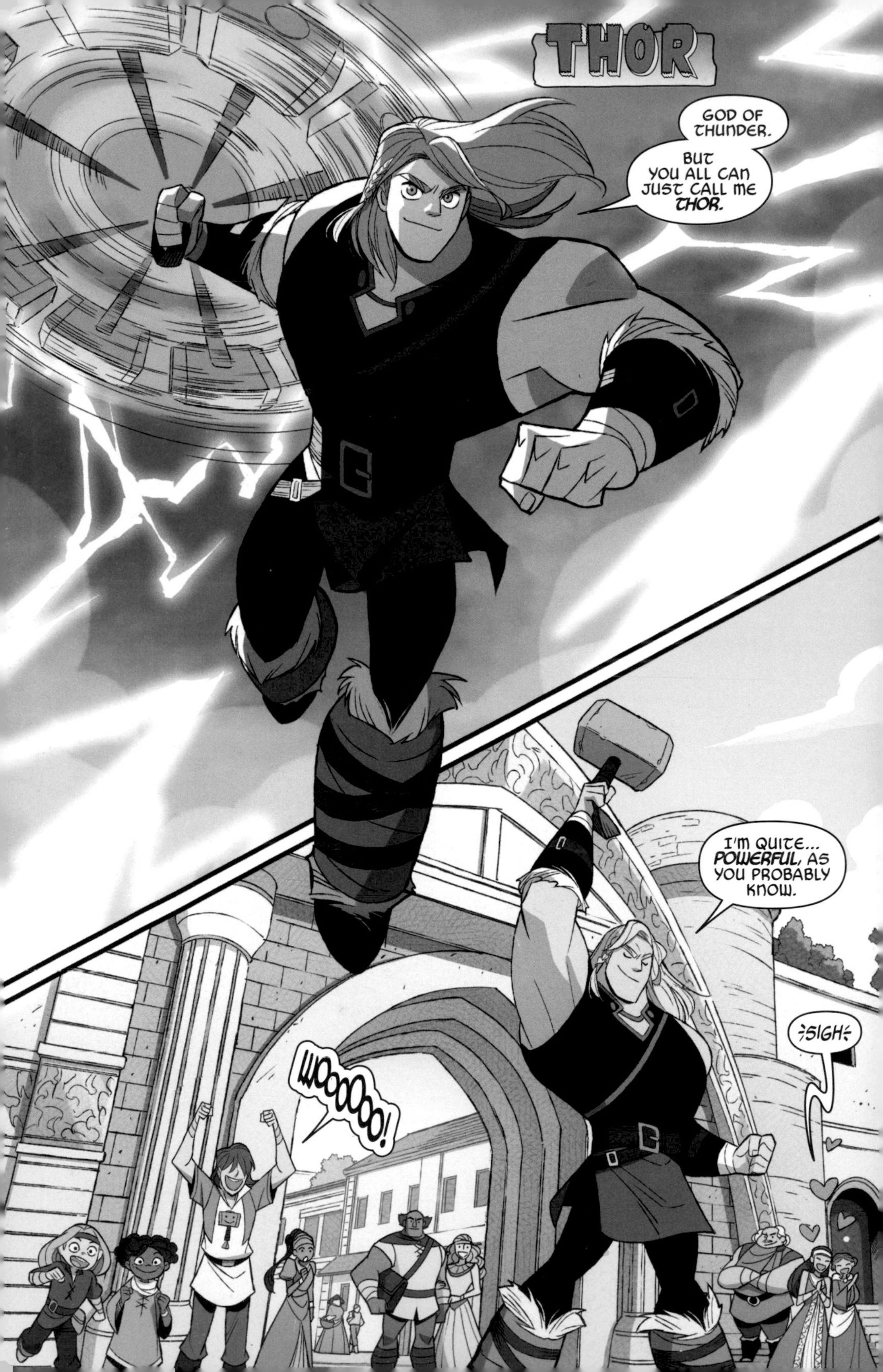
THOR
GOD OF THUNDER.
BUT YOU ALL CAN JUST CALL ME THOR.
I'M QUITE... POWERFUL, AS YOU PROBABLY KNOW.
WOOOOOO!
SIGH

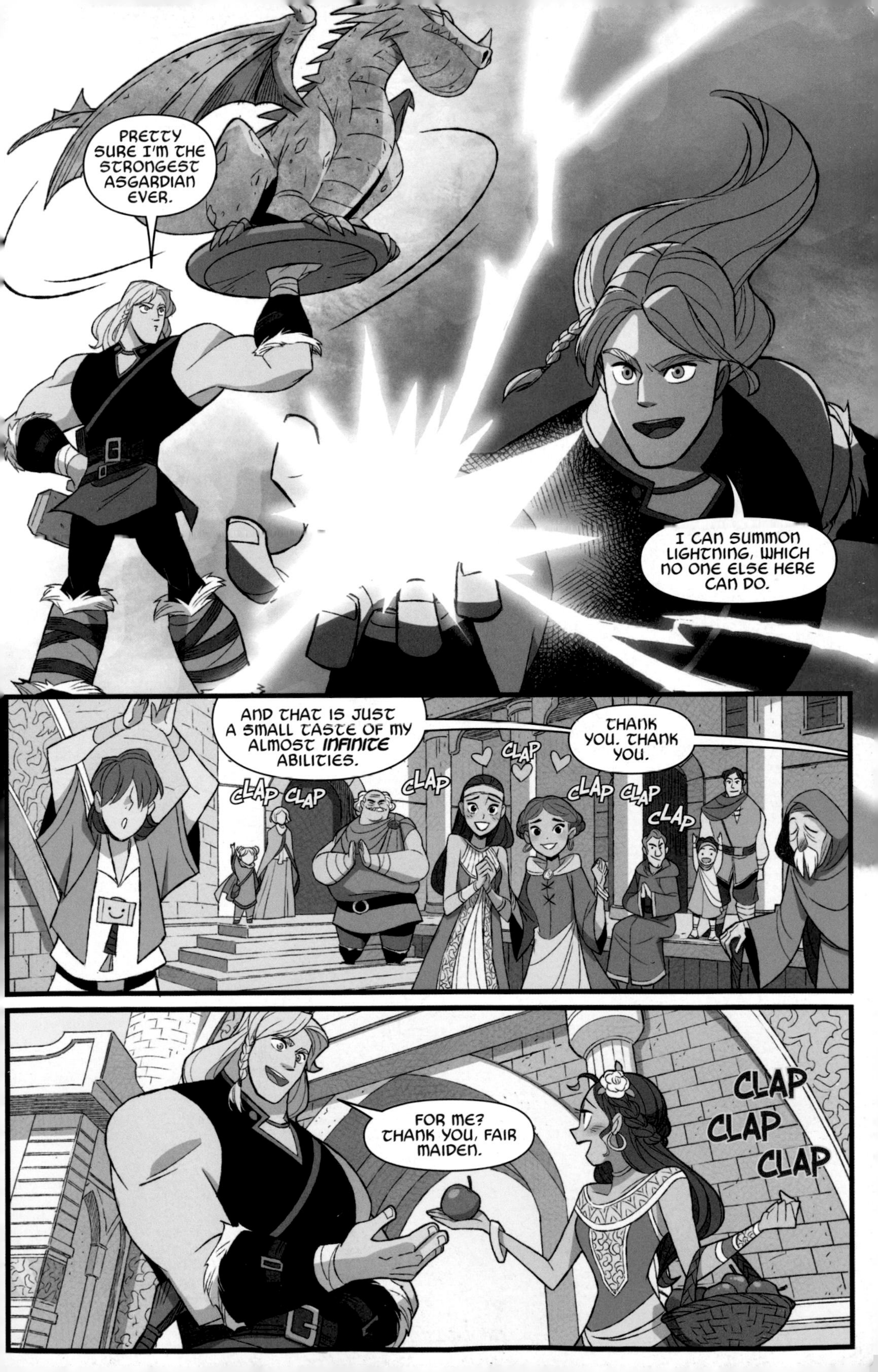
PRETTY SURE I'M THE STRONGEST ASGARDIAN EVER.
I CAN SUMMON LIGHTNING, WHICH NO ONE ELSE HERE CAN DO.
AND THAT IS JUST A SMALL TASTE OF MY ALMOST *INFINITE* ABILITIES.
THANK YOU. THANK YOU.
CLAP CLAP
CLAP
CLAP
CLAP CLAP
CLAP
FOR ME? THANK YOU, FAIR MAIDEN.
CLAP
CLAP
CLAP

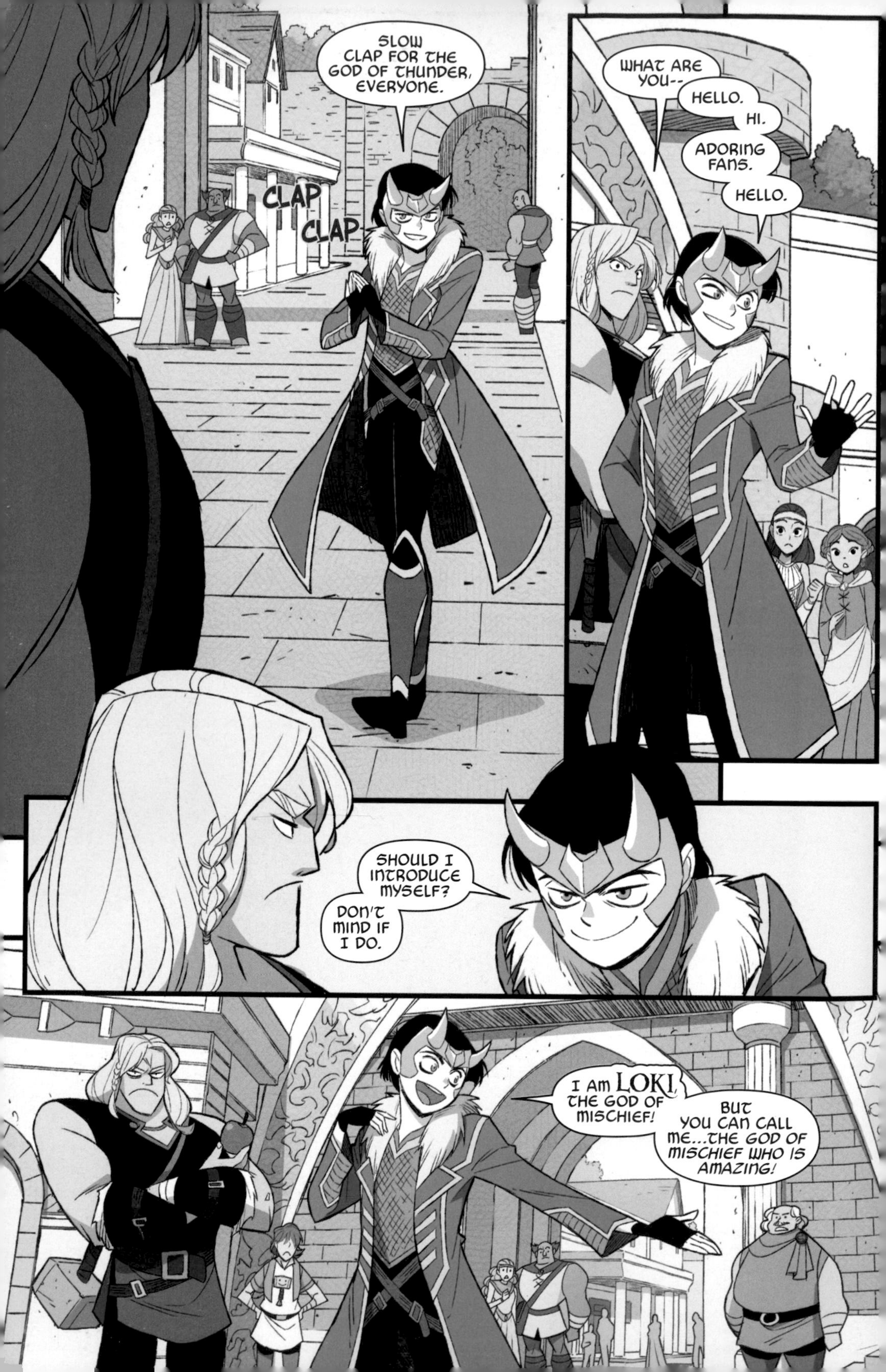
SLOW CLAP FOR THE GOD OF THUNDER, EVERYONE.
CLAP
CLAP
WHAT ARE YOU--
HELLO.
HI.
ADORING FANS.
HELLO.
SHOULD I INTRODUCE MYSELF?
DON'T MIND IF I DO.
I AM LOKI, THE GOD OF MISCHIEF!
BUT YOU CAN CALL ME...THE GOD OF MISCHIEF WHO IS AMAZING!

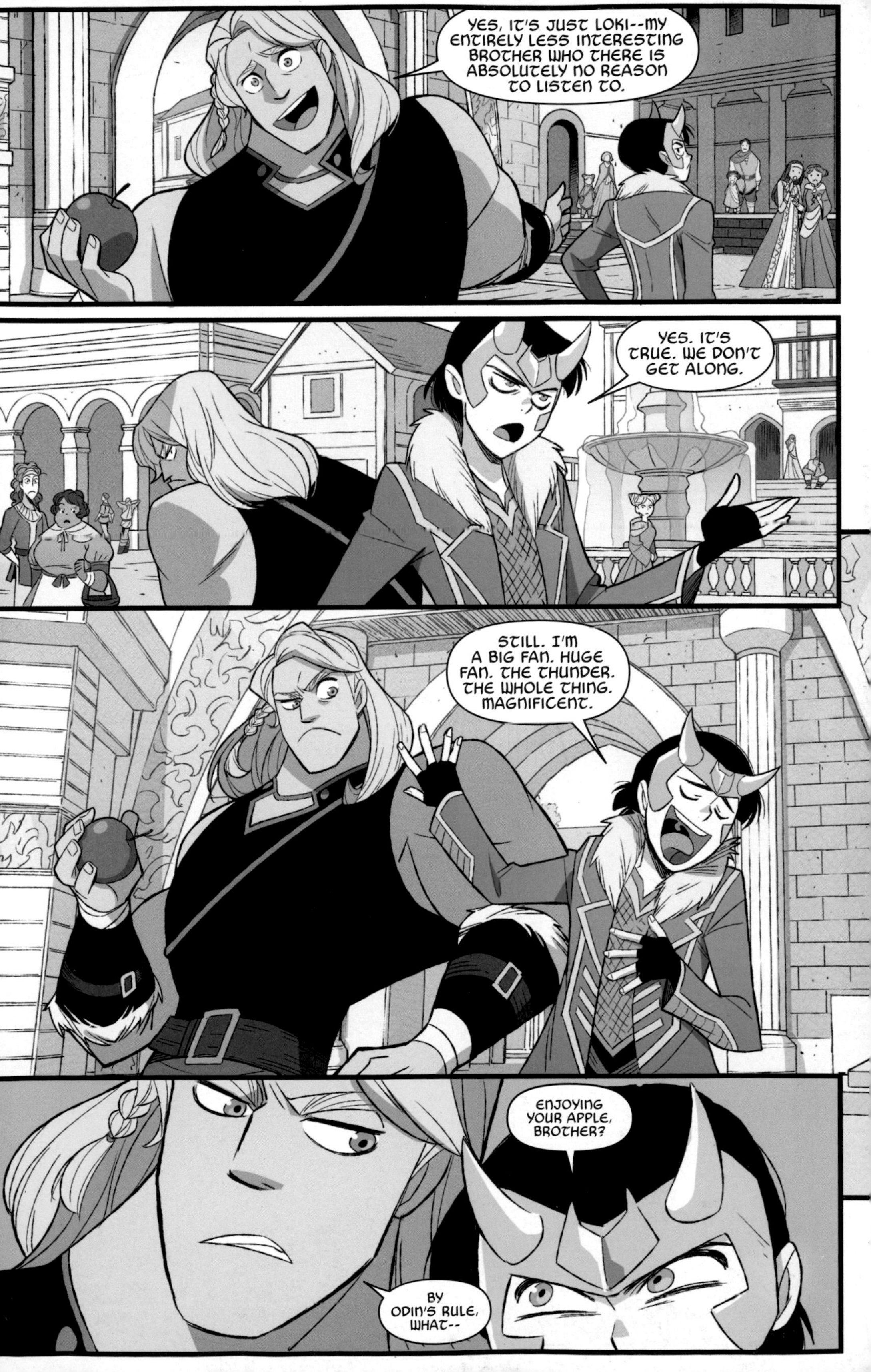
YES, IT'S JUST LOKI--MY ENTIRELY LESS INTERESTING BROTHER WHO THERE IS ABSOLUTELY NO REASON TO LISTEN TO.
YES. IT'S TRUE. WE DON'T GET ALONG.
STILL. I'M A BIG FAN. HUGE FAN. THE THUNDER. THE WHOLE THING. MAGNIFICENT.
ENJOYING YOUR APPLE, BROTHER?
BY ODIN'S RULE, WHAT--

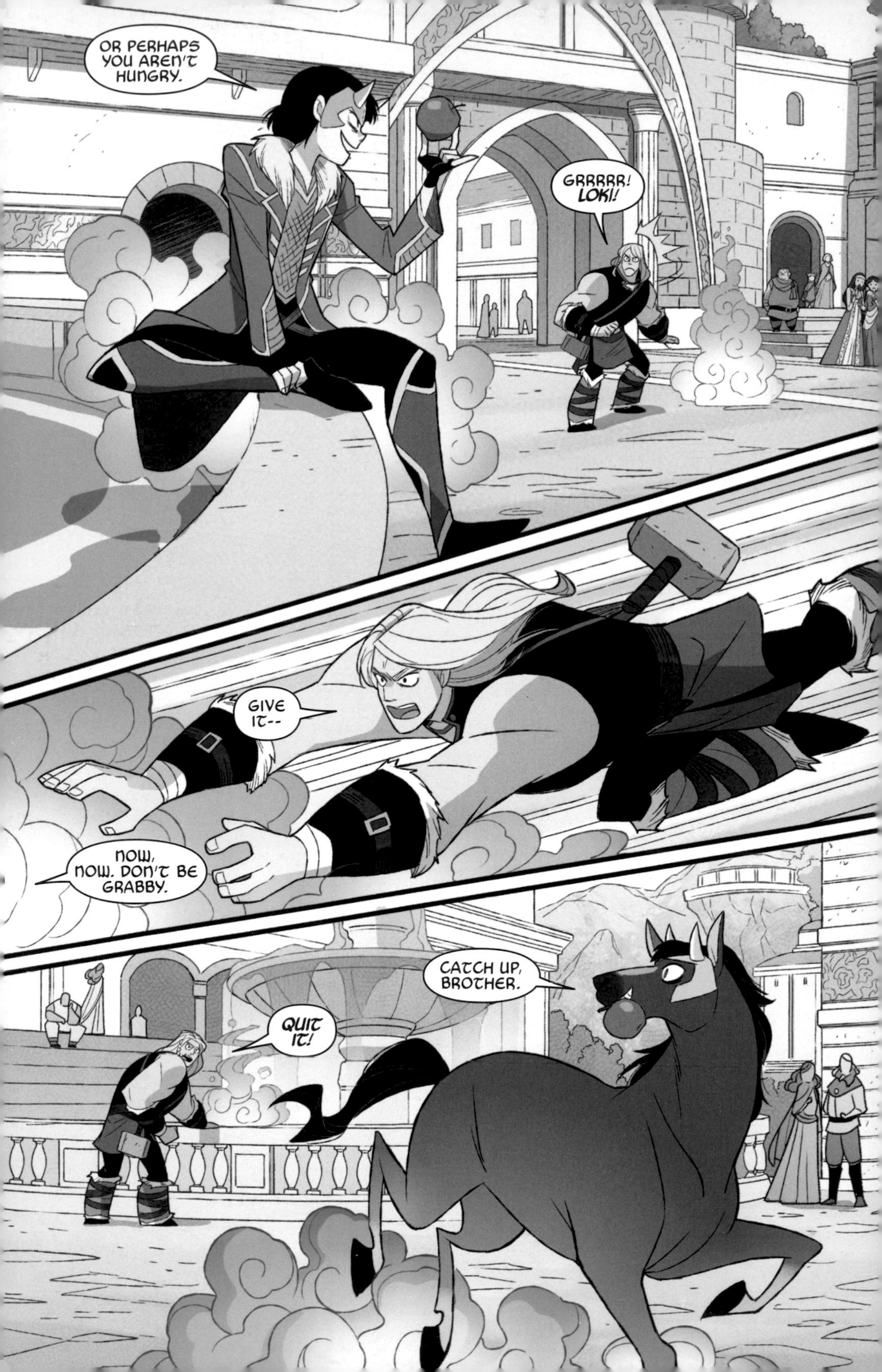
OR PERHAPS YOU AREN'T HUNGRY.
GRRRRR! LOKI!
GIVE IT--
NOW, NOW. DON'T BE GRABBY.
CATCH UP, BROTHER.
QUIT IT!

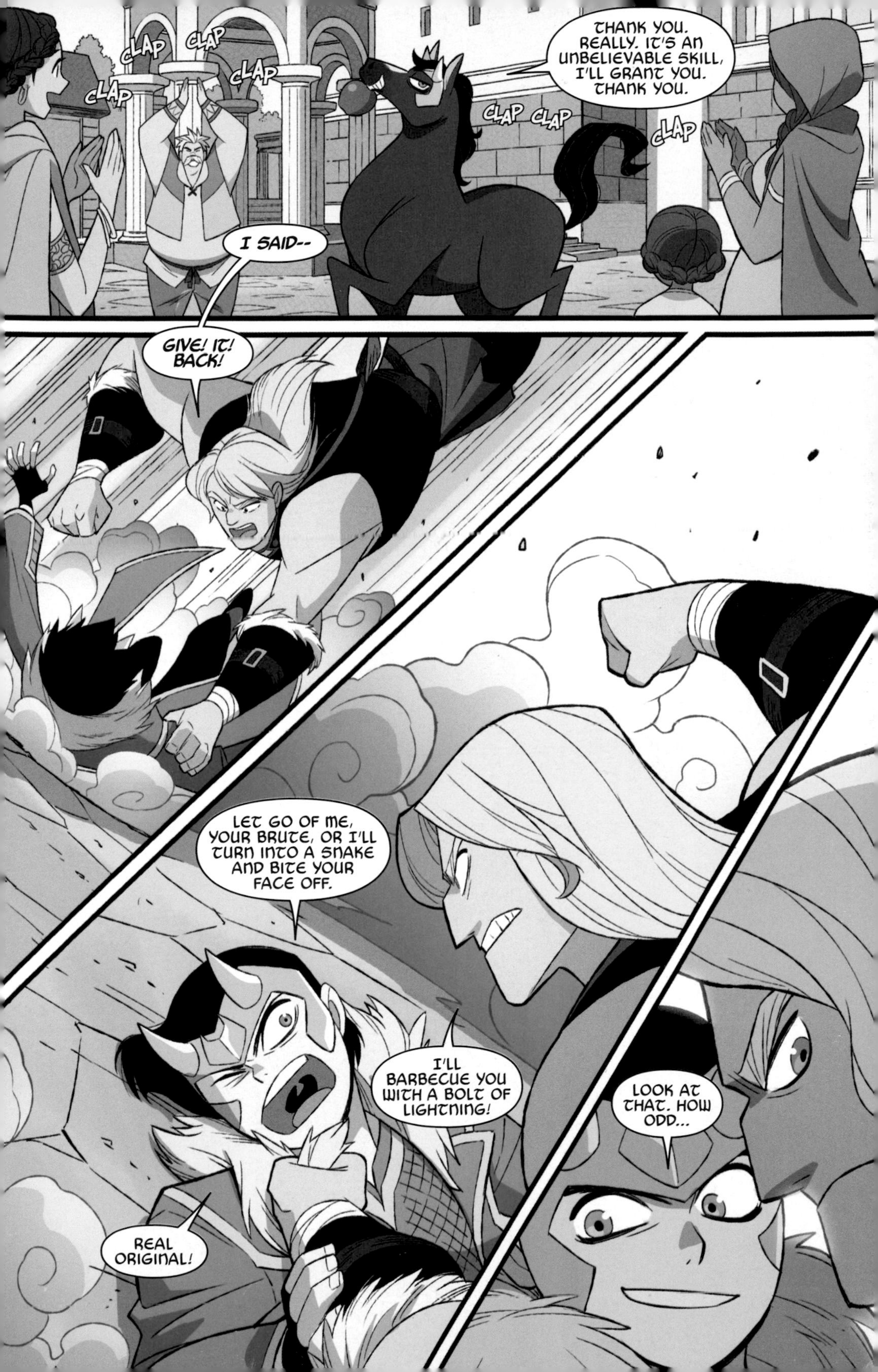
CLAP
CLAP
CLAP
CLAP
THANK YOU. REALLY. IT'S AN UNBELIEVABLE SKILL, I'LL GRANT YOU. THANK YOU.
CLAP
CLAP
CLAP
I SAID--
GIVE! IT! BACK!
LET GO OF ME, YOUR BRUTE, OR I'LL TURN INTO A SNAKE AND BITE YOUR FACE OFF.
I'LL BARBECUE YOU WITH A BOLT OF LIGHTNING!
REAL ORIGINAL!
LOOK AT THAT. HOW ODD...

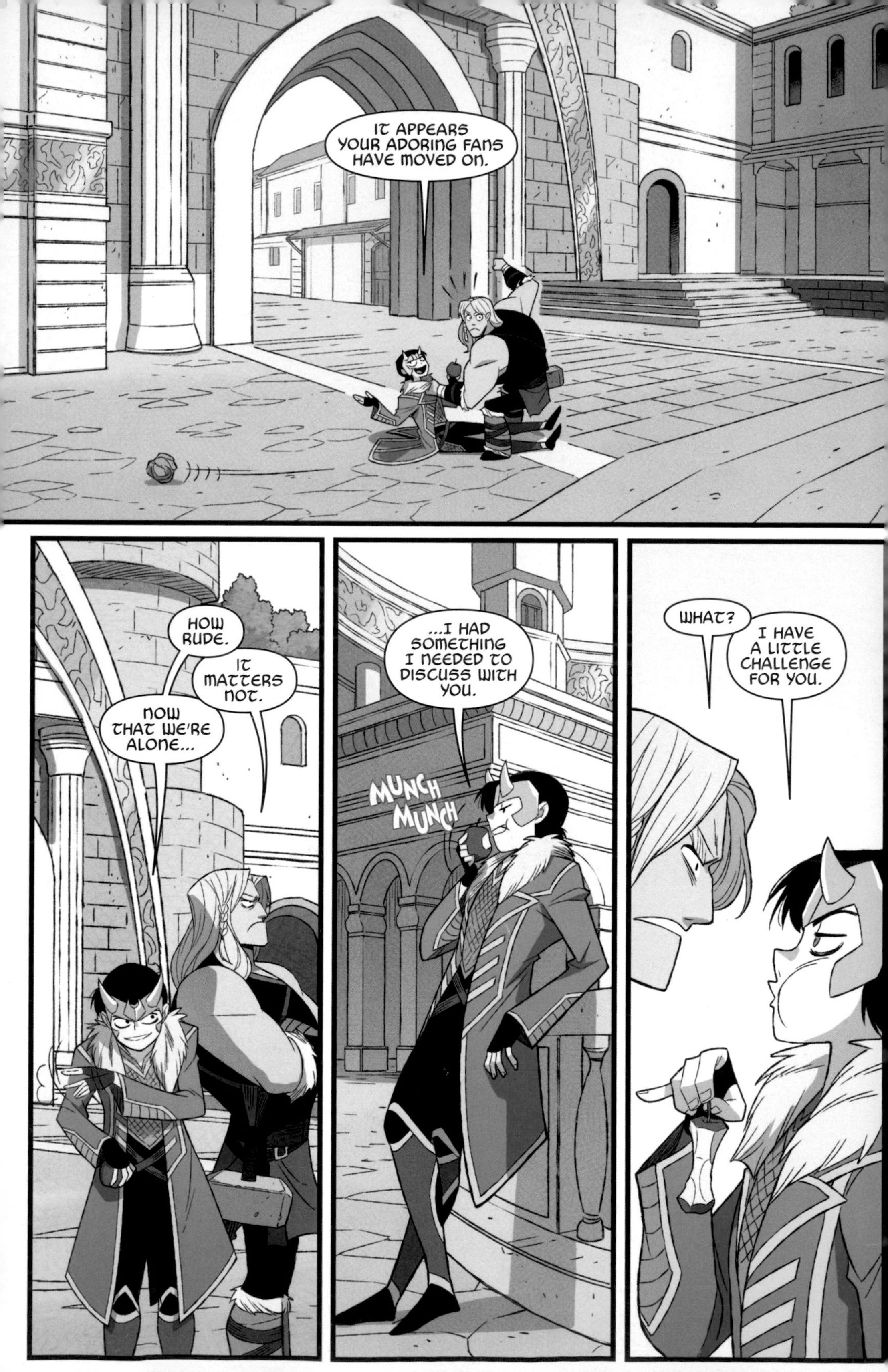
IT APPEARS YOUR ADORING FANS HAVE MOVED ON.
HOW RUDE.
IT MATTERS NOT.
NOW THAT WE'RE ALONE...
...I HAD SOMETHING I NEEDED TO DISCUSS WITH YOU.
MUNCH MUNCH
WHAT?
I HAVE A LITTLE CHALLENGE FOR YOU.

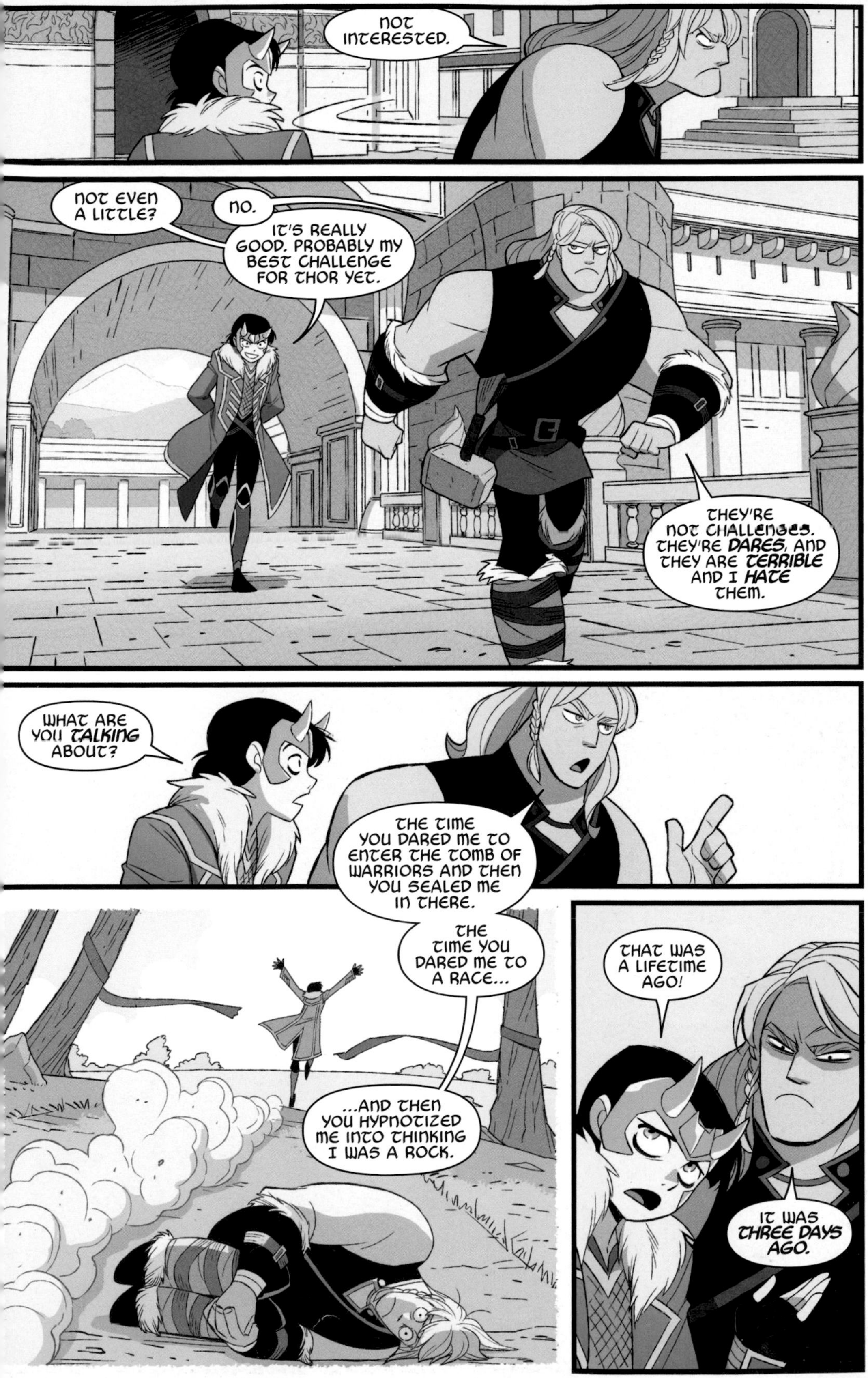
NOT INTERESTED.
NOT EVEN A LITTLE?
NO.
IT'S REALLY GOOD. PROBABLY MY BEST CHALLENGE FOR THOR YET.
THEY'RE NOT CHALLENGES. THEY'RE *DARES*, AND THEY ARE *TERRIBLE* AND I *HATE* THEM.
WHAT ARE YOU *TALKING* ABOUT?
THE TIME YOU DARED ME TO ENTER THE TOMB OF WARRIORS AND THEN YOU SEALED ME IN THERE.
THE TIME YOU DARED ME TO A RACE...
...AND THEN YOU HYPNOTIZED ME INTO THINKING I WAS A ROCK.
THAT WAS A LIFETIME AGO!
IT WAS *THREE DAYS AGO.*

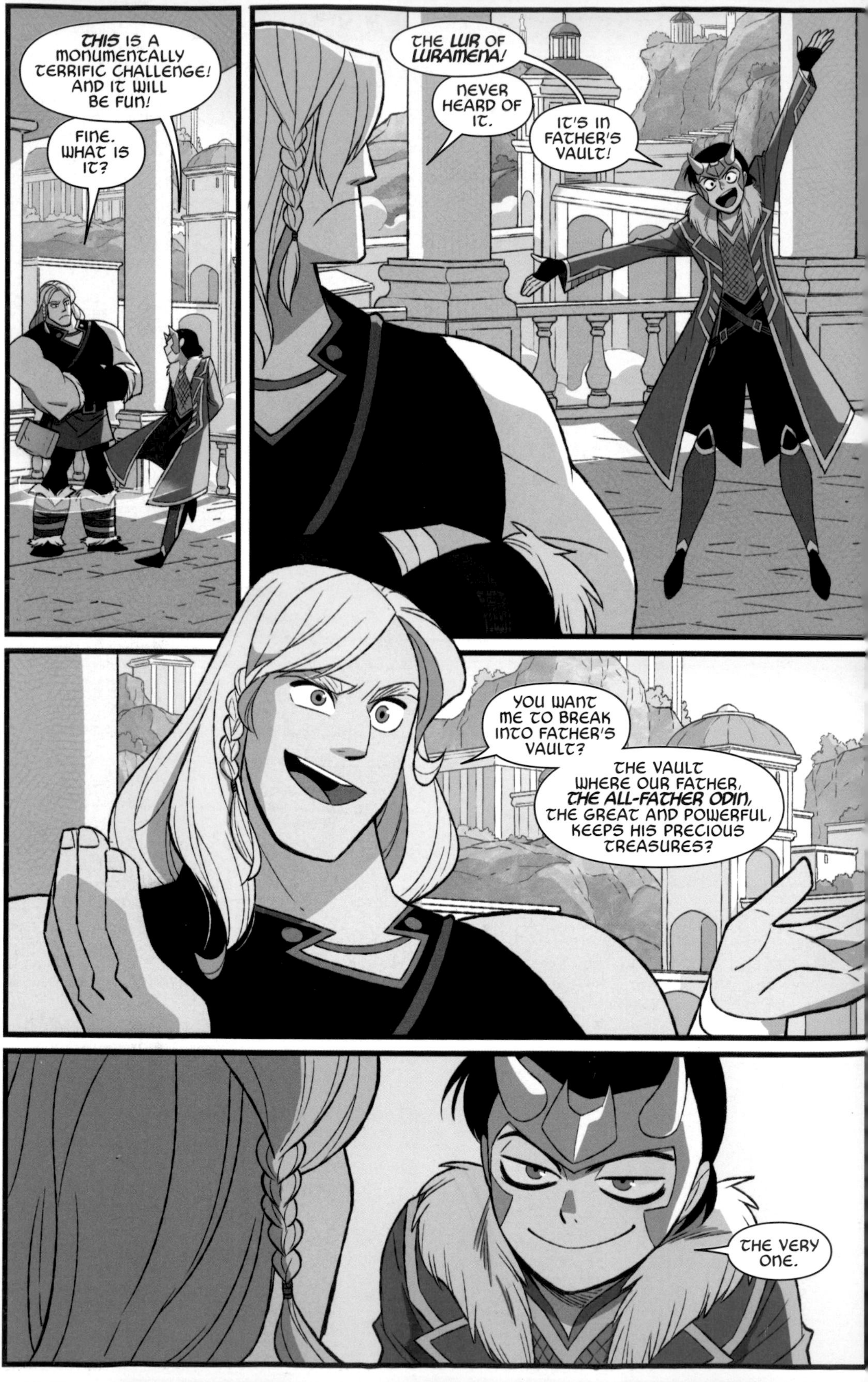
THIS IS A MONUMENTALLY TERRIFIC CHALLENGE! AND IT WILL BE FUN!
FINE. WHAT IS IT?
THE LUR OF LURAMENA!
NEVER HEARD OF IT.
IT'S IN FATHER'S VAULT!
YOU WANT ME TO BREAK INTO FATHER'S VAULT?
THE VAULT WHERE OUR FATHER, THE ALL-FATHER ODIN, THE GREAT AND POWERFUL, KEEPS HIS PRECIOUS TREASURES?
THE VERY ONE.

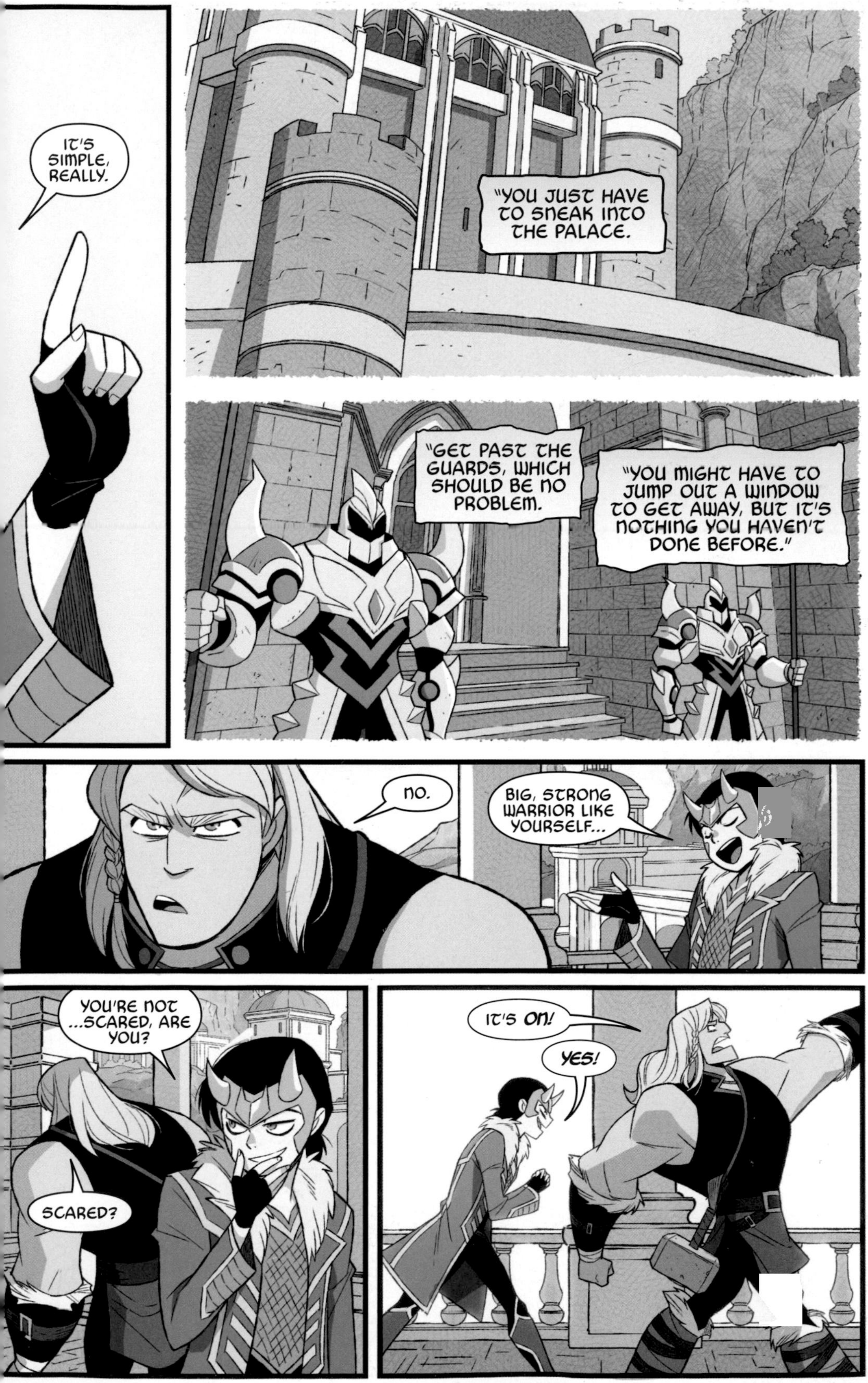
IT'S SIMPLE, REALLY.
"YOU JUST HAVE TO SNEAK INTO THE PALACE.
"GET PAST THE GUARDS, WHICH SHOULD BE NO PROBLEM.
"YOU MIGHT HAVE TO JUMP OUT A WINDOW TO GET AWAY, BUT IT'S NOTHING YOU HAVEN'T DONE BEFORE."
NO.
BIG, STRONG WARRIOR LIKE YOURSELF...
YOU'RE NOT ...SCARED, ARE YOU?
SCARED?
IT'S ON!
YES!

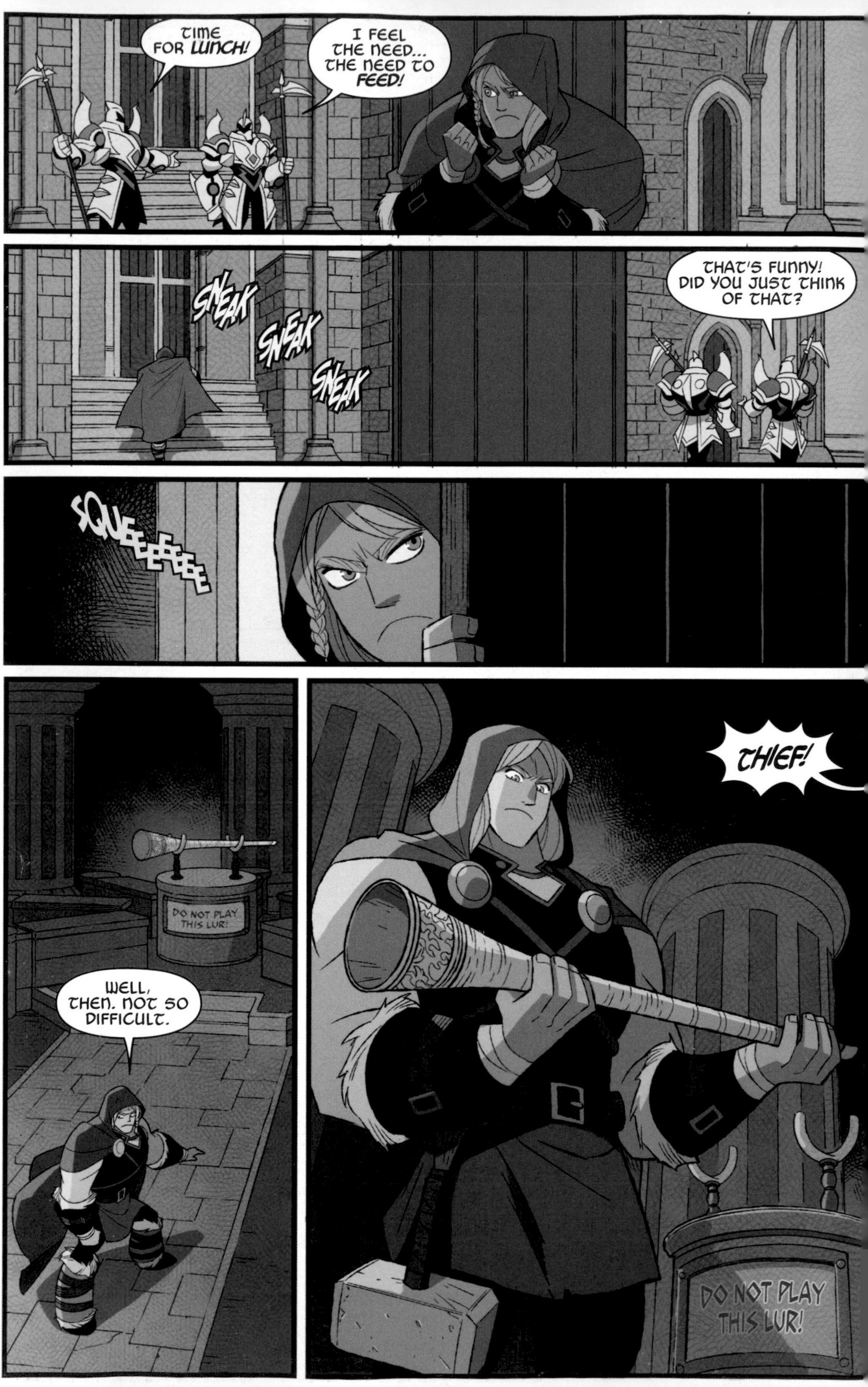
TIME FOR LUNCH!
I FEEL THE NEED... THE NEED TO FEED!
SNEAK
SNEAK
SNEAK
THAT'S FUNNY! DID YOU JUST THINK OF THAT?
SQUEEEEEEE
DO NOT PLAY THIS LUR!
WELL, THEN. NOT SO DIFFICULT.
THIEF!
DO NOT PLAY THIS LUR!

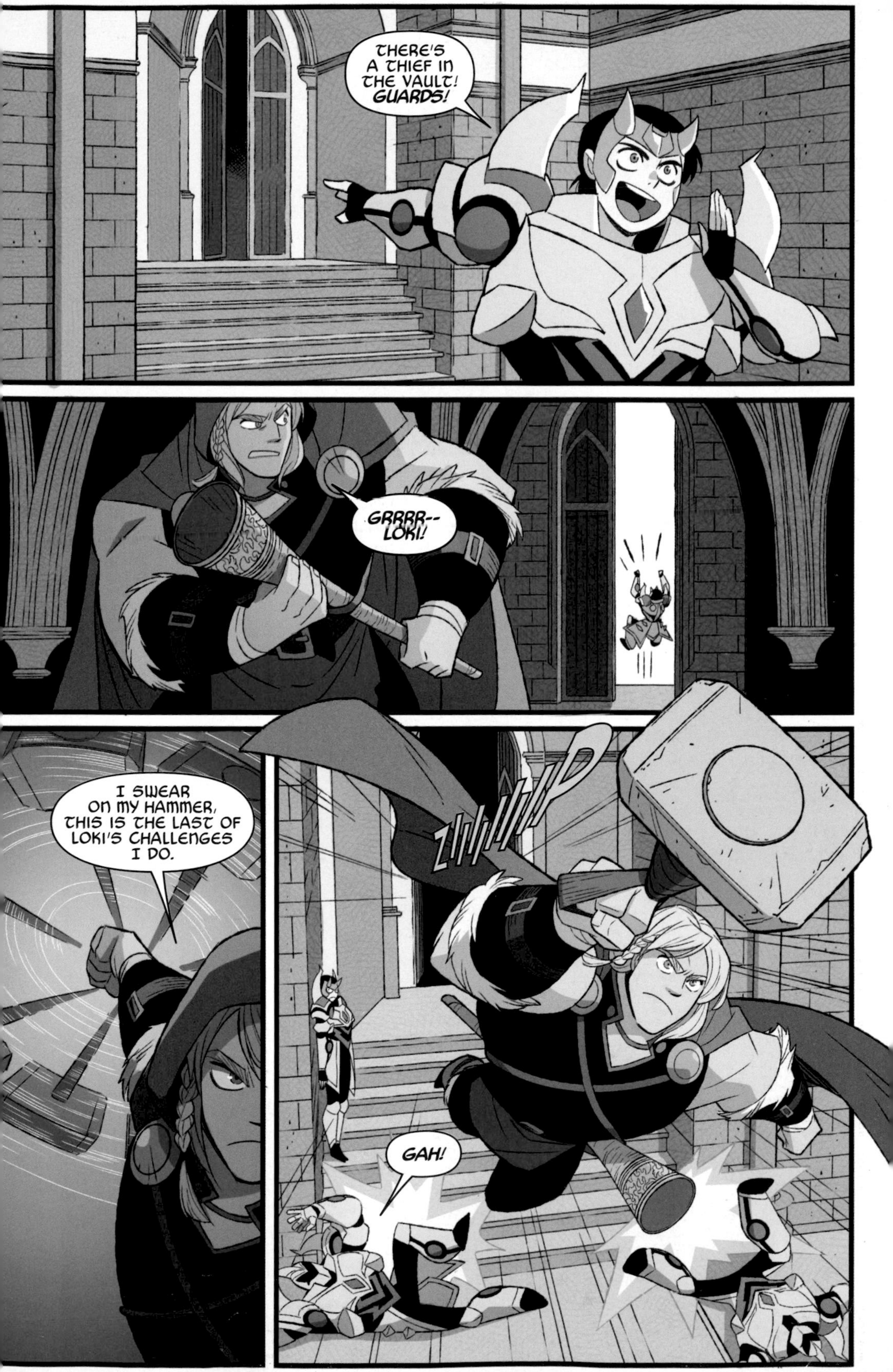
THERE'S A THIEF IN THE VAULT! GUARDS!
GRRRR-- LOKI!
I SWEAR ON MY HAMMER, THIS IS THE LAST OF LOKI'S CHALLENGES I DO.
ZWHUMP
GAH!

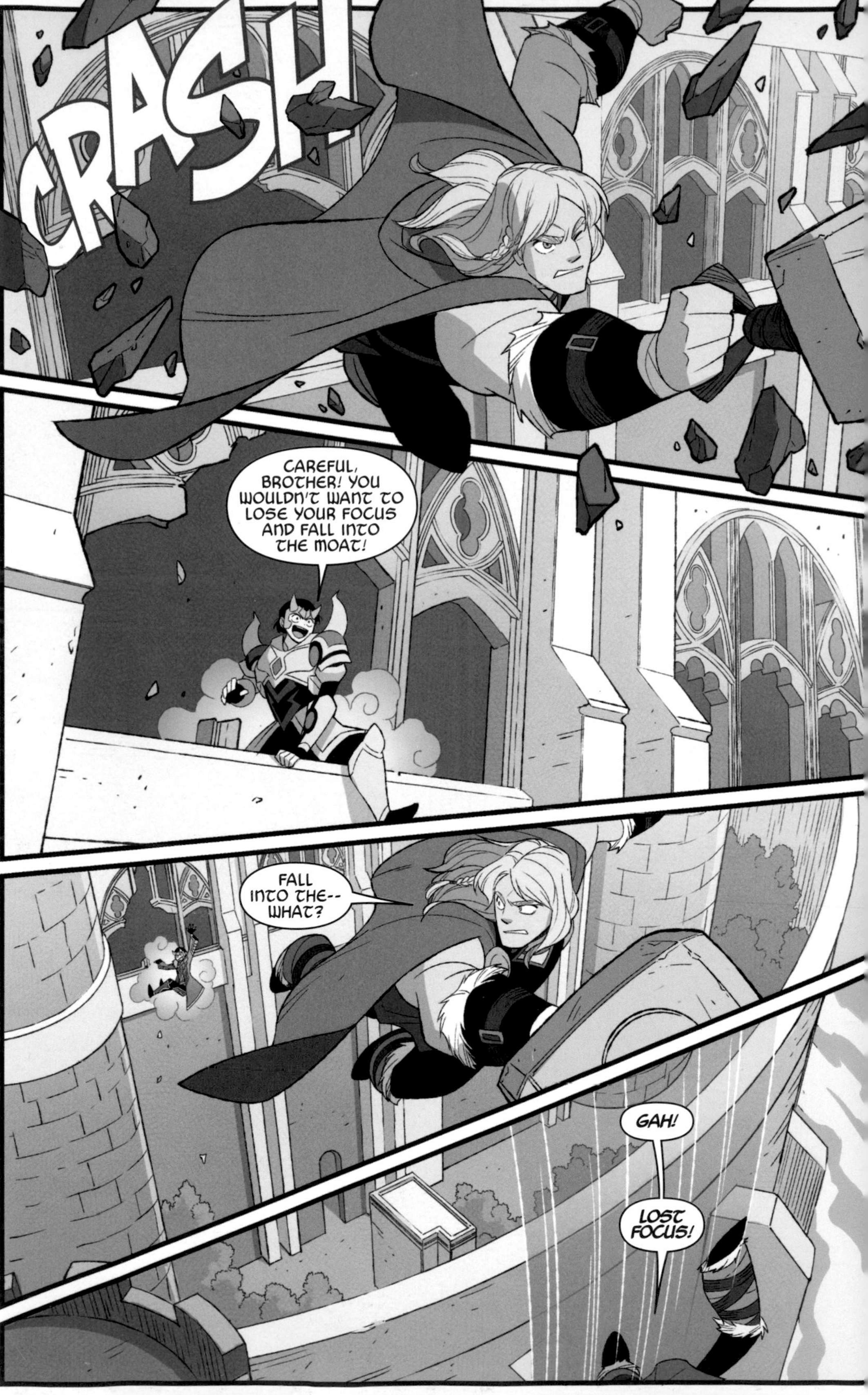
CRASH!
CAREFUL, BROTHER! YOU WOULDN'T WANT TO LOSE YOUR FOCUS AND FALL INTO THE MOAT!
FALL INTO THE-- WHAT?
GAH!
LOST FOCUS!

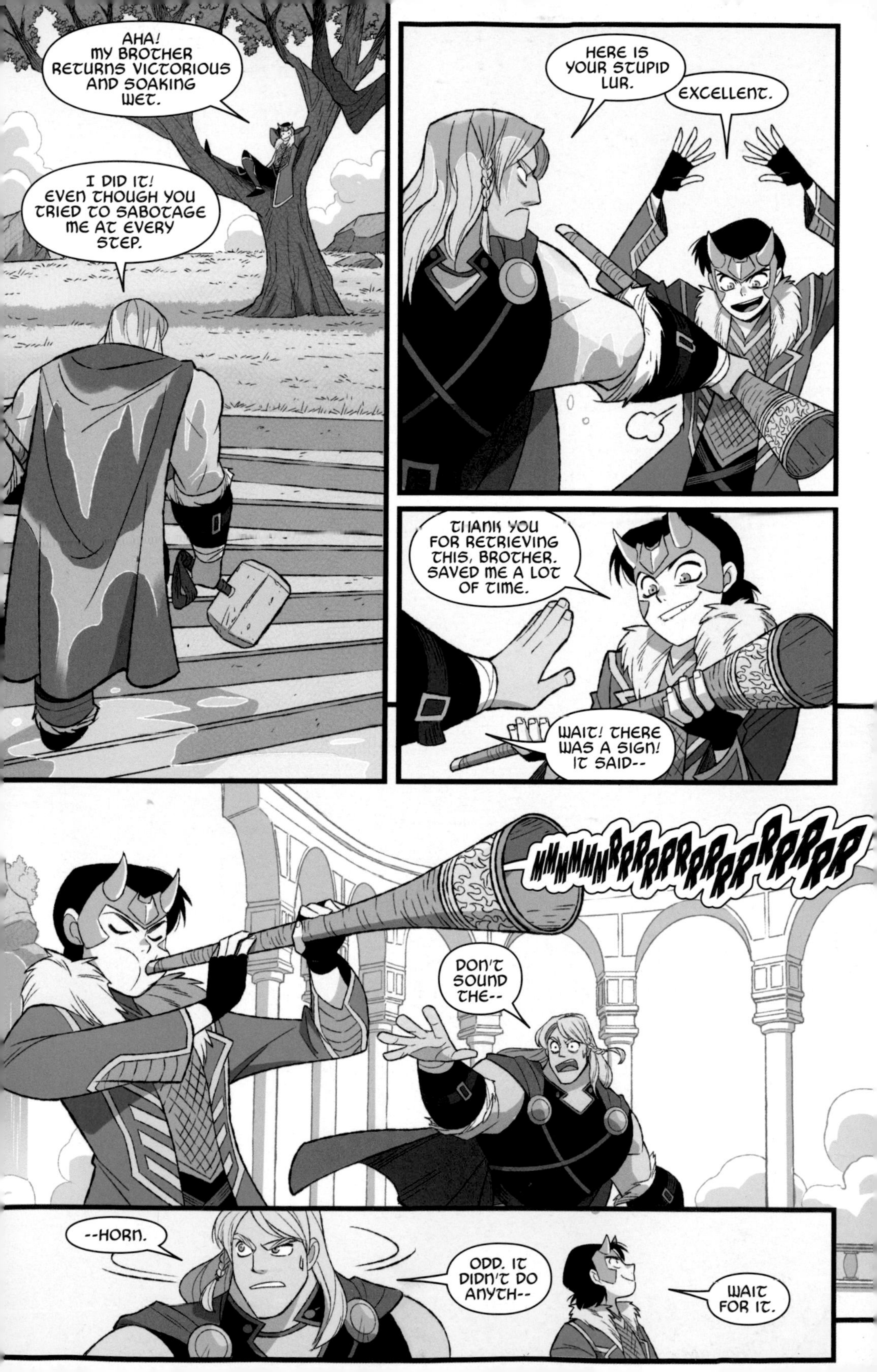

AHA! MY BROTHER RETURNS VICTORIOUS AND SOAKING WET.
I DID IT! EVEN THOUGH YOU TRIED TO SABOTAGE ME AT EVERY STEP.
HERE IS YOUR STUPID LUR.
EXCELLENT.
THANK YOU FOR RETRIEVING THIS, BROTHER. SAVED ME A LOT OF TIME.
WAIT! THERE WAS A SIGN! IT SAID--
HMMMMMRRRRRRRRRRRRRRRRR
DON'T SOUND THE--
--HORN.
ODD. IT DIDN'T DO ANYTH--
WAIT FOR IT.

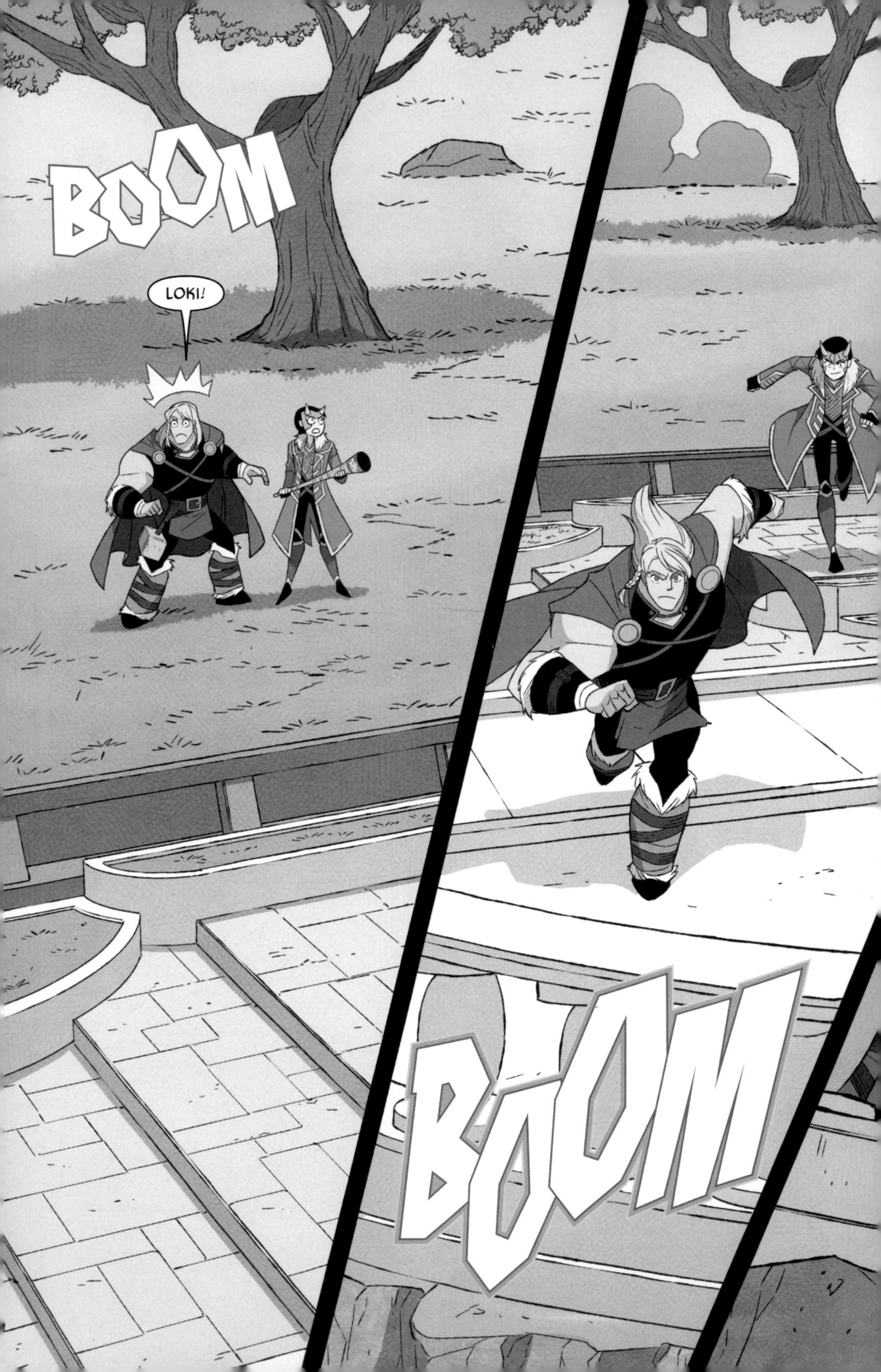
BOOM
LOKI!
BOOM

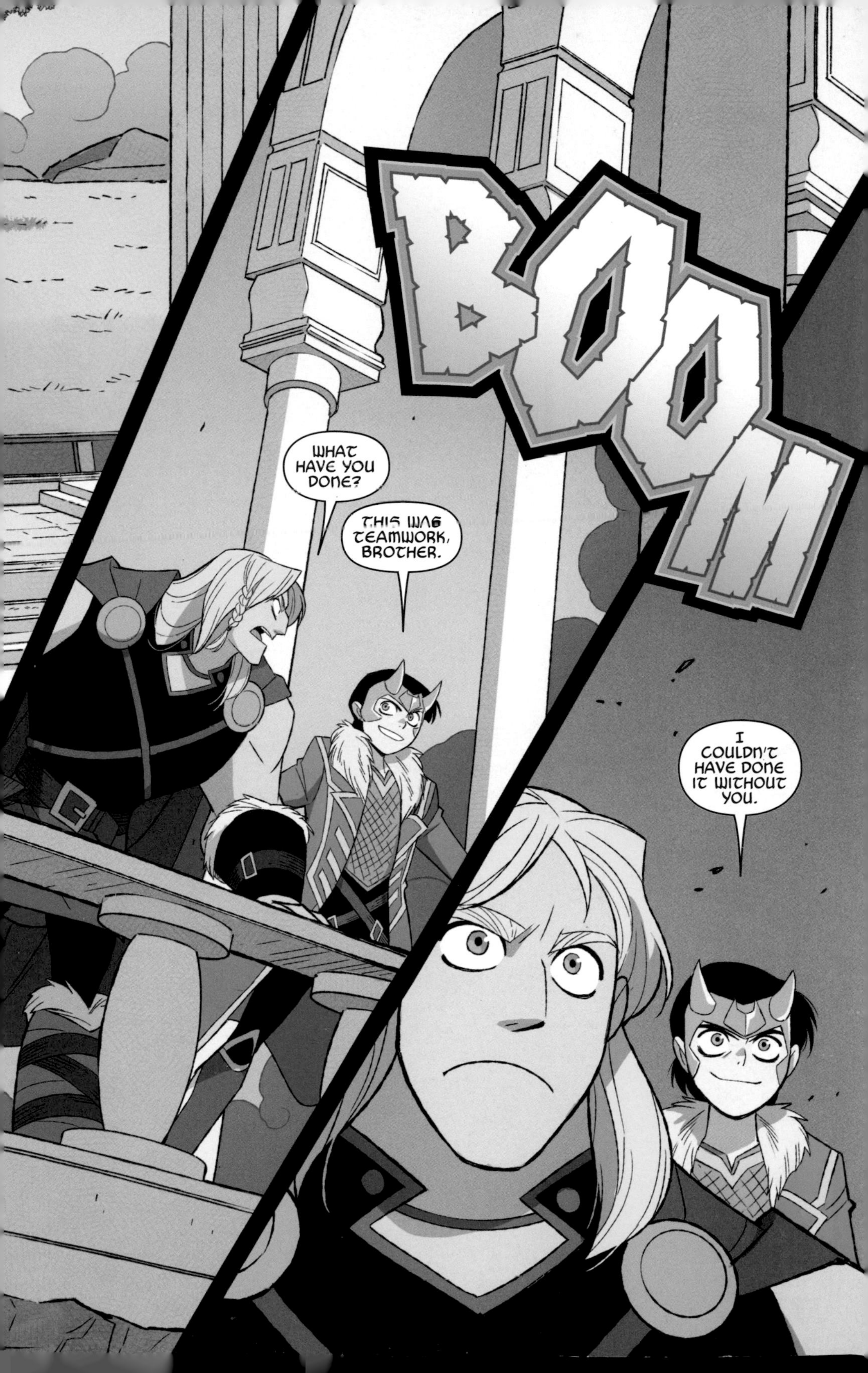
BOOM
WHAT HAVE YOU DONE?
THIS WAS TEAMWORK, BROTHER.
I COULDN'T HAVE DONE IT WITHOUT YOU.

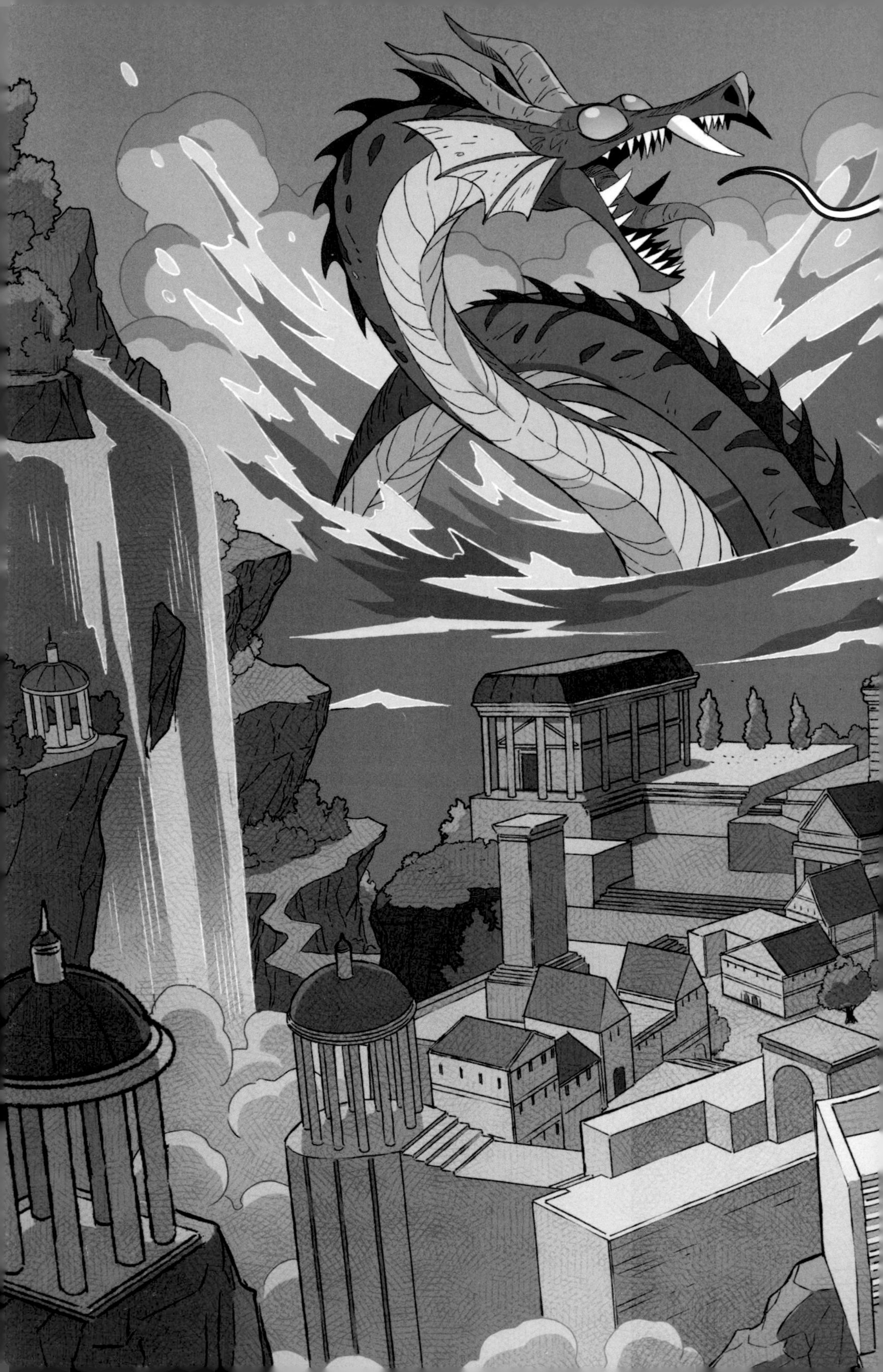

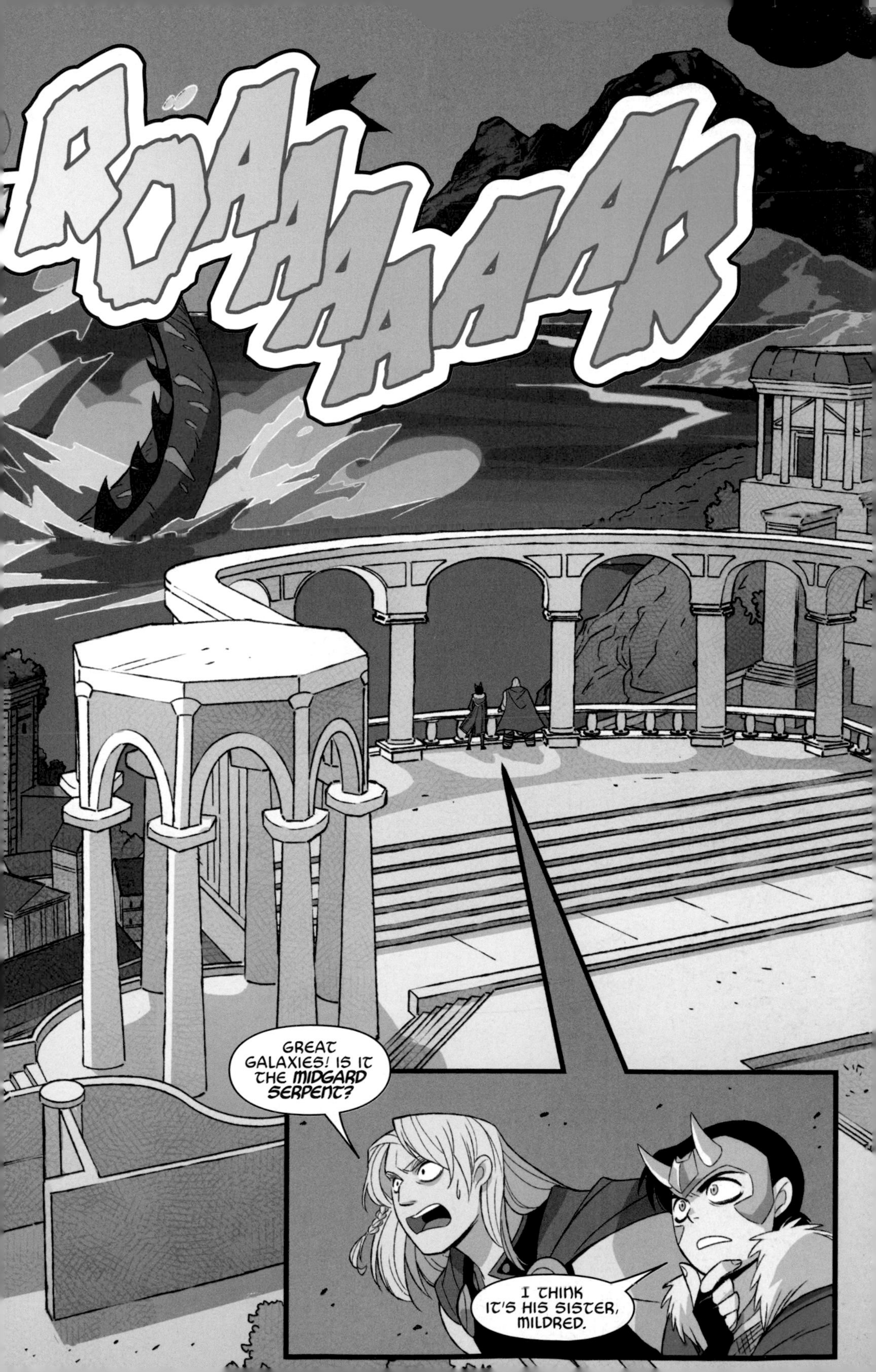
ROAAAAAAR
GREAT GALAXIES! IS IT THE MIDGARD SERPENT?
I THINK IT'S HIS SISTER, MILDRED.

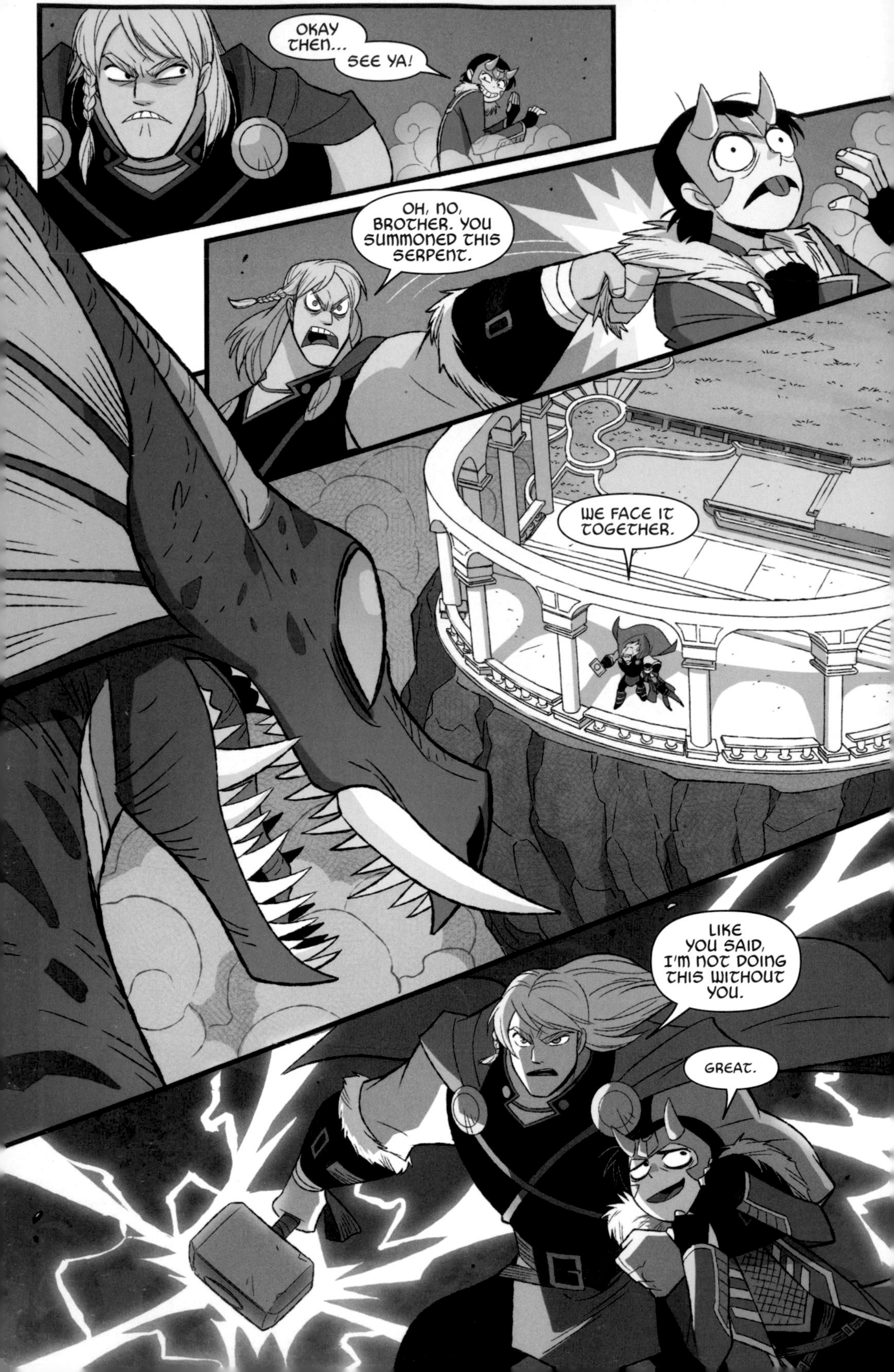
OKAY THEN... SEE YA!
OH, NO, BROTHER. YOU SUMMONED THIS SERPENT.
WE FACE IT TOGETHER.
LIKE YOU SAID, I'M NOT DOING THIS WITHOUT YOU.
GREAT.

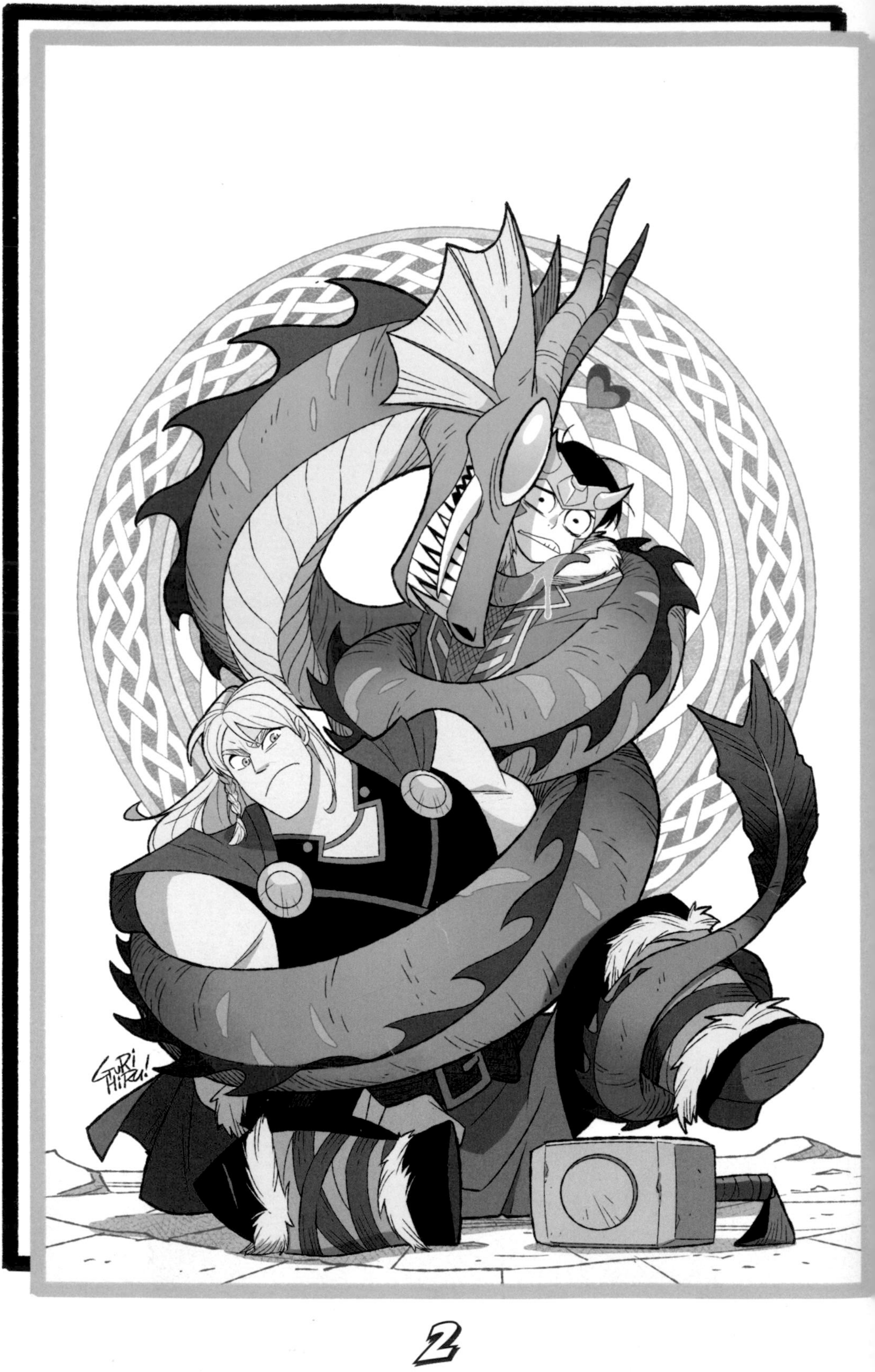
GURI HIRU!

2

RETURNING TO OUR STORY IN PROGRESS!

IT APPEARS THAT THE NOBLE BUT TROUBLESOME BROTHERS THOR AND LOKI, AFTER STEALING A MAGICAL LUR FROM THEIR FATHER ODIN'S VAULT OF MAGICAL AND IMPORTANT THINGS, HAVE SUMMONED THE SISTER OF THE MIDGARD SERPENT.

I'M SURE THEY'LL OVERCOME THEIR DIFFERENCES AND WORK TOGETHER AND EVERYTHING WILL BE FINE.

THIS IS ALL YOUR FAULT.

WHOEVER'S FAULT IT IS, AND I'M NOT CONCEDING ANYTHING...

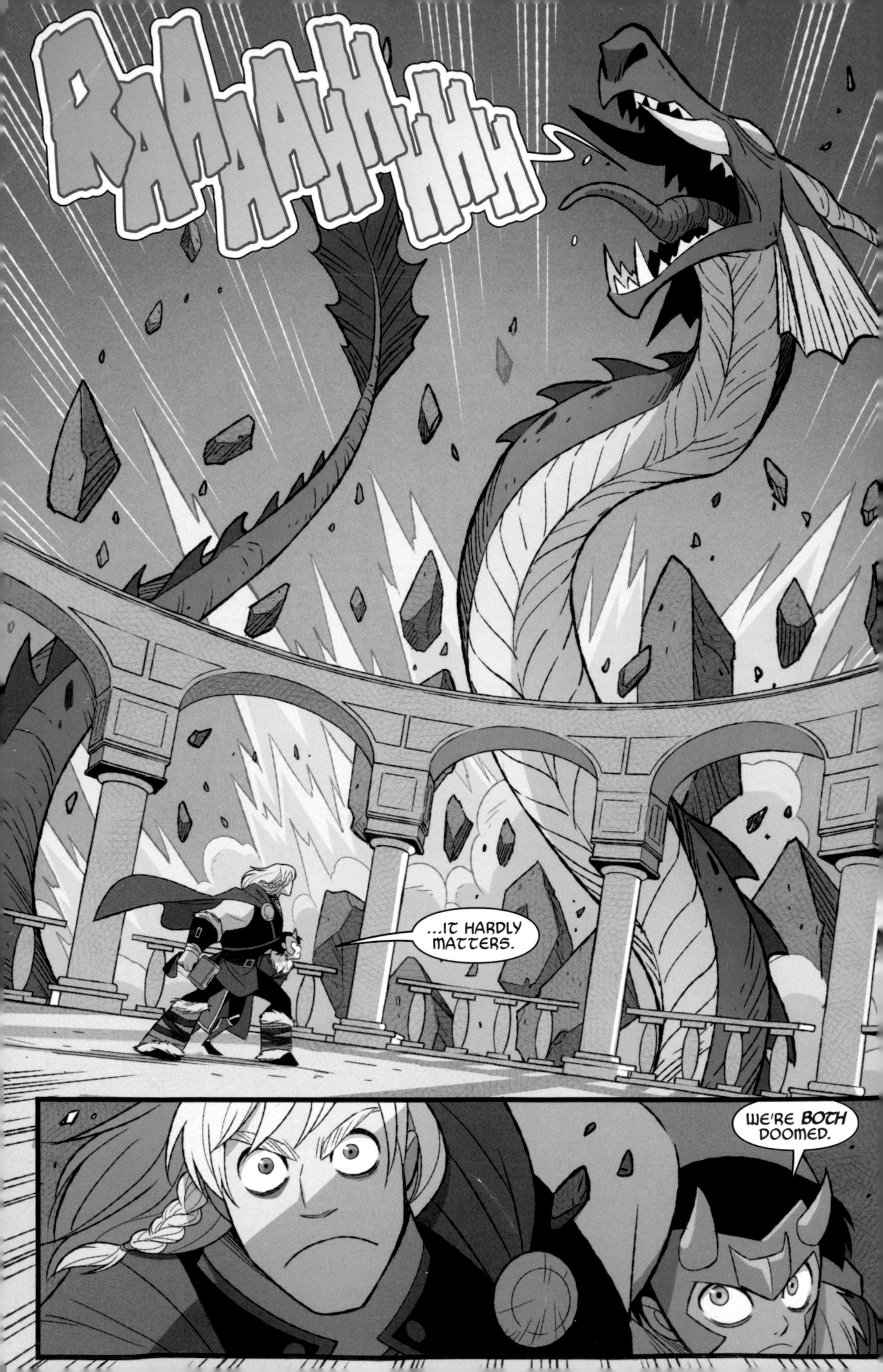
RAAAAHHHHHHH
...IT HARDLY MATTERS.
WE'RE BOTH DOOMED.

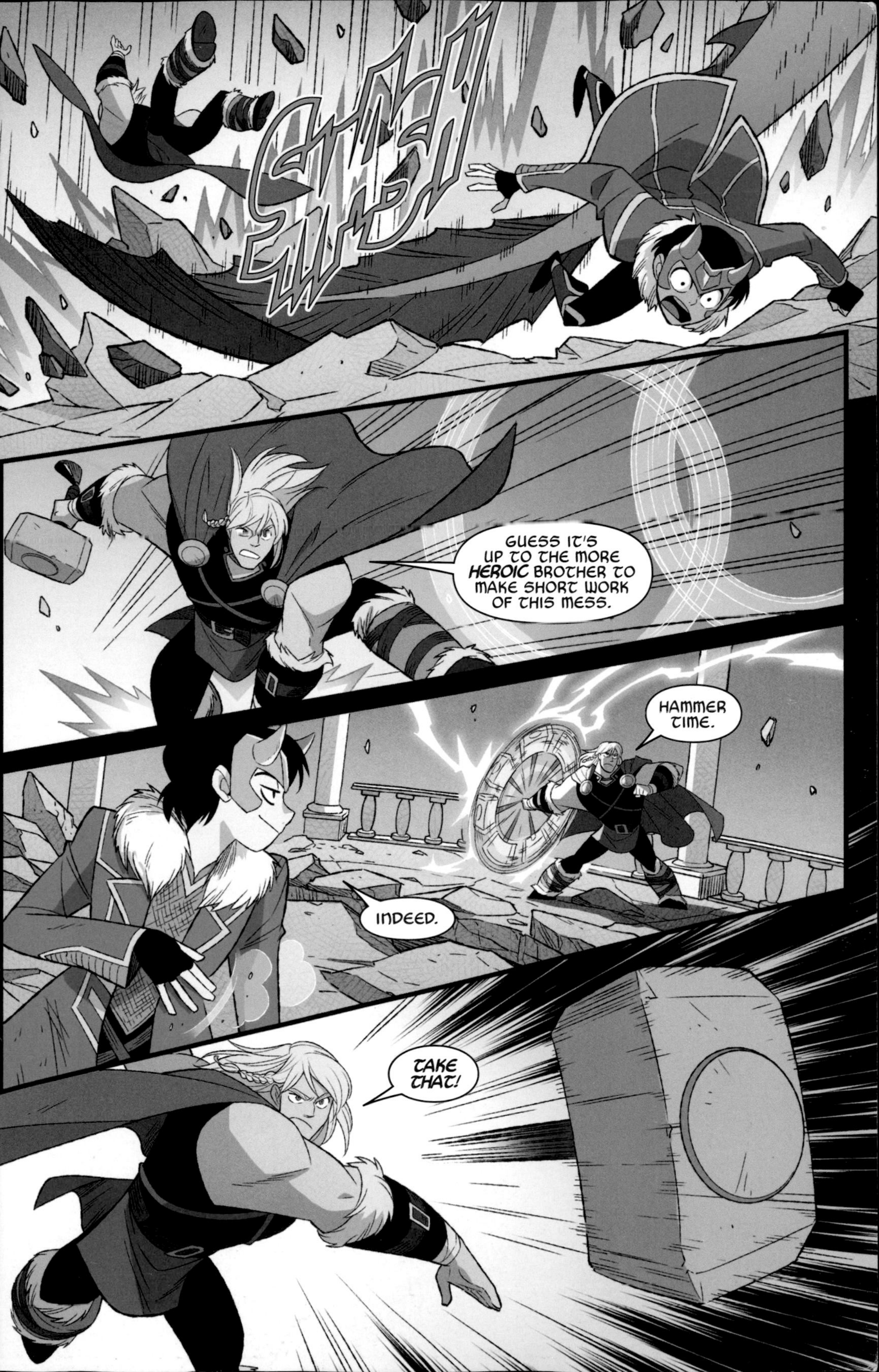
GUESS IT'S UP TO THE MORE HEROIC BROTHER TO MAKE SHORT WORK OF THIS MESS.
HAMMER TIME.
INDEED.
TAKE THAT!

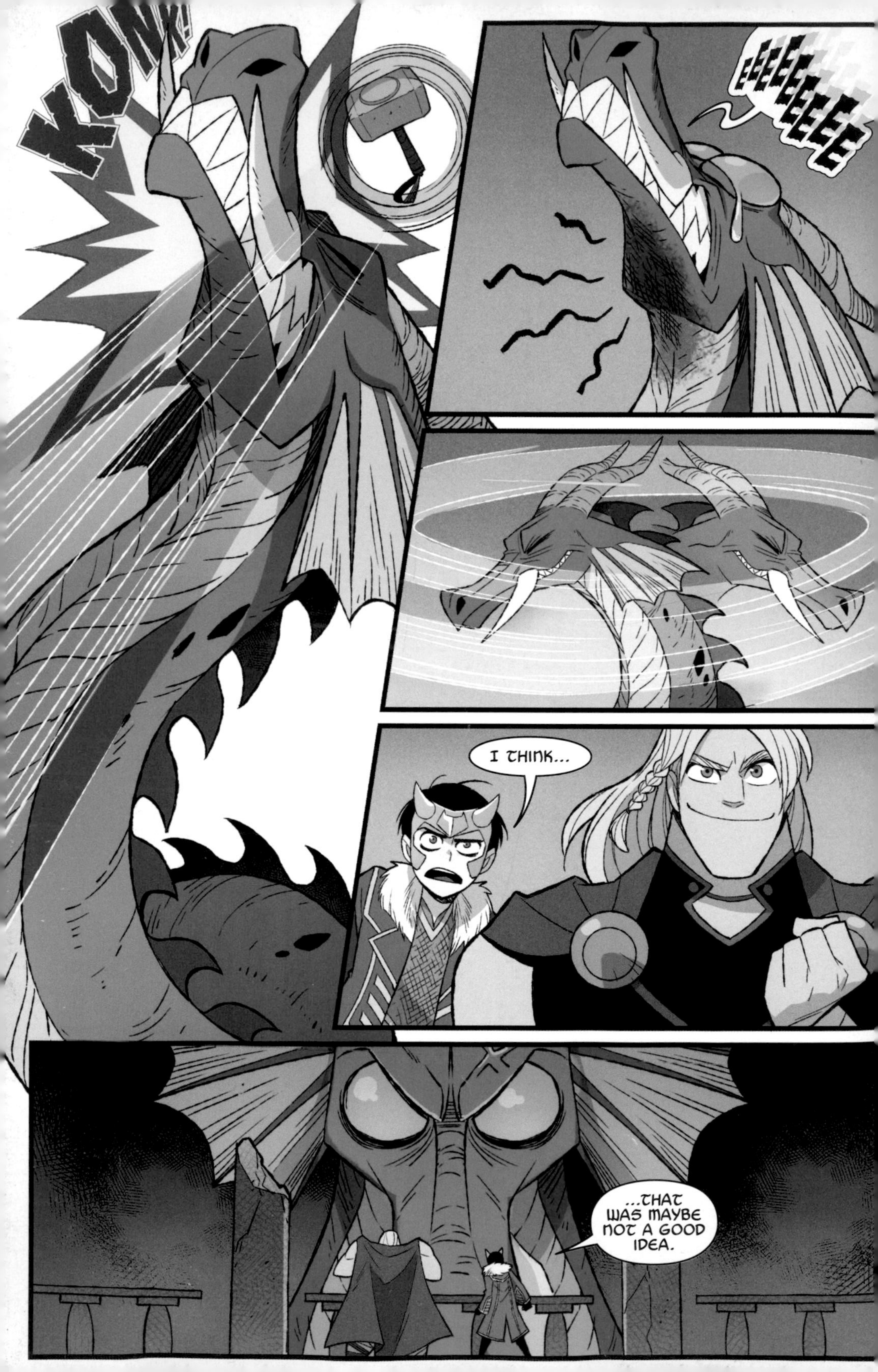
KONK!
EEEEEEEEE
I THINK...
...THAT WAS MAYBE NOT A GOOD IDEA.

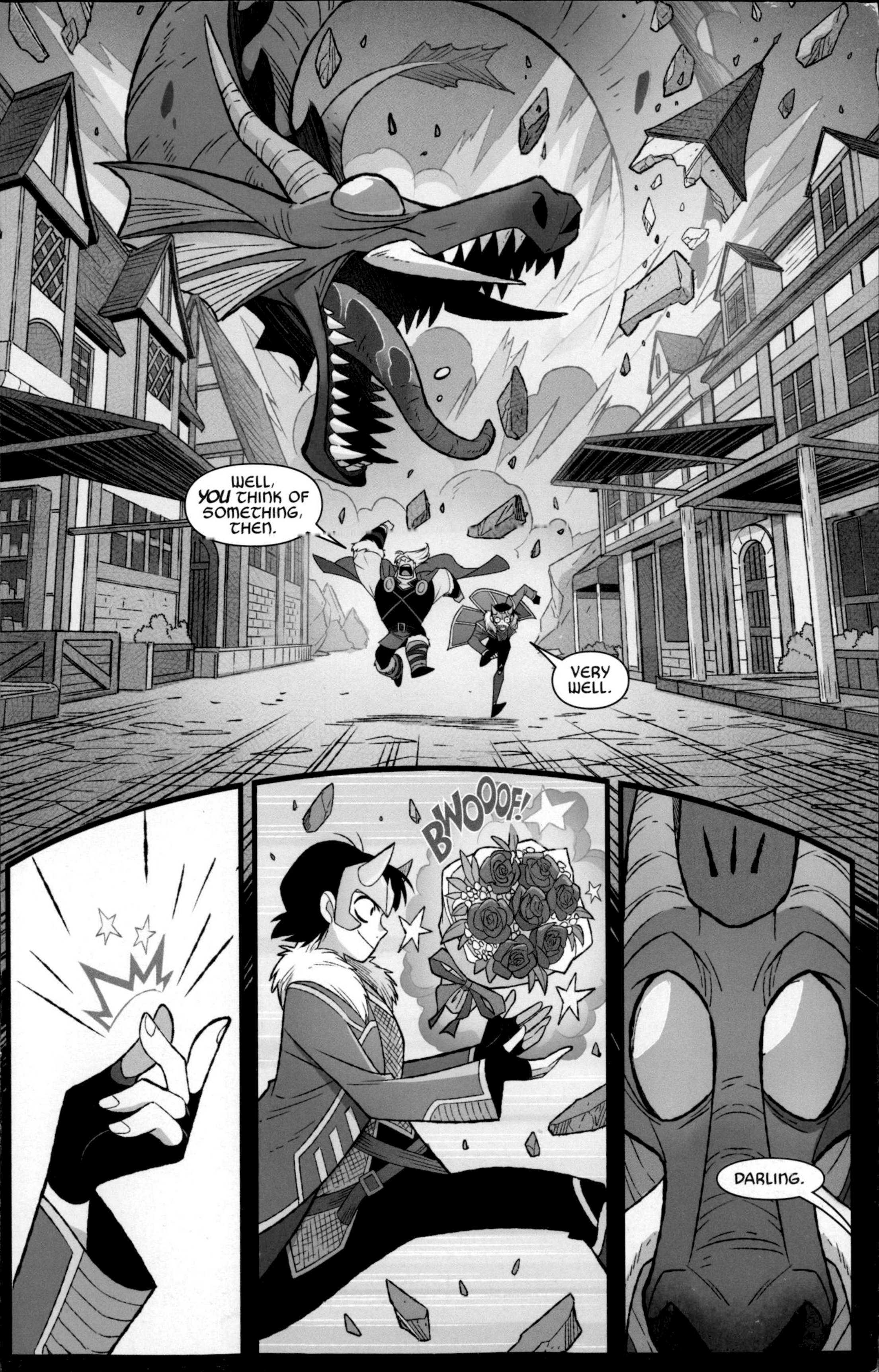
WELL, YOU THINK OF SOMETHING, THEN.
VERY WELL.
BWOOOF!
DARLING.

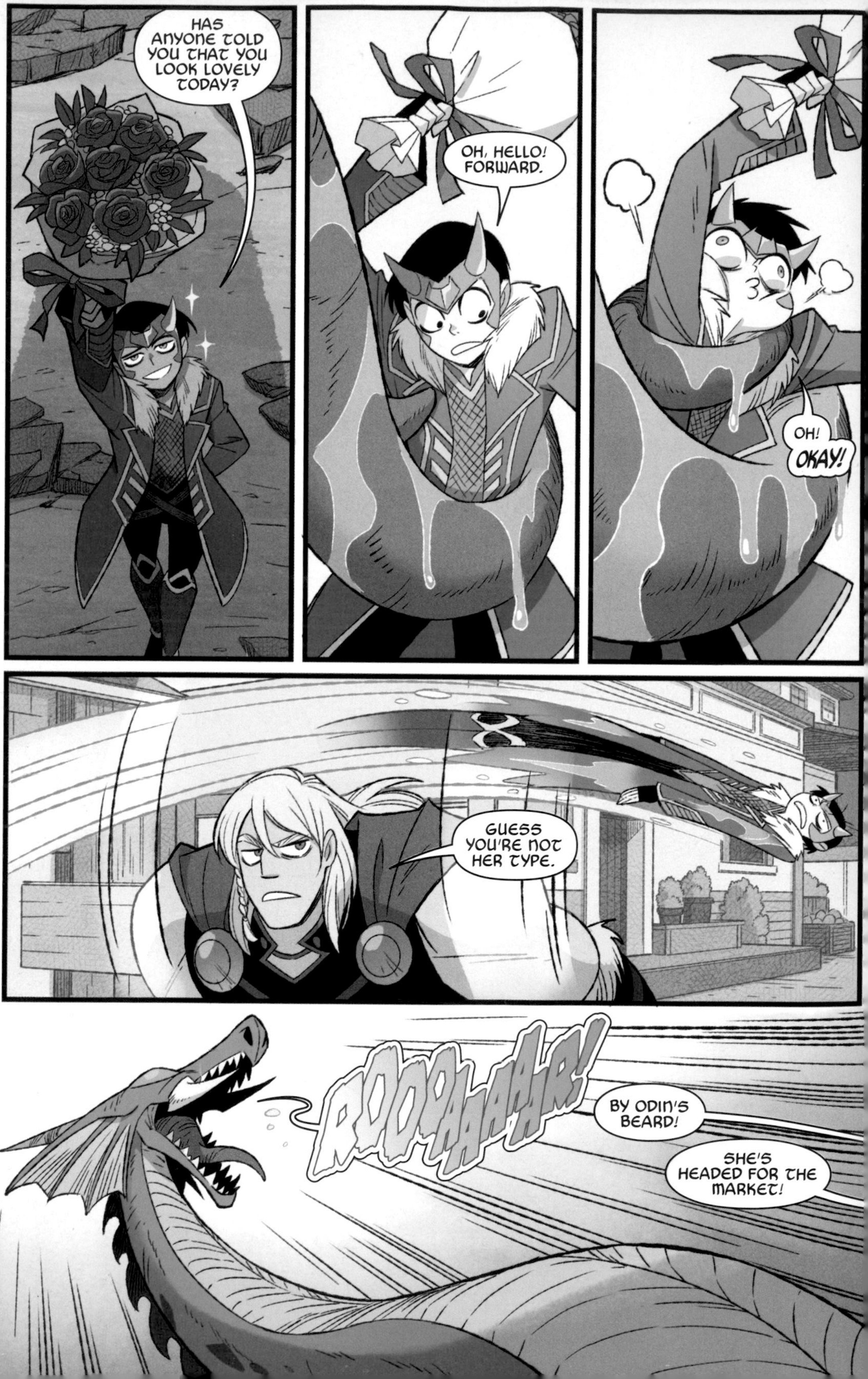
HAS ANYONE TOLD YOU THAT YOU LOOK LOVELY TODAY?
OH, HELLO! FORWARD.
OH! OKAY!
GUESS YOU'RE NOT HER TYPE.
ROOOAAAAAR!
BY ODIN'S BEARD!
SHE'S HEADED FOR THE MARKET!

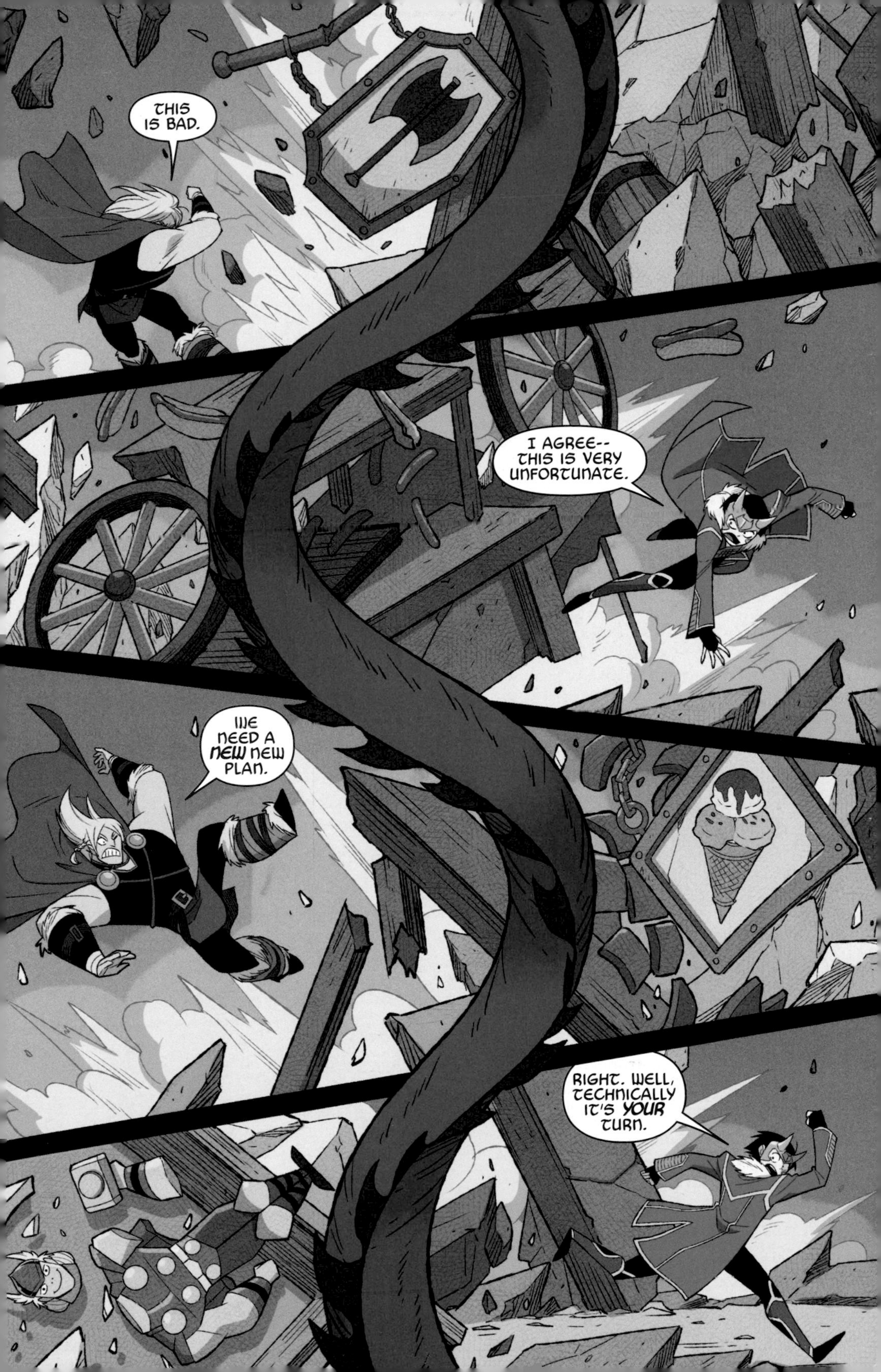
THIS IS BAD.
I AGREE-- THIS IS VERY UNFORTUNATE.
WE NEED A NEW NEW PLAN.
RIGHT. WELL, TECHNICALLY IT'S YOUR TURN.

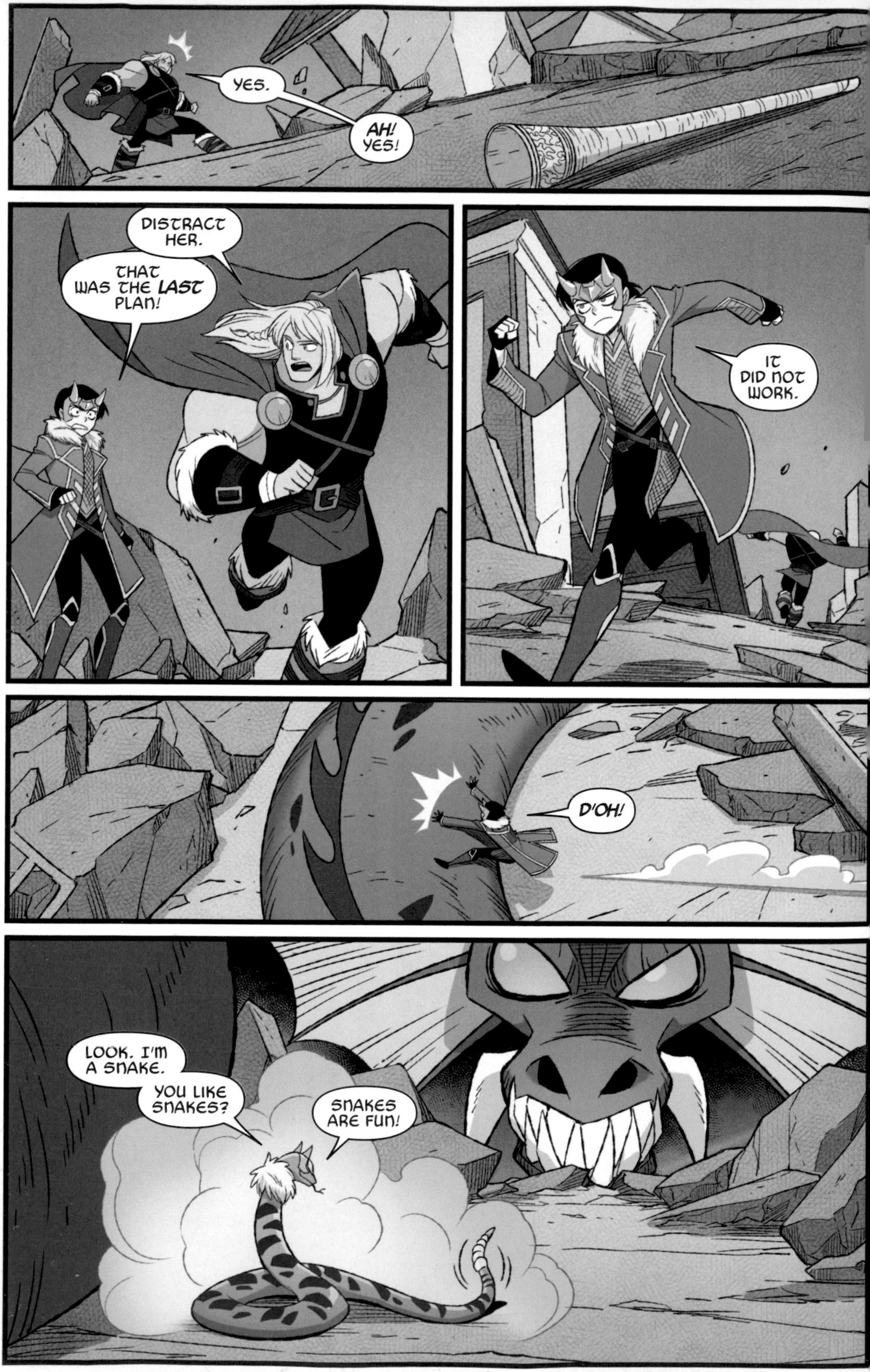
YES.
AH! YES!
DISTRACT HER.
THAT WAS THE LAST PLAN!
IT DID NOT WORK.
D'OH!
LOOK. I'M A SNAKE.
YOU LIKE SNAKES?
SNAKES ARE FUN!

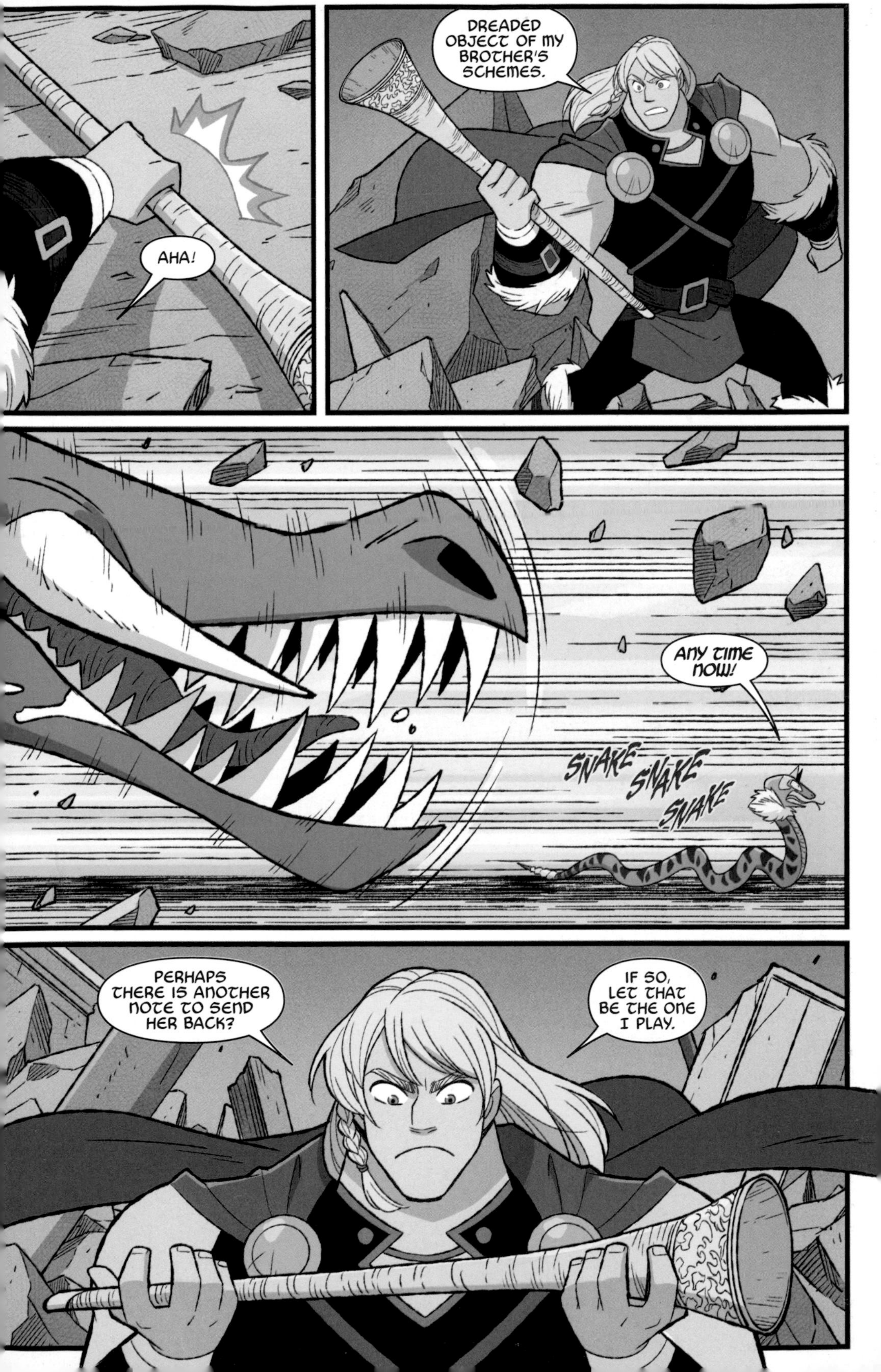
AHA!
DREADED OBJECT OF MY BROTHER'S SCHEMES.
ANY TIME NOW!
SNAKE SNAKE SNAKE
PERHAPS THERE IS ANOTHER NOTE TO SEND HER BACK?
IF SO, LET THAT BE THE ONE I PLAY.

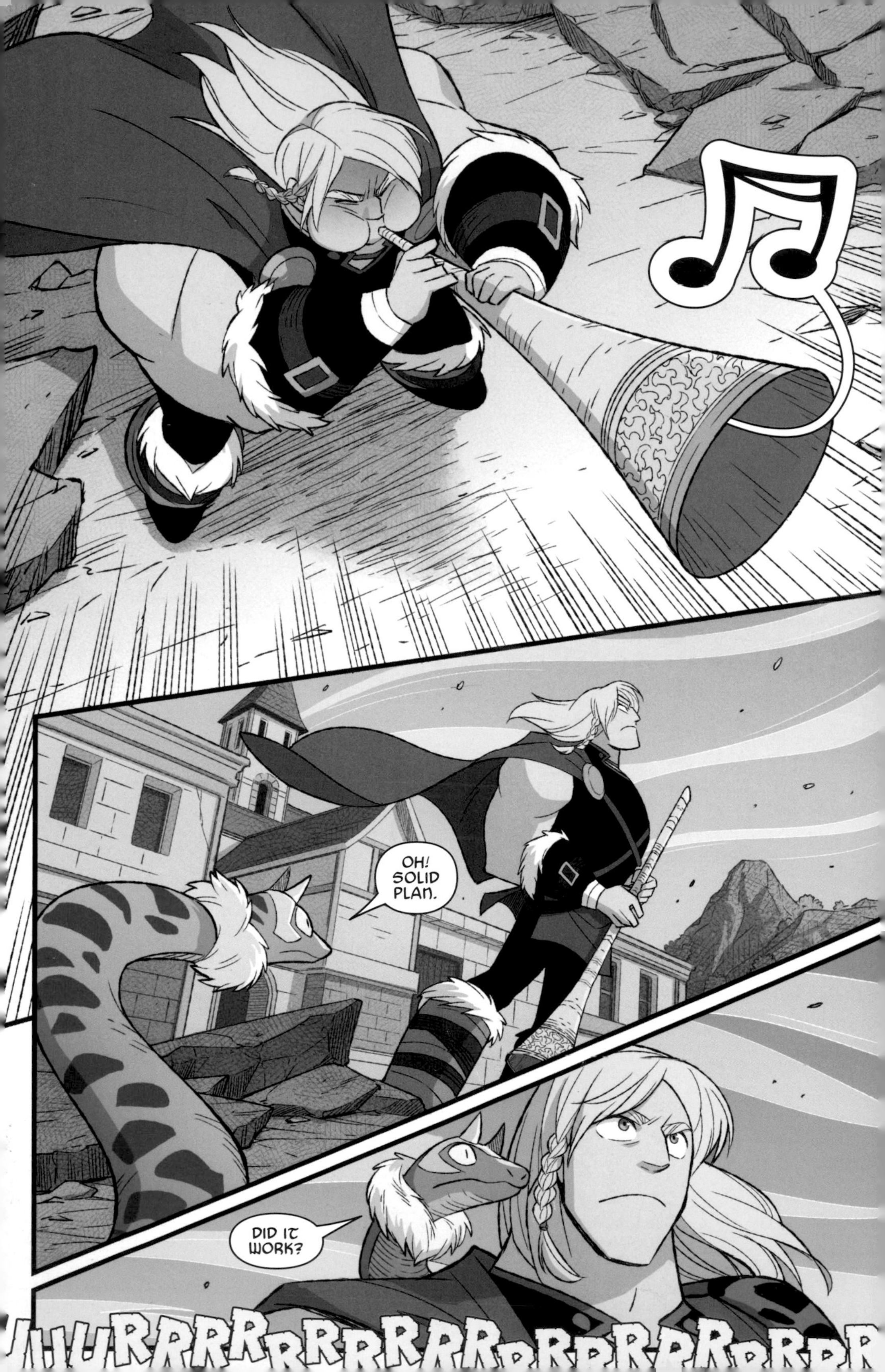
OH! SOLID PLAN.
DID IT WORK?
IIIURRRRRRRRRRRRRRRRRRR

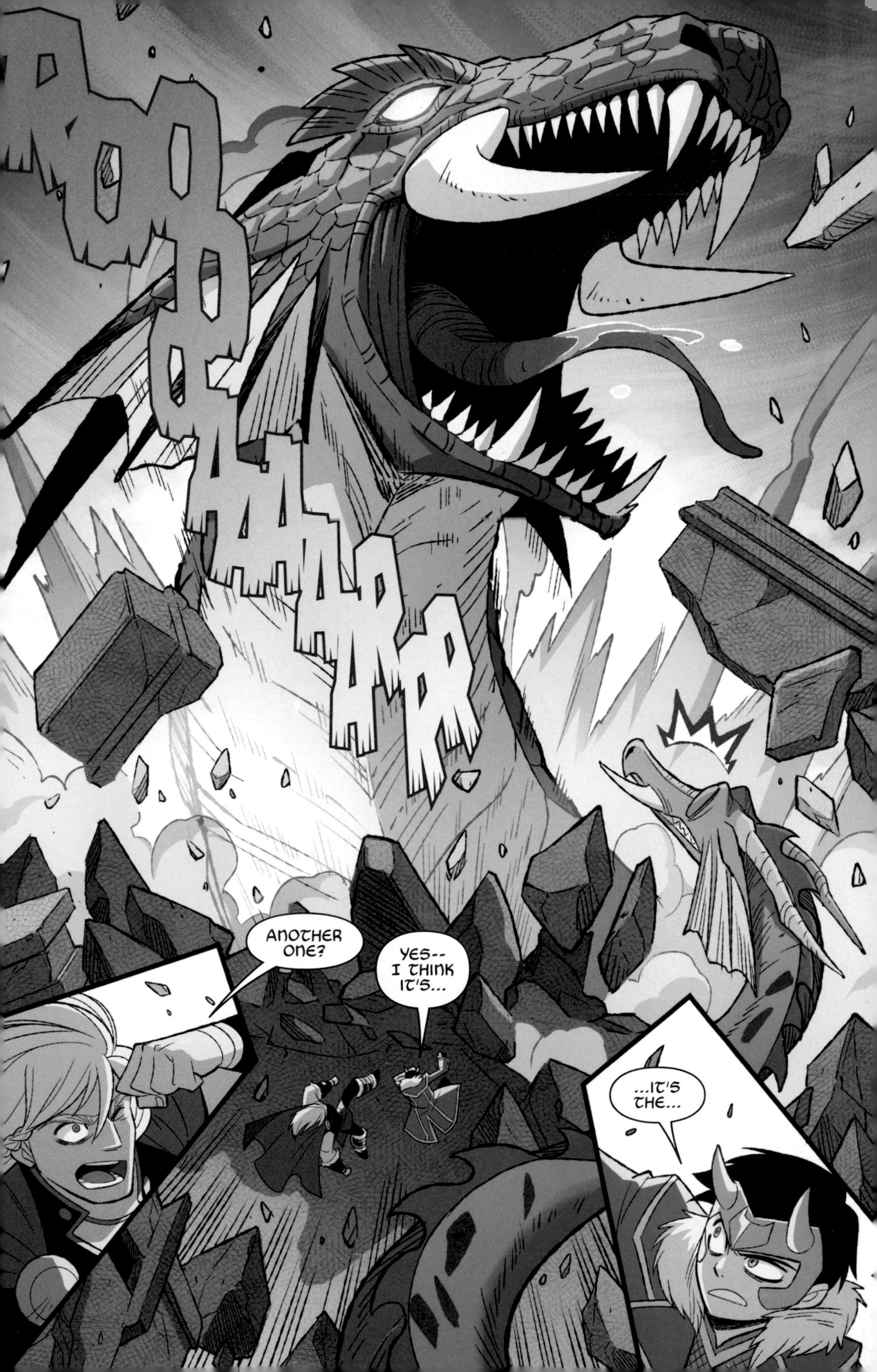

ROOOAAARR
ANOTHER ONE?
YES-- I THINK IT'S...
...IT'S THE...

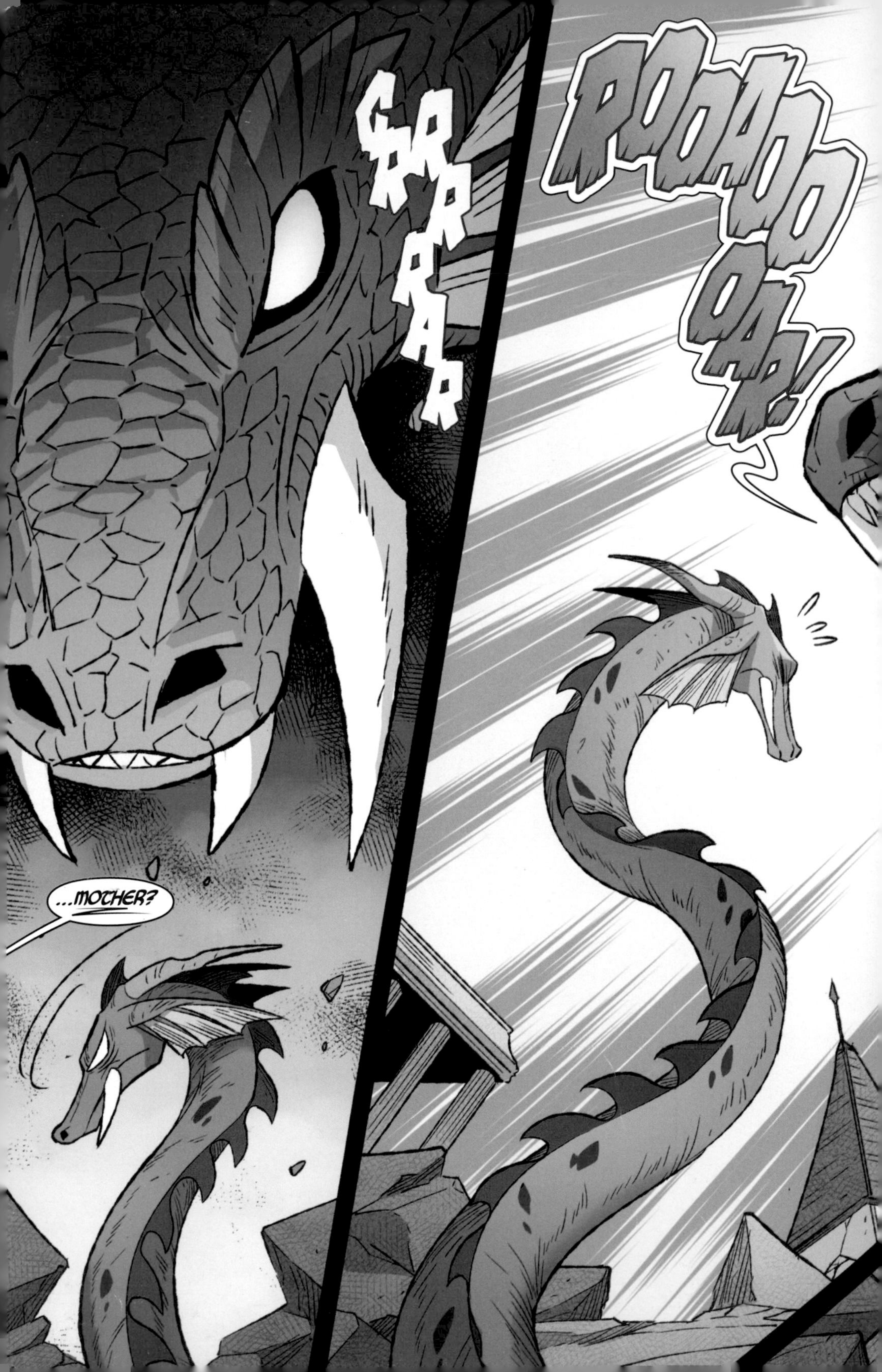
GRRRRAR
...MOTHER?
ROOAOOOAR!

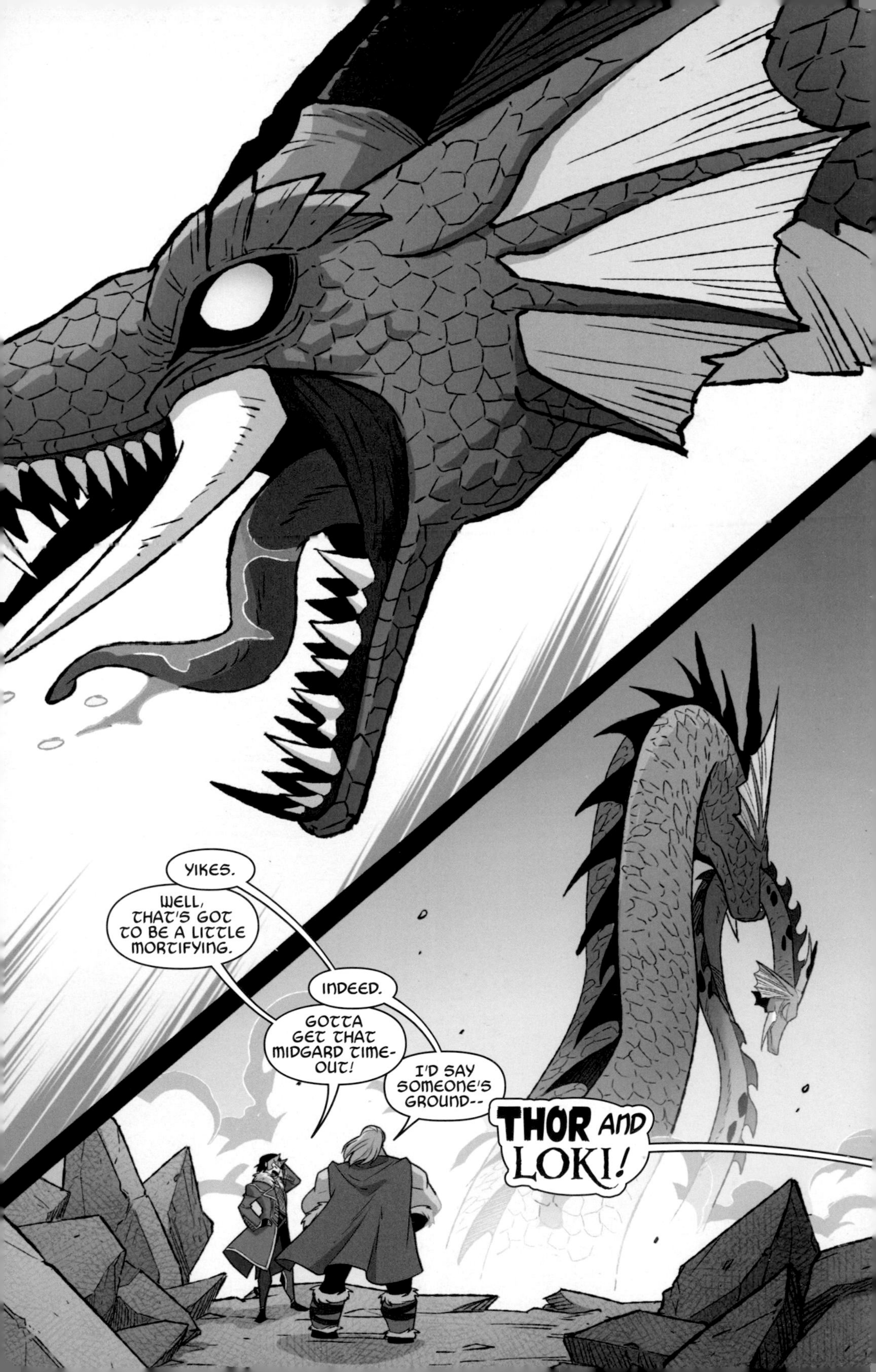

YIKES.
WELL, THAT'S GOT TO BE A LITTLE MORTIFYING.
INDEED.
GOTTA GET THAT MIDGARD TIME-OUT!
I'D SAY SOMEONE'S GROUND--
THOR AND LOKI!

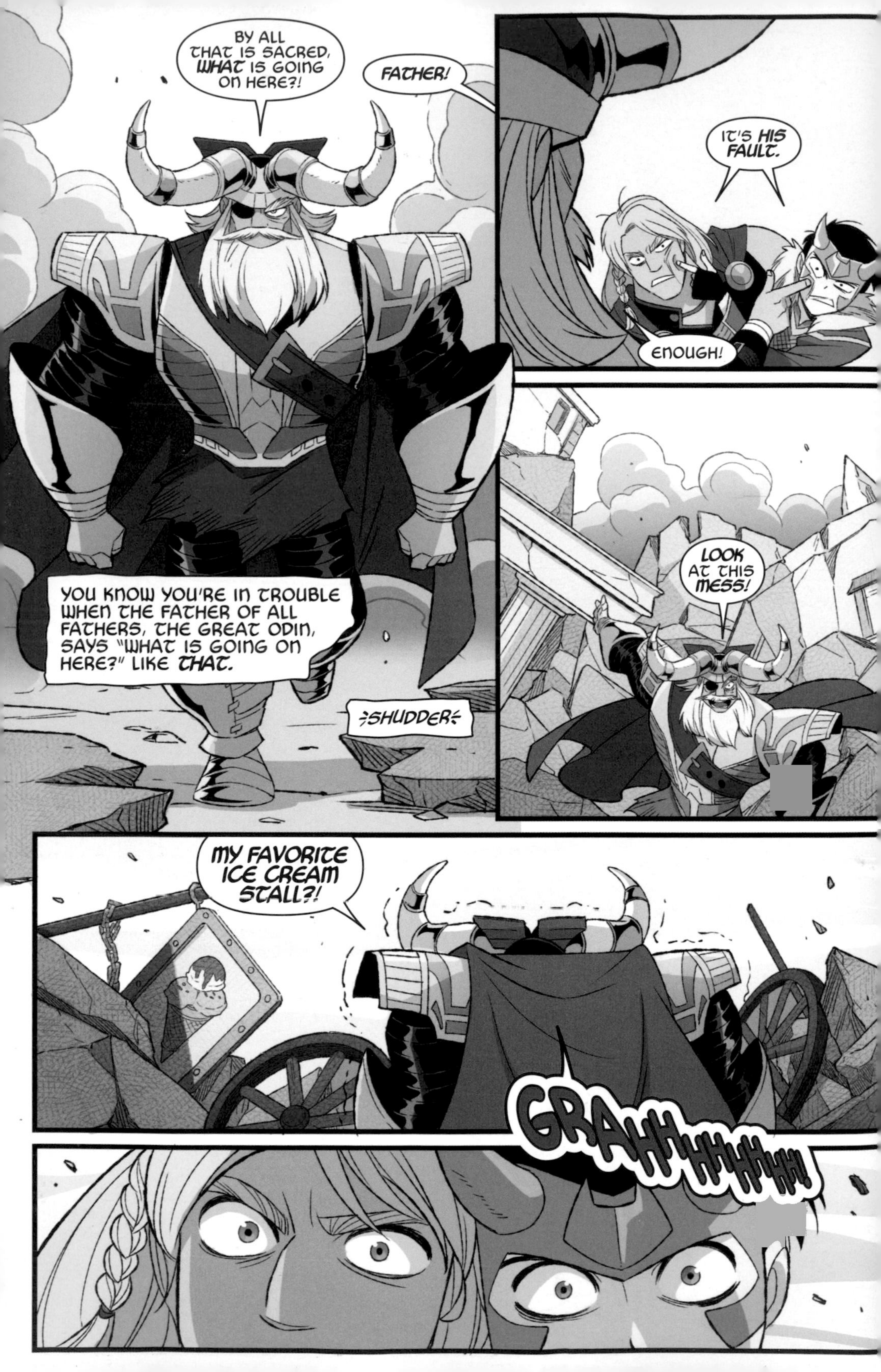
BY ALL THAT IS SACRED, WHAT IS GOING ON HERE?!
FATHER!
IT'S HIS FAULT.
ENOUGH!
YOU KNOW YOU'RE IN TROUBLE WHEN THE FATHER OF ALL FATHERS, THE GREAT ODIN, SAYS "WHAT IS GOING ON HERE?" LIKE THAT.
SHUDDER
LOOK AT THIS MESS!
MY FAVORITE ICE CREAM STALL?!
GRAHHHHHHHH!

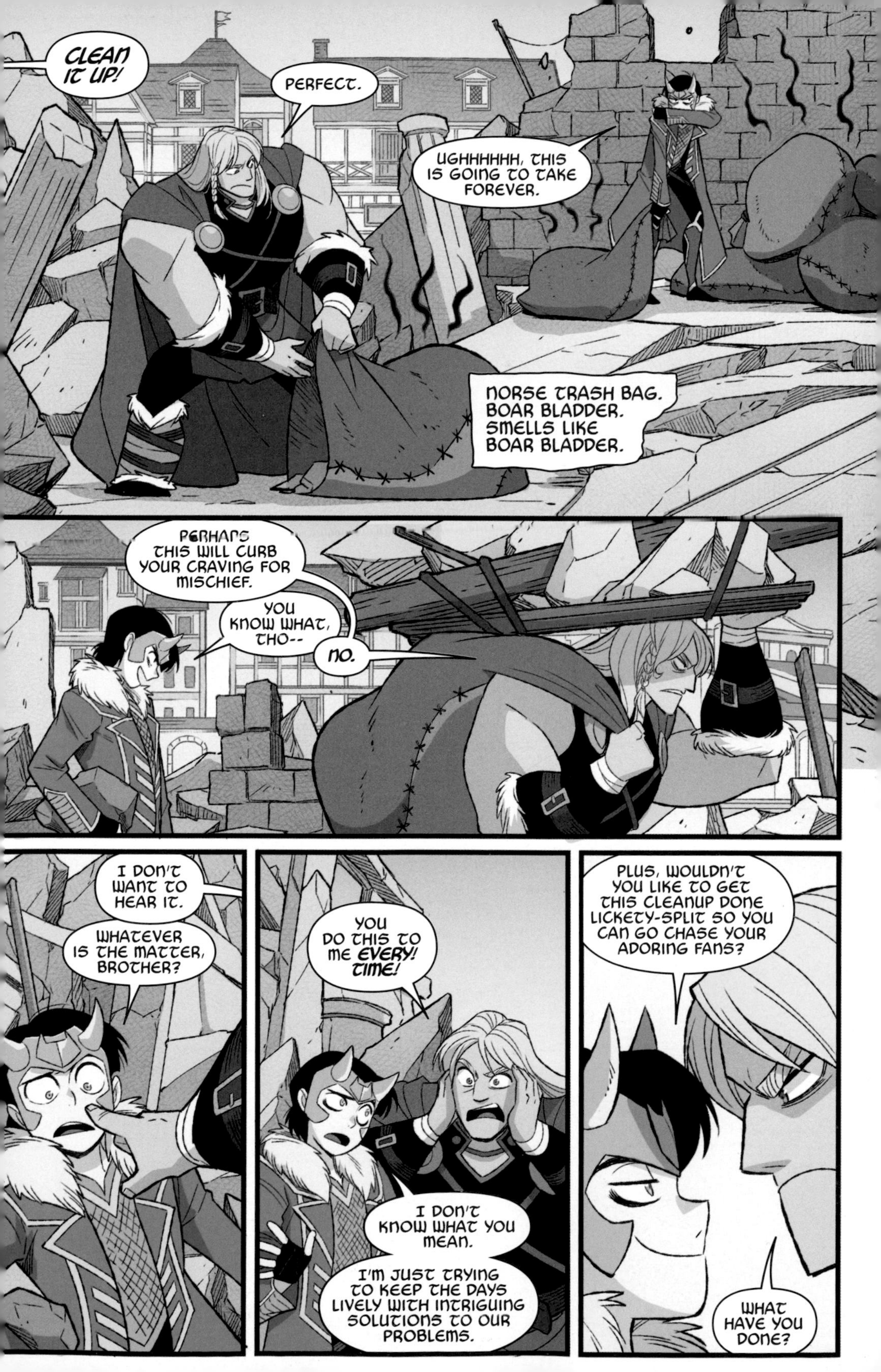

CLEAN IT UP!
PERFECT.
UGHHHHHH, THIS IS GOING TO TAKE FOREVER.
NORSE TRASH BAG. BOAR BLADDER. SMELLS LIKE BOAR BLADDER.
PERHAPS THIS WILL CURB YOUR CRAVING FOR MISCHIEF.
YOU KNOW WHAT, THO--
NO.
I DON'T WANT TO HEAR IT.
WHATEVER IS THE MATTER, BROTHER?
YOU DO THIS TO ME EVERY! TIME!
I DON'T KNOW WHAT YOU MEAN.
I'M JUST TRYING TO KEEP THE DAYS LIVELY WITH INTRIGUING SOLUTIONS TO OUR PROBLEMS.
PLUS, WOULDN'T YOU LIKE TO GET THIS CLEANUP DONE LICKETY-SPLIT SO YOU CAN GO CHASE YOUR ADORING FANS?
WHAT HAVE YOU DONE?

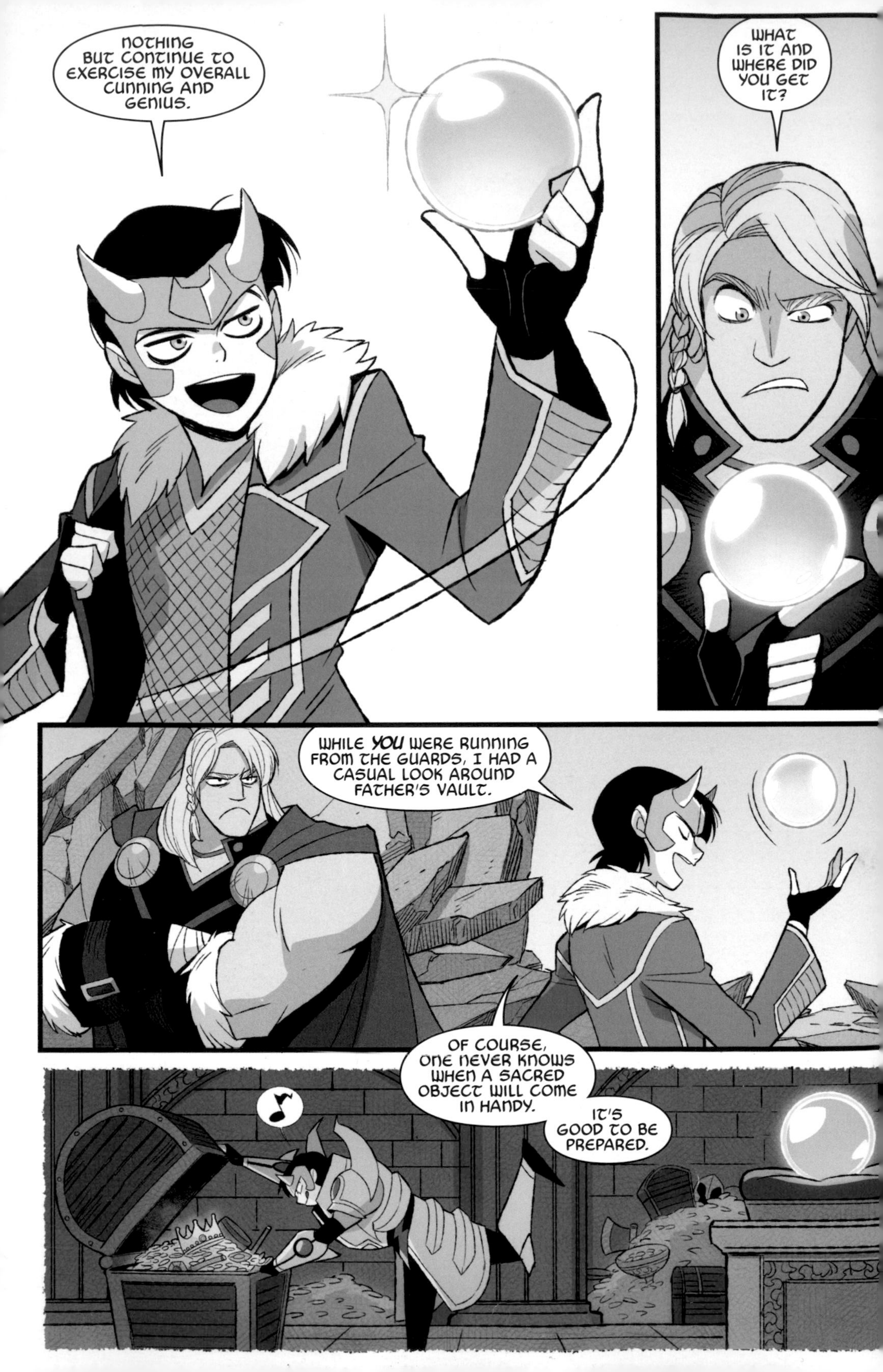
NOTHING BUT CONTINUE TO EXERCISE MY OVERALL CUNNING AND GENIUS.
WHAT IS IT AND WHERE DID YOU GET IT?
WHILE *YOU* WERE RUNNING FROM THE GUARDS, I HAD A CASUAL LOOK AROUND FATHER'S VAULT.
OF COURSE, ONE NEVER KNOWS WHEN A SACRED OBJECT WILL COME IN HANDY.
IT'S GOOD TO BE PREPARED.

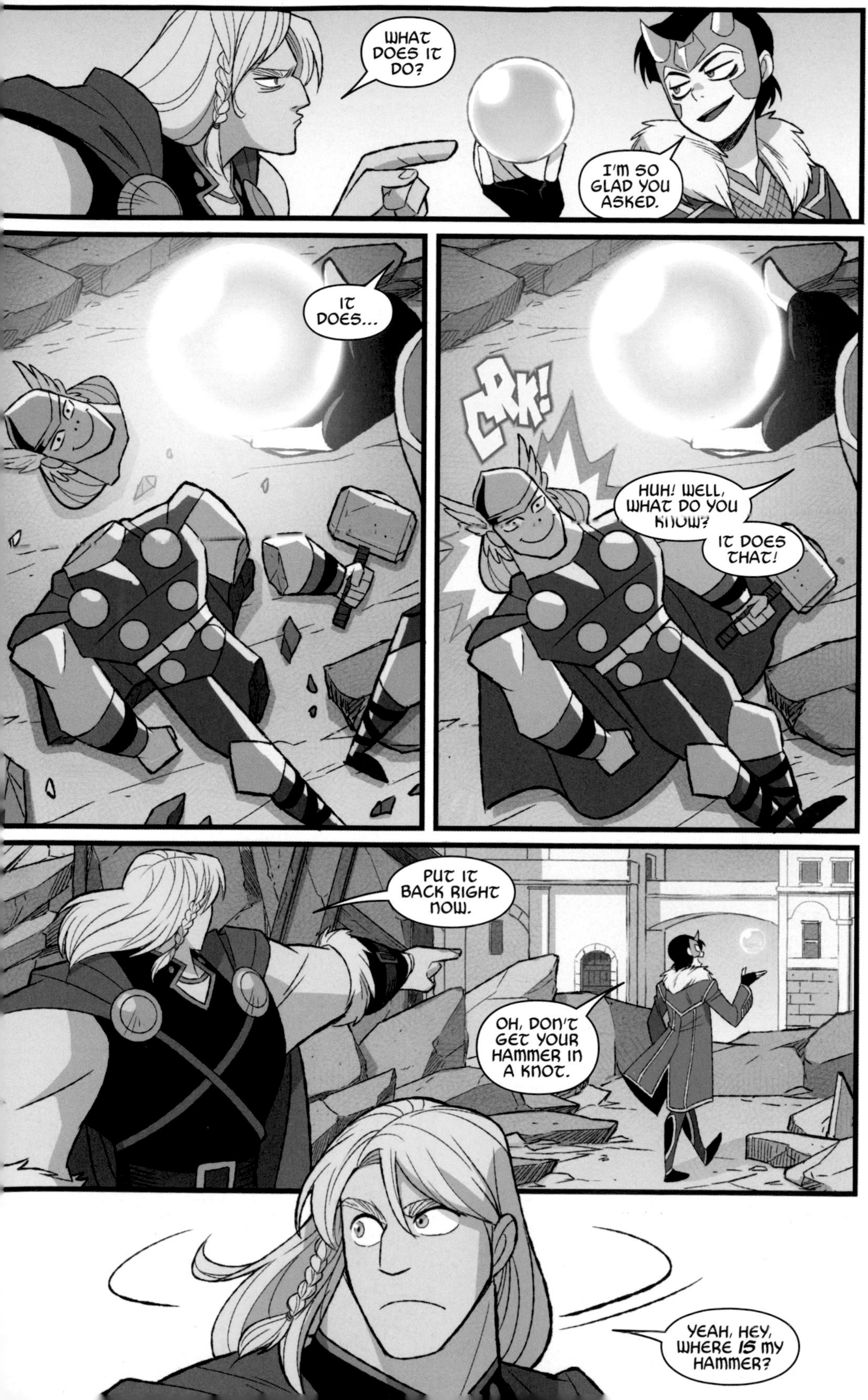
WHAT DOES IT DO?
I'M SO GLAD YOU ASKED.
IT DOES...
CRK!
HUH! WELL, WHAT DO YOU KNOW?
IT DOES THAT!
PUT IT BACK RIGHT NOW.
OH, DON'T GET YOUR HAMMER IN A KNOT.
YEAH, HEY, WHERE IS MY HAMMER?

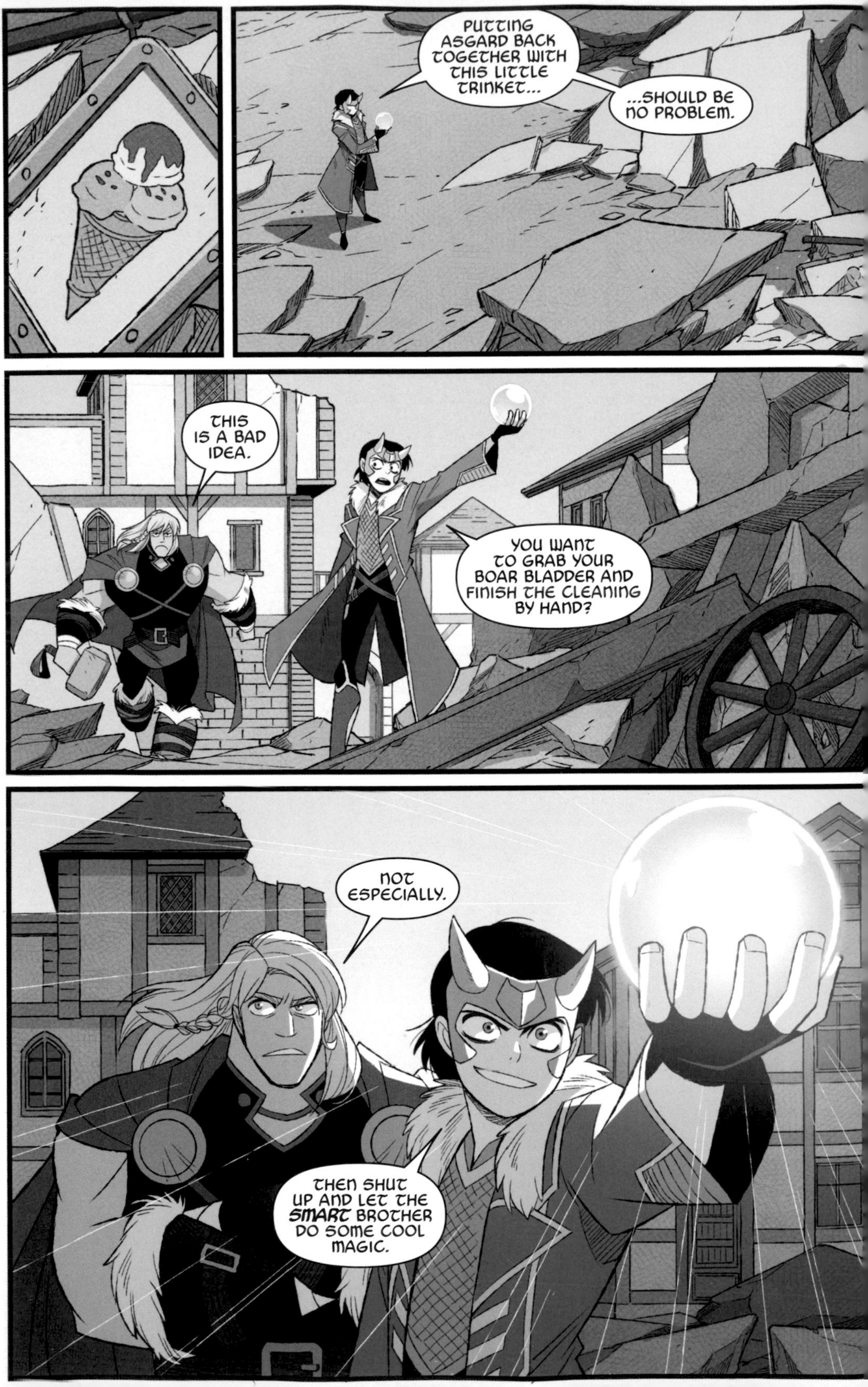
PUTTING ASGARD BACK TOGETHER WITH THIS LITTLE TRINKET...
...SHOULD BE NO PROBLEM.
THIS IS A BAD IDEA.
YOU WANT TO GRAB YOUR BOAR BLADDER AND FINISH THE CLEANING BY HAND?
NOT ESPECIALLY.
THEN SHUT UP AND LET THE SMART BROTHER DO SOME COOL MAGIC.

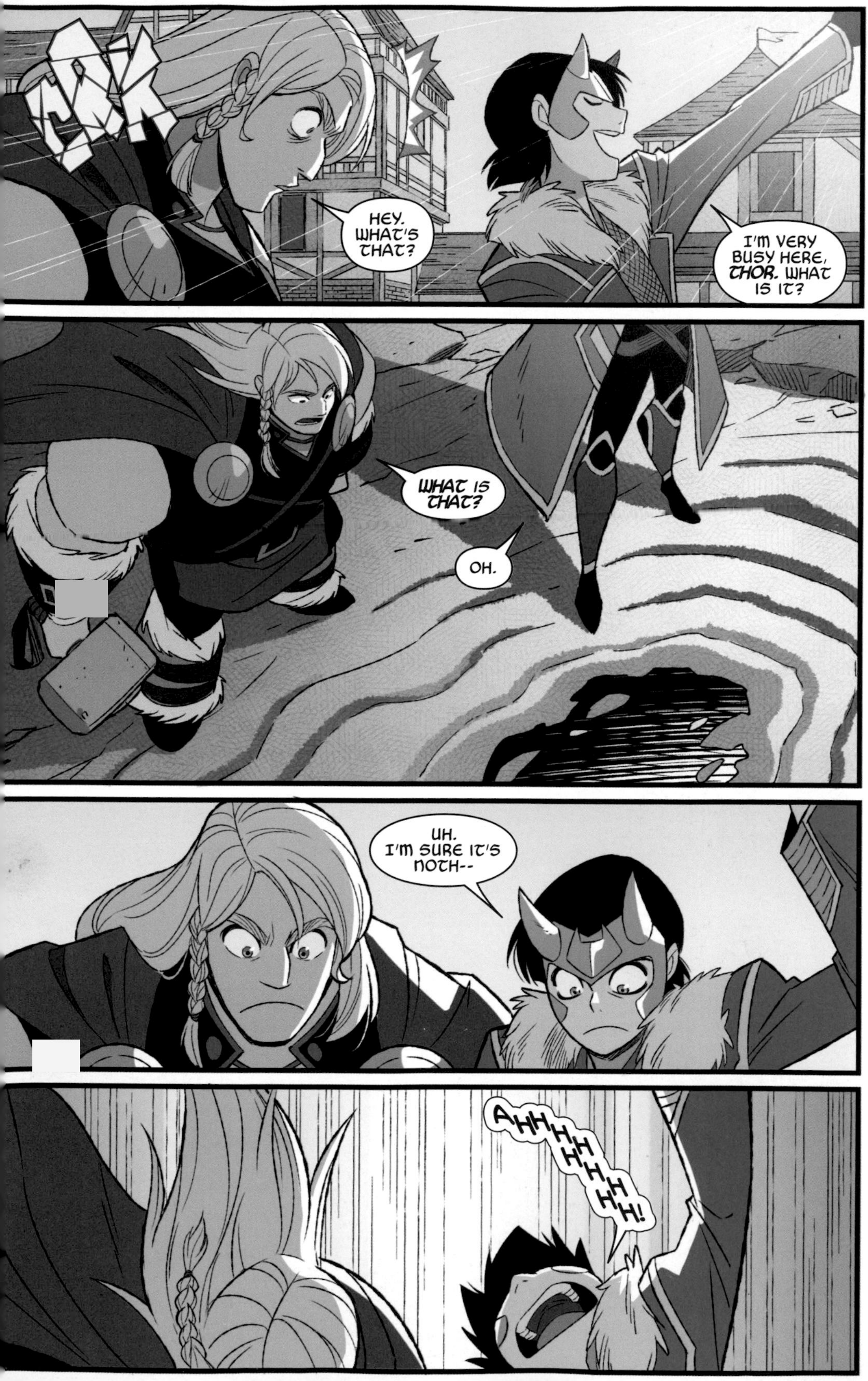

CRAK
HEY. WHAT'S THAT?
I'M VERY BUSY HERE, THOR. WHAT IS IT?
WHAT IS THAT?
OH.
UH. I'M SURE IT'S NOTH--
AHHHHHHHHHH!

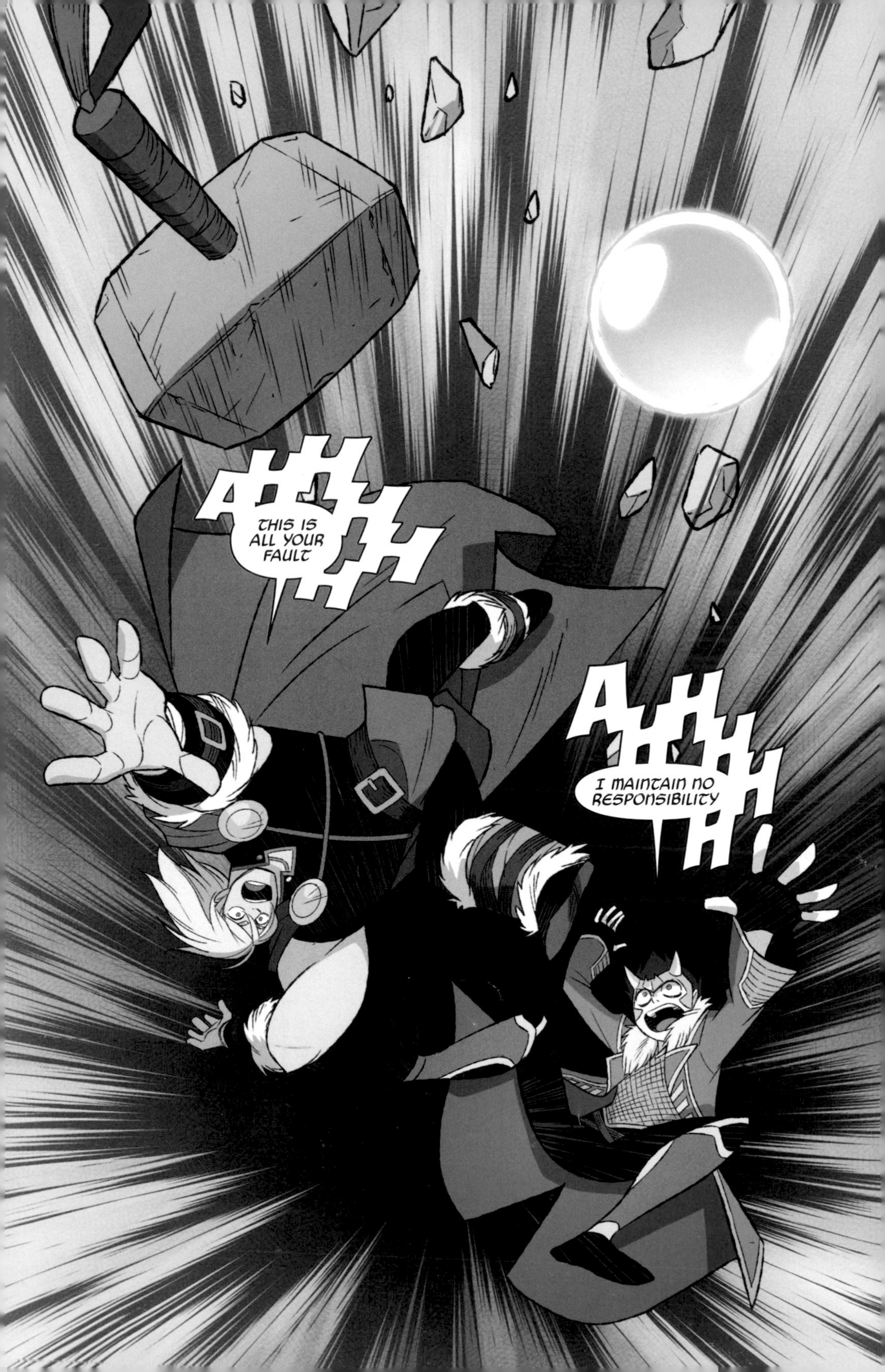
AAHHHH
THIS IS ALL YOUR FAULT
AAHHHH!
I MAINTAIN NO RESPONSIBILITY

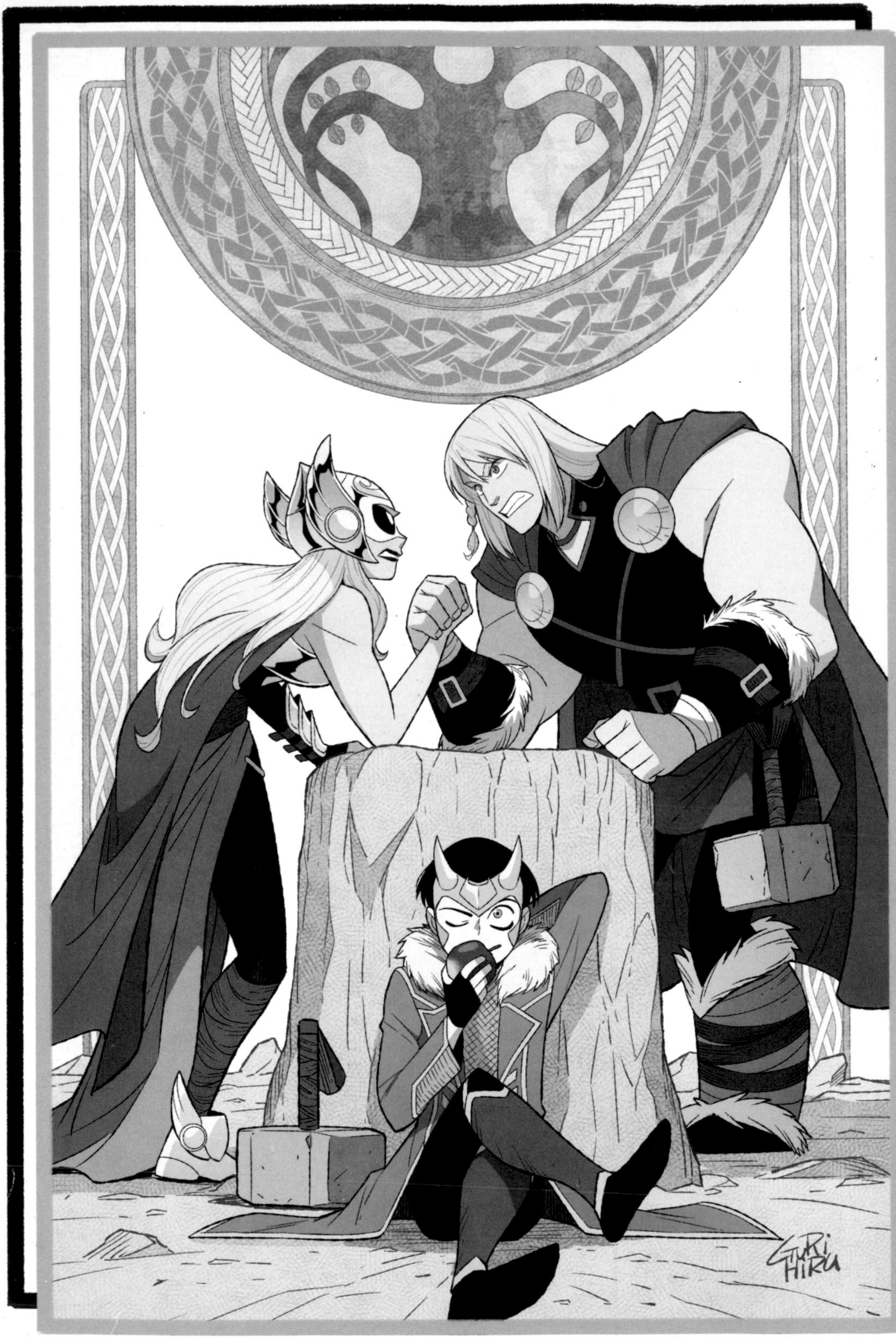
GURIHIRU

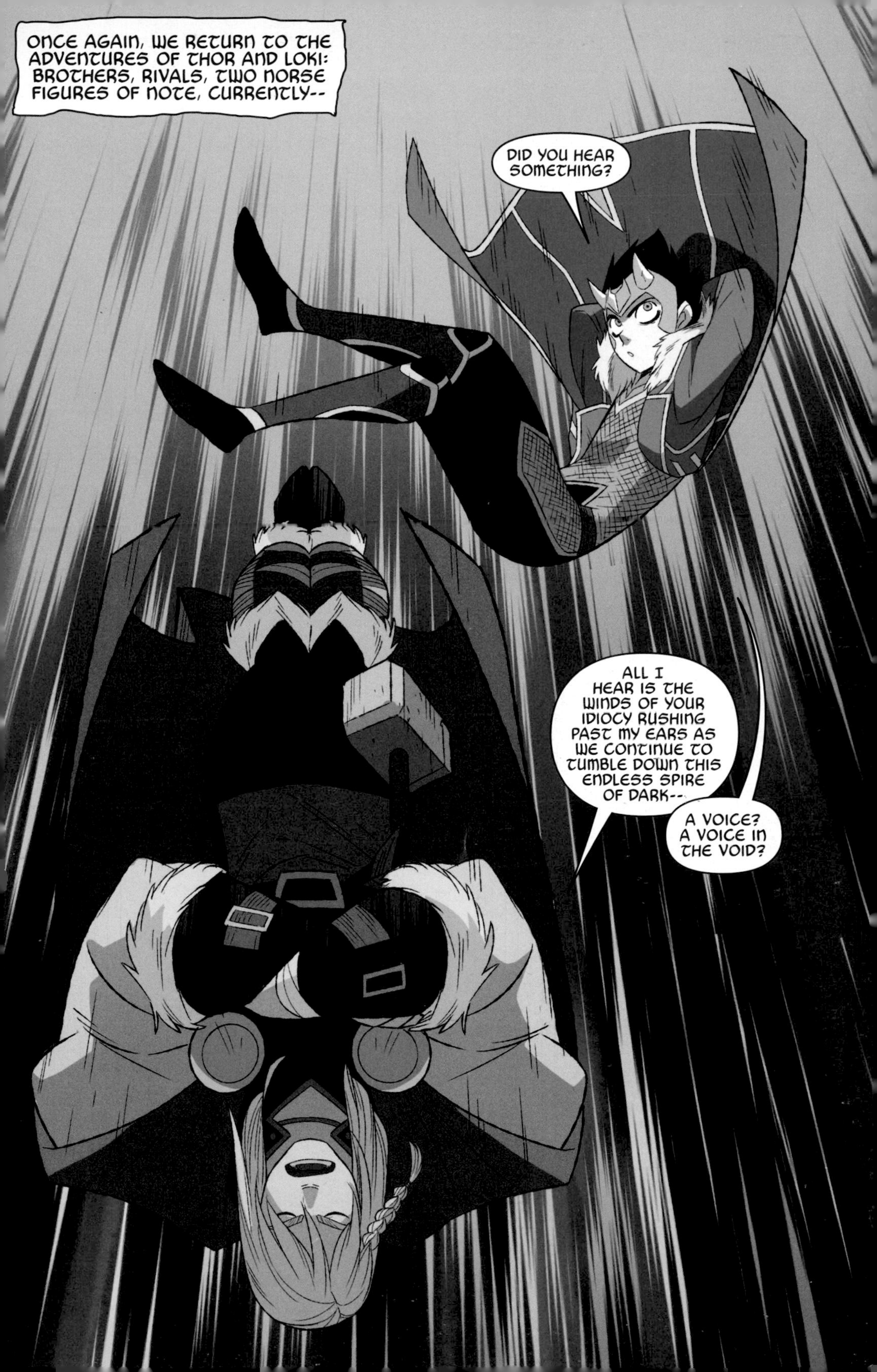
ONCE AGAIN, WE RETURN TO THE ADVENTURES OF THOR AND LOKI: BROTHERS, RIVALS, TWO NORSE FIGURES OF NOTE, CURRENTLY--
DID YOU HEAR SOMETHING?
ALL I HEAR IS THE WINDS OF YOUR IDIOCY RUSHING PAST MY EARS AS WE CONTINUE TO TUMBLE DOWN THIS ENDLESS SPIRE OF DARK--
A VOICE? A VOICE IN THE VOID?

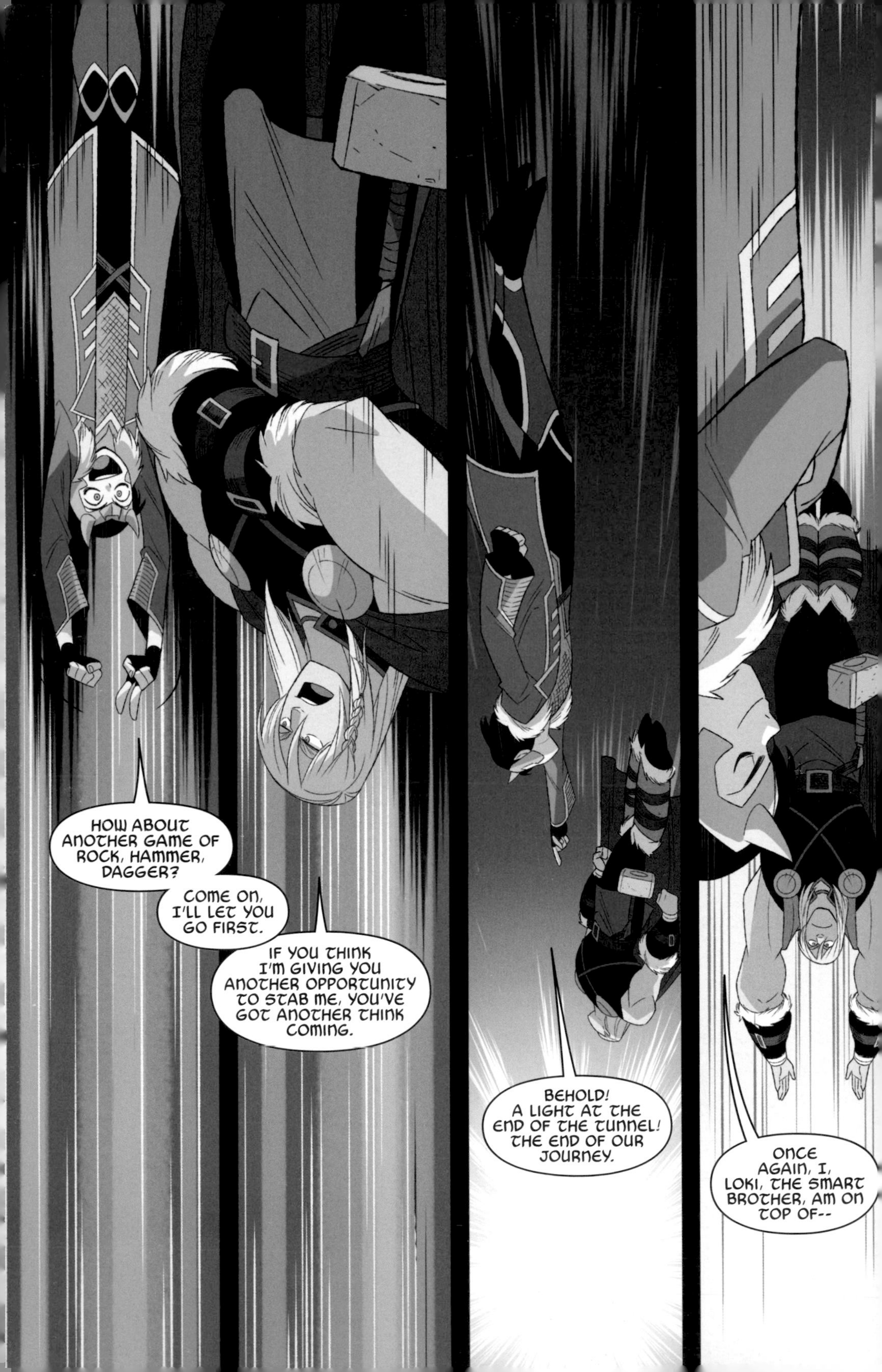
HOW ABOUT ANOTHER GAME OF ROCK, HAMMER, DAGGER?
COME ON, I'LL LET YOU GO FIRST.
IF YOU THINK I'M GIVING YOU ANOTHER OPPORTUNITY TO STAB ME, YOU'VE GOT ANOTHER THINK COMING.
BEHOLD! A LIGHT AT THE END OF THE TUNNEL! THE END OF OUR JOURNEY.
ONCE AGAIN, I, LOKI, THE SMART BROTHER, AM ON TOP OF--

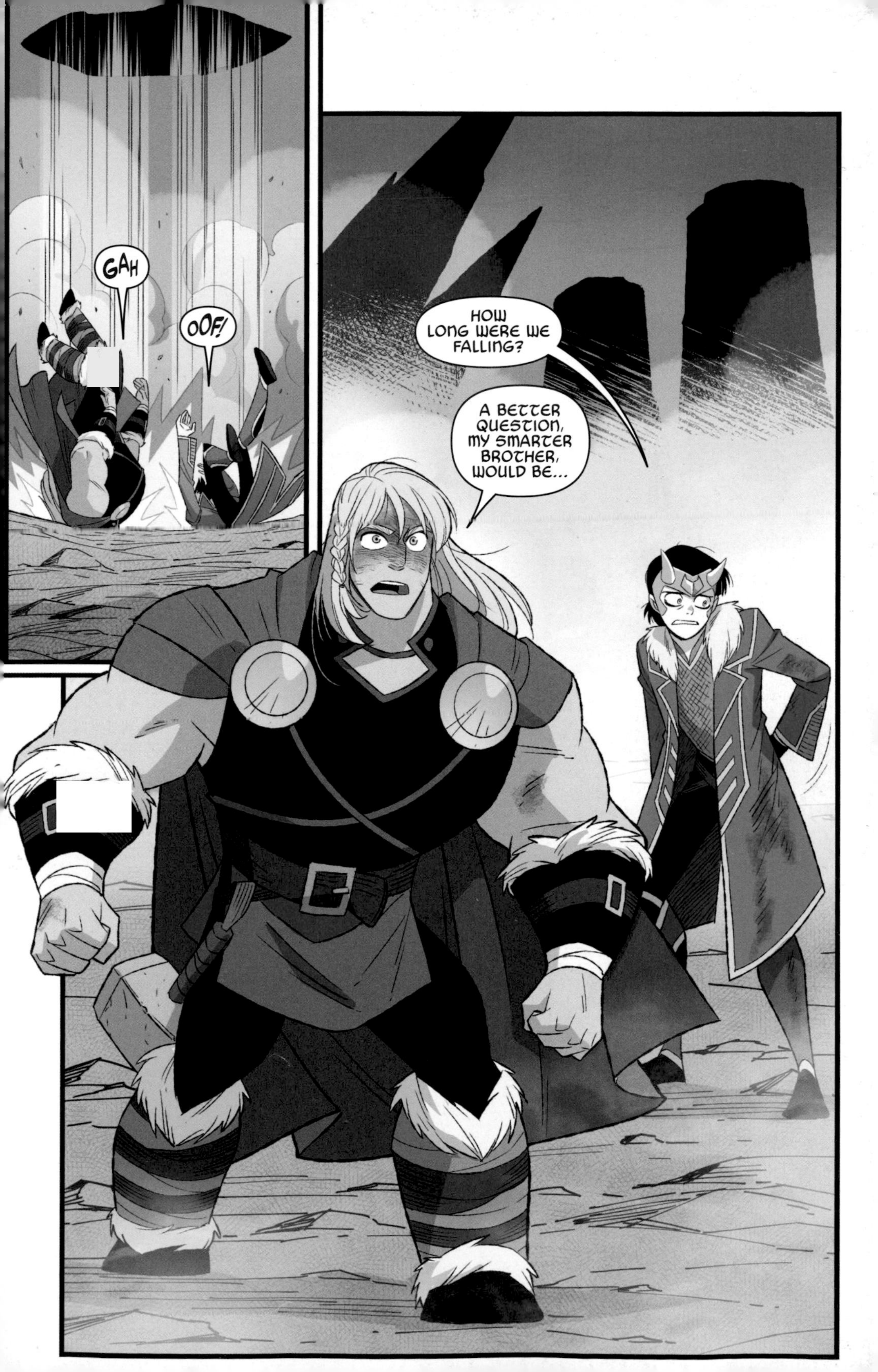
GAH
OOF!
HOW LONG WERE WE FALLING?
A BETTER QUESTION, MY SMARTER BROTHER, WOULD BE...

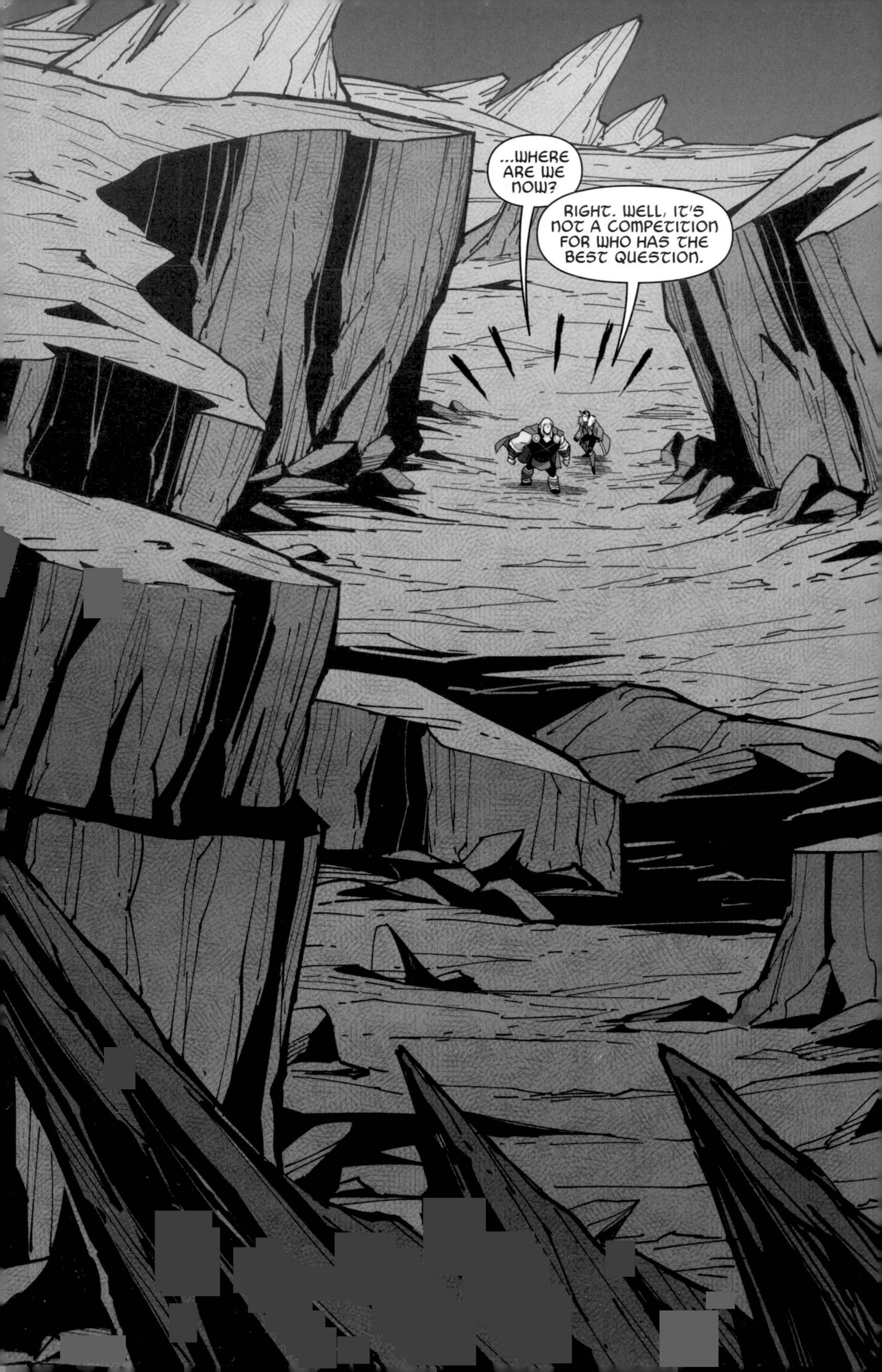
...WHERE ARE WE NOW?
RIGHT. WELL, IT'S NOT A COMPETITION FOR WHO HAS THE BEST QUESTION.

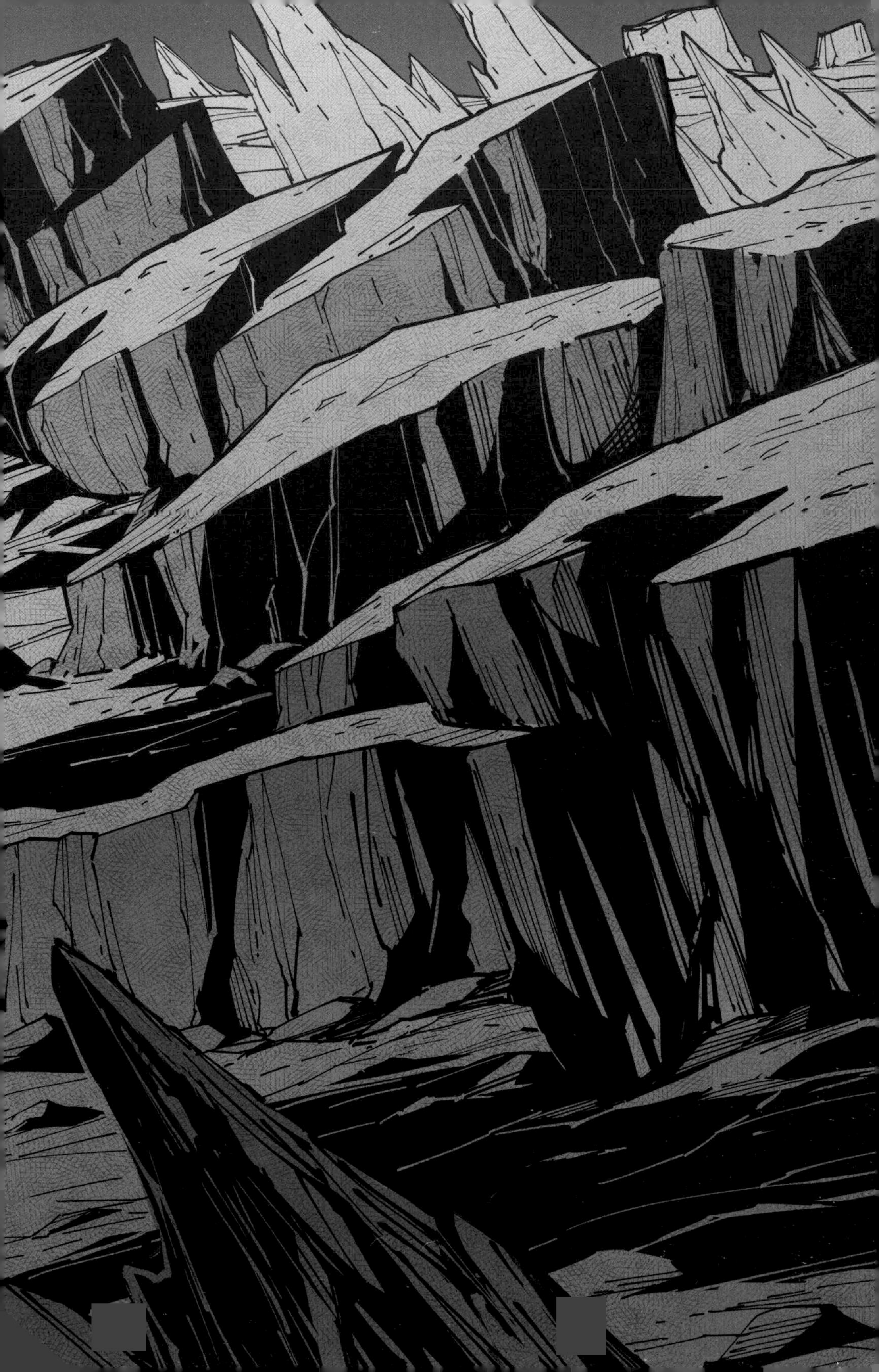

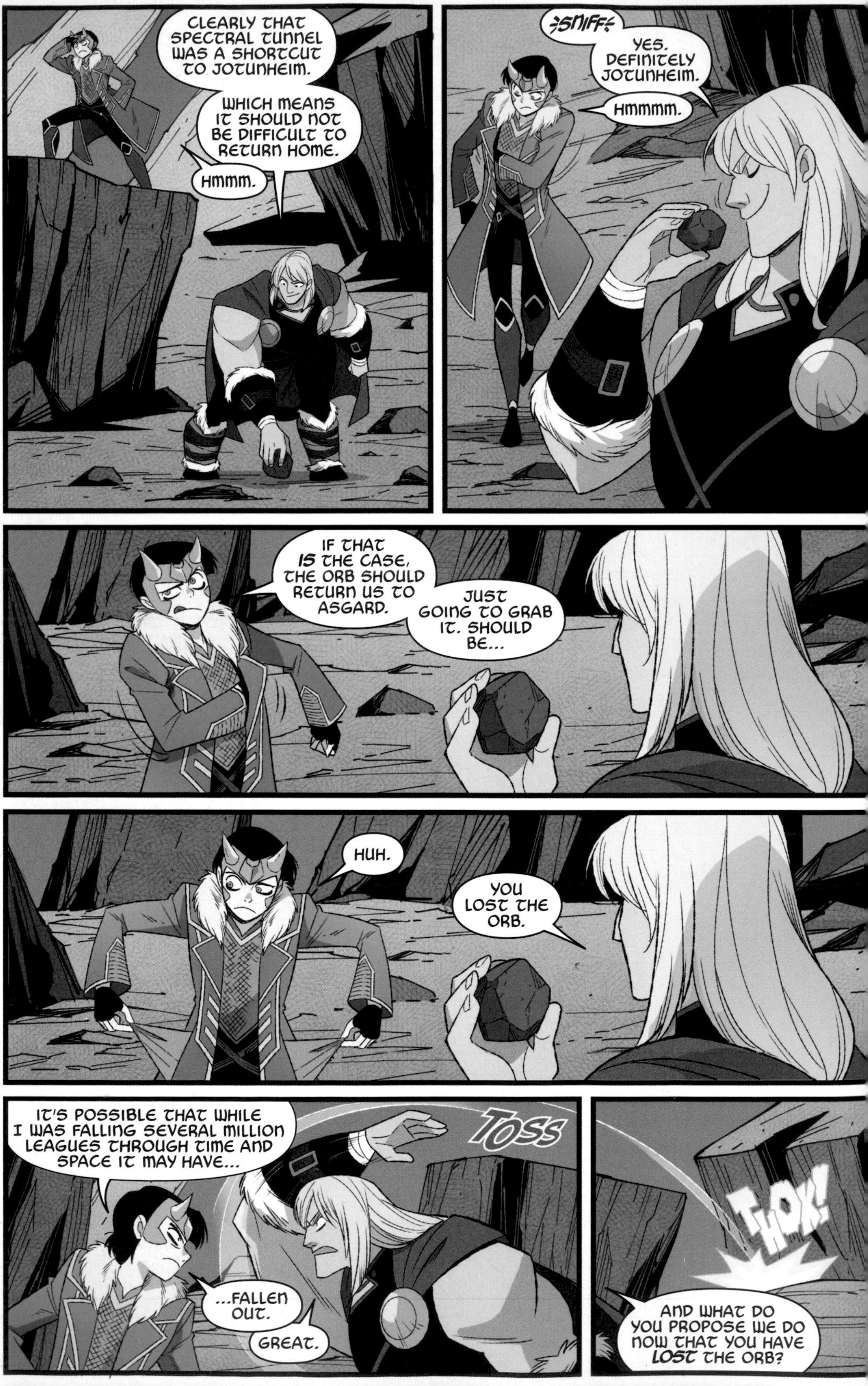
CLEARLY THAT SPECTRAL TUNNEL WAS A SHORTCUT TO JOTUNHEIM.
WHICH MEANS IT SHOULD NOT BE DIFFICULT TO RETURN HOME.
HMMM.
SNIFF
YES. DEFINITELY JOTUNHEIM.
HMMMM.
IF THAT IS THE CASE, THE ORB SHOULD RETURN US TO ASGARD.
JUST GOING TO GRAB IT. SHOULD BE...
HUH.
YOU LOST THE ORB.
IT'S POSSIBLE THAT WHILE I WAS FALLING SEVERAL MILLION LEAGUES THROUGH TIME AND SPACE IT MAY HAVE...
TOSS
...FALLEN OUT.
GREAT.
THOK!
AND WHAT DO YOU PROPOSE WE DO NOW THAT YOU HAVE LOST THE ORB?

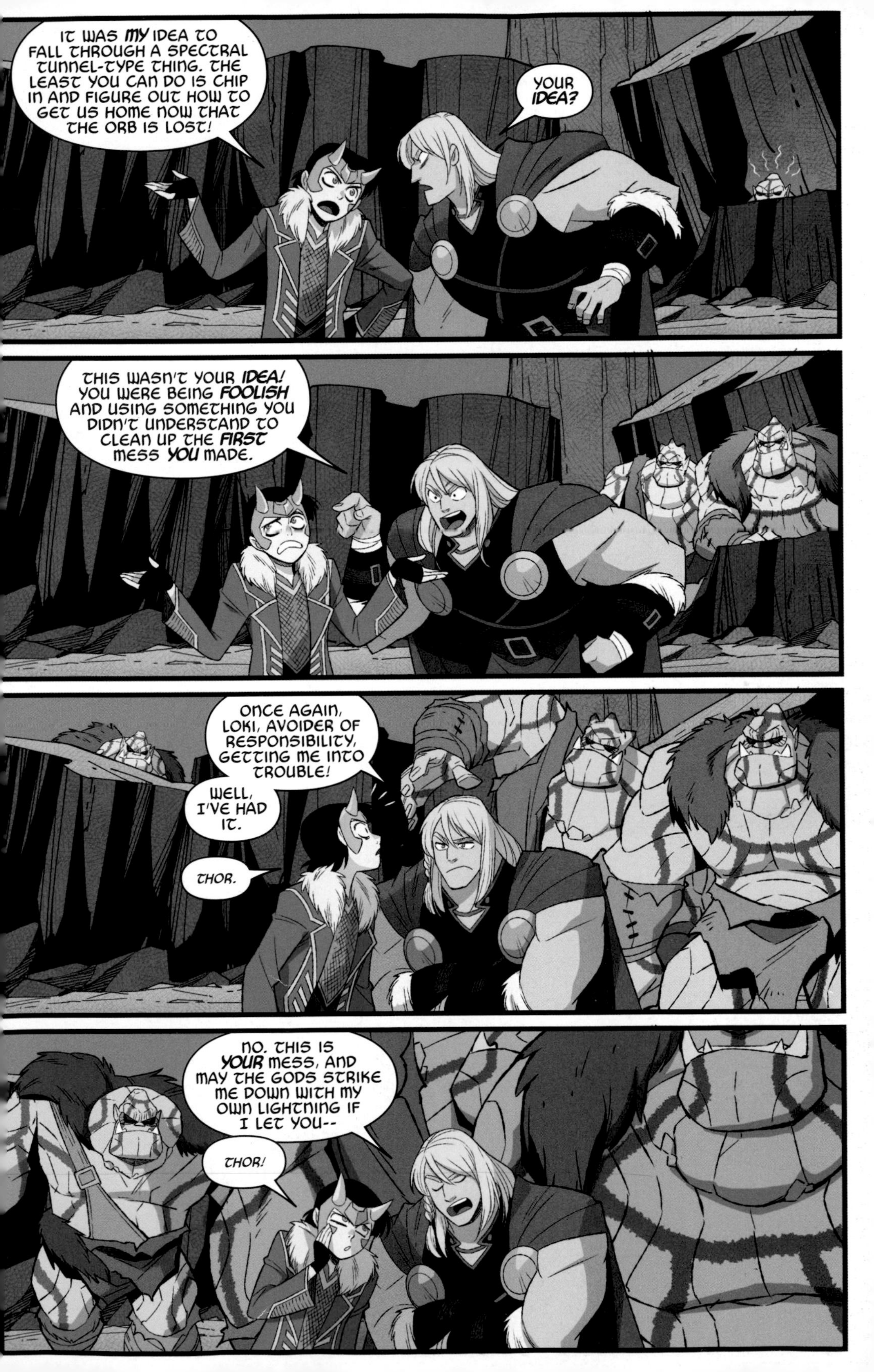
IT WAS MY IDEA TO FALL THROUGH A SPECTRAL TUNNEL-TYPE THING. THE LEAST YOU CAN DO IS CHIP IN AND FIGURE OUT HOW TO GET US HOME NOW THAT THE ORB IS LOST!
YOUR IDEA?
THIS WASN'T YOUR IDEA! YOU WERE BEING FOOLISH AND USING SOMETHING YOU DIDN'T UNDERSTAND TO CLEAN UP THE FIRST MESS YOU MADE.
ONCE AGAIN, LOKI, AVOIDER OF RESPONSIBILITY, GETTING ME INTO TROUBLE!
WELL, I'VE HAD IT.
THOR.
NO. THIS IS YOUR MESS, AND MAY THE GODS STRIKE ME DOWN WITH MY OWN LIGHTNING IF I LET YOU--
THOR!

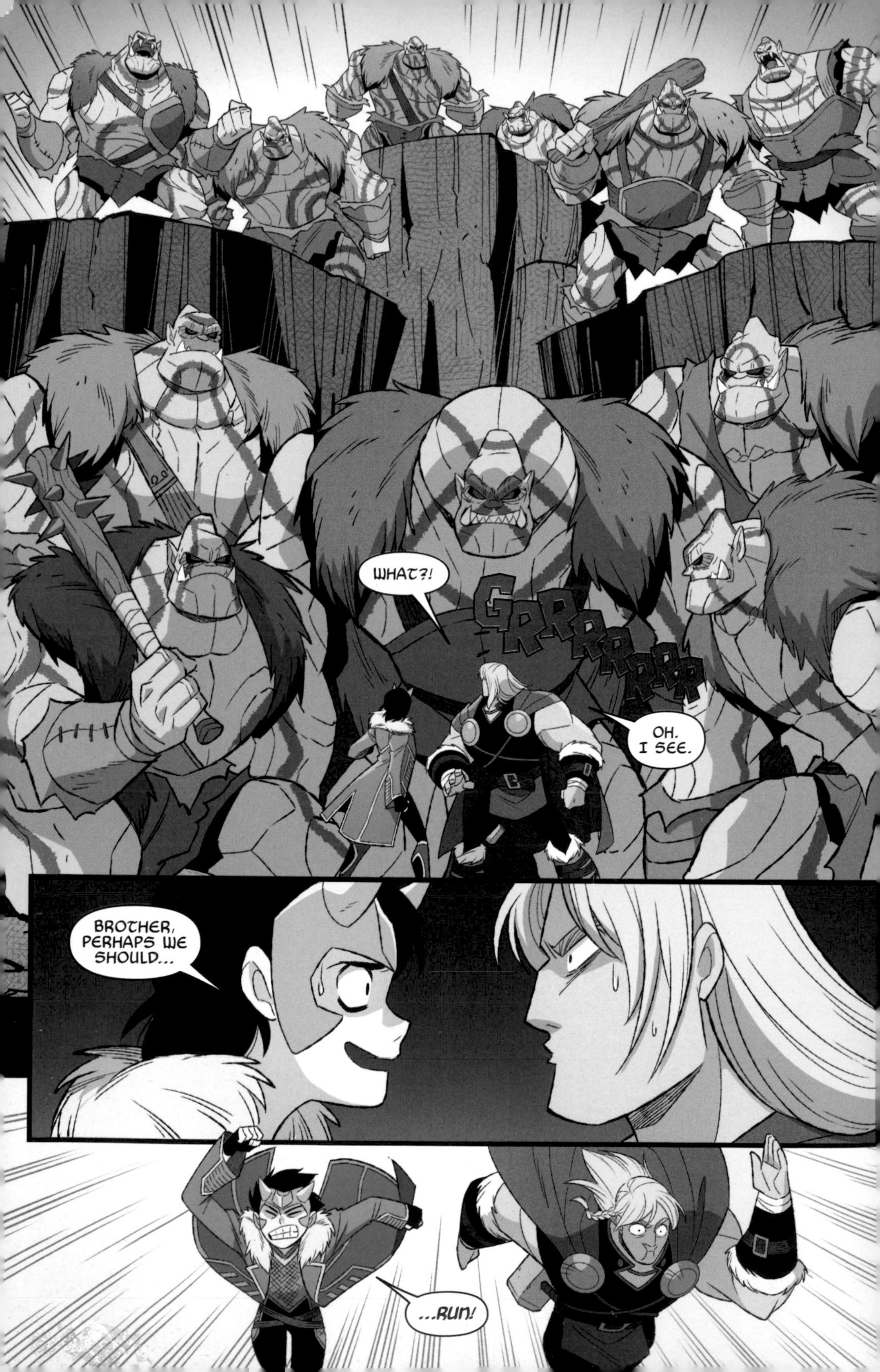
WHAT?!
GRRRRRRRR
OH. I SEE.
BROTHER, PERHAPS WE SHOULD...
...RUN!

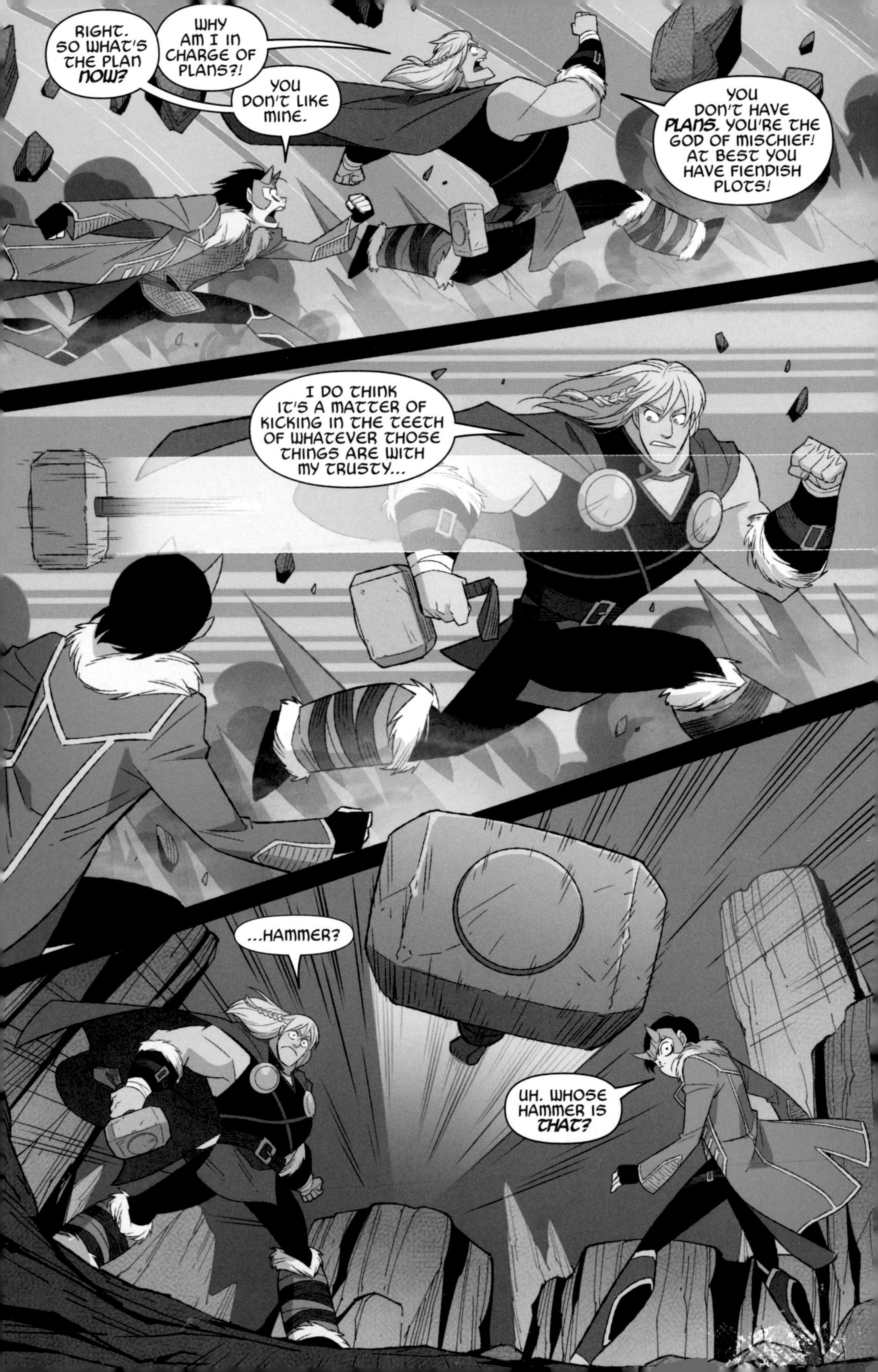
RIGHT. SO WHAT'S THE PLAN *NOW?*
WHY AM I IN CHARGE OF PLANS?!
YOU DON'T LIKE MINE.
YOU DON'T HAVE **PLANS.** YOU'RE THE GOD OF MISCHIEF! AT BEST YOU HAVE FIENDISH PLOTS!
I DO THINK IT'S A MATTER OF KICKING IN THE TEETH OF WHATEVER THOSE THINGS ARE WITH MY TRUSTY...
...HAMMER?
UH. WHOSE HAMMER IS *THAT?*

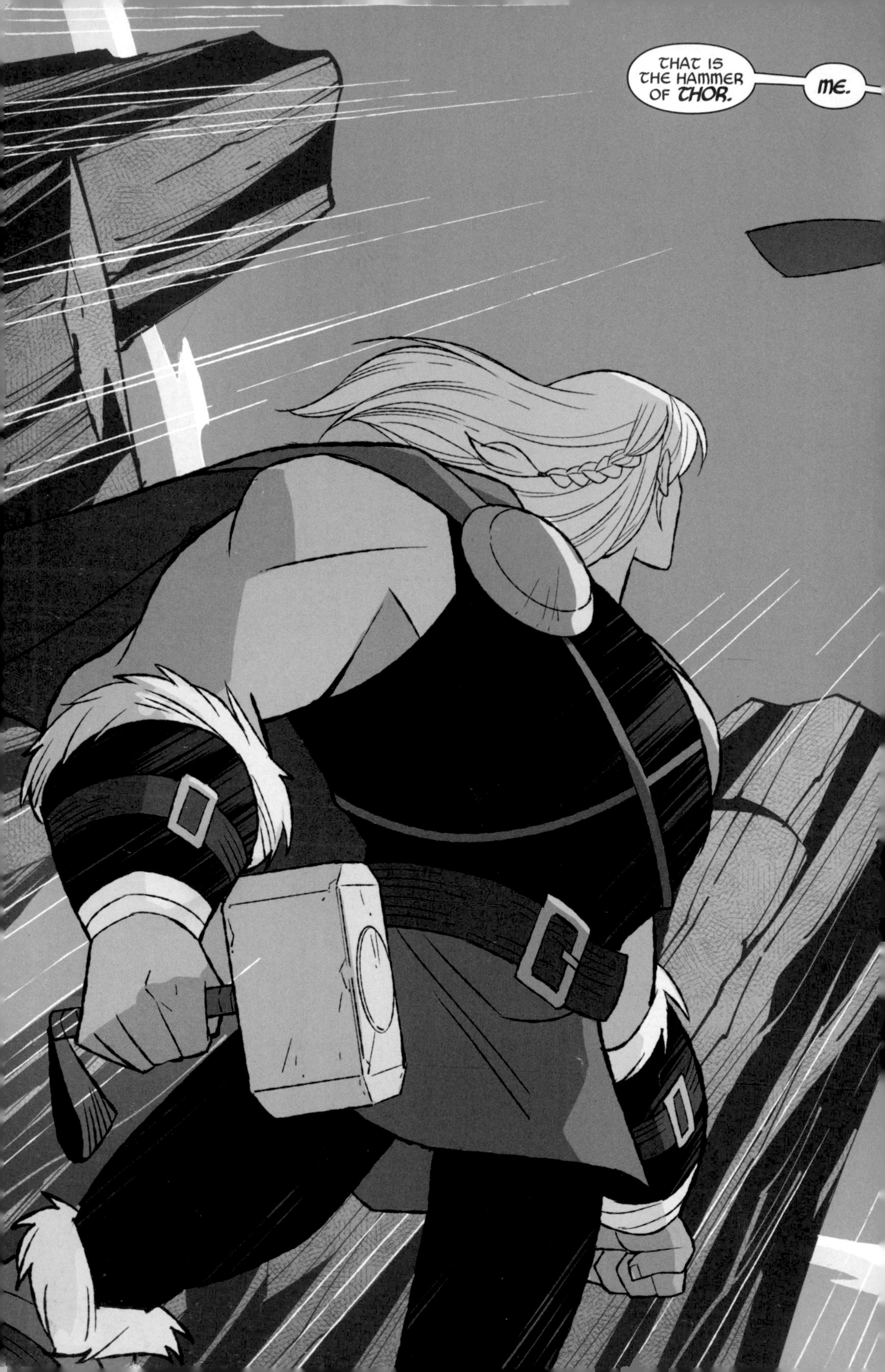
THAT IS THE HAMMER OF THOR.
ME.

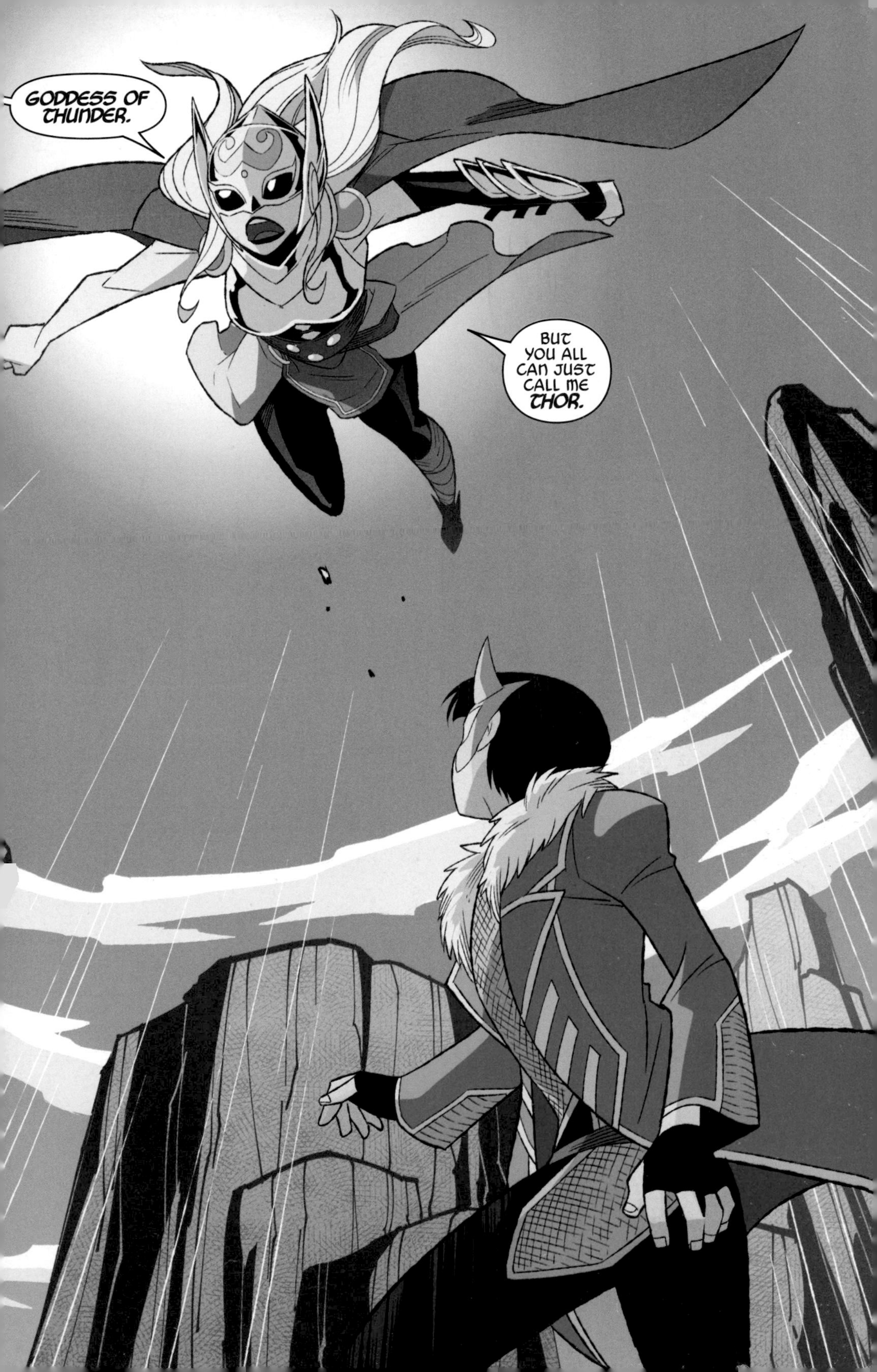
GODDESS OF THUNDER.
BUT YOU ALL CAN JUST CALL ME THOR.

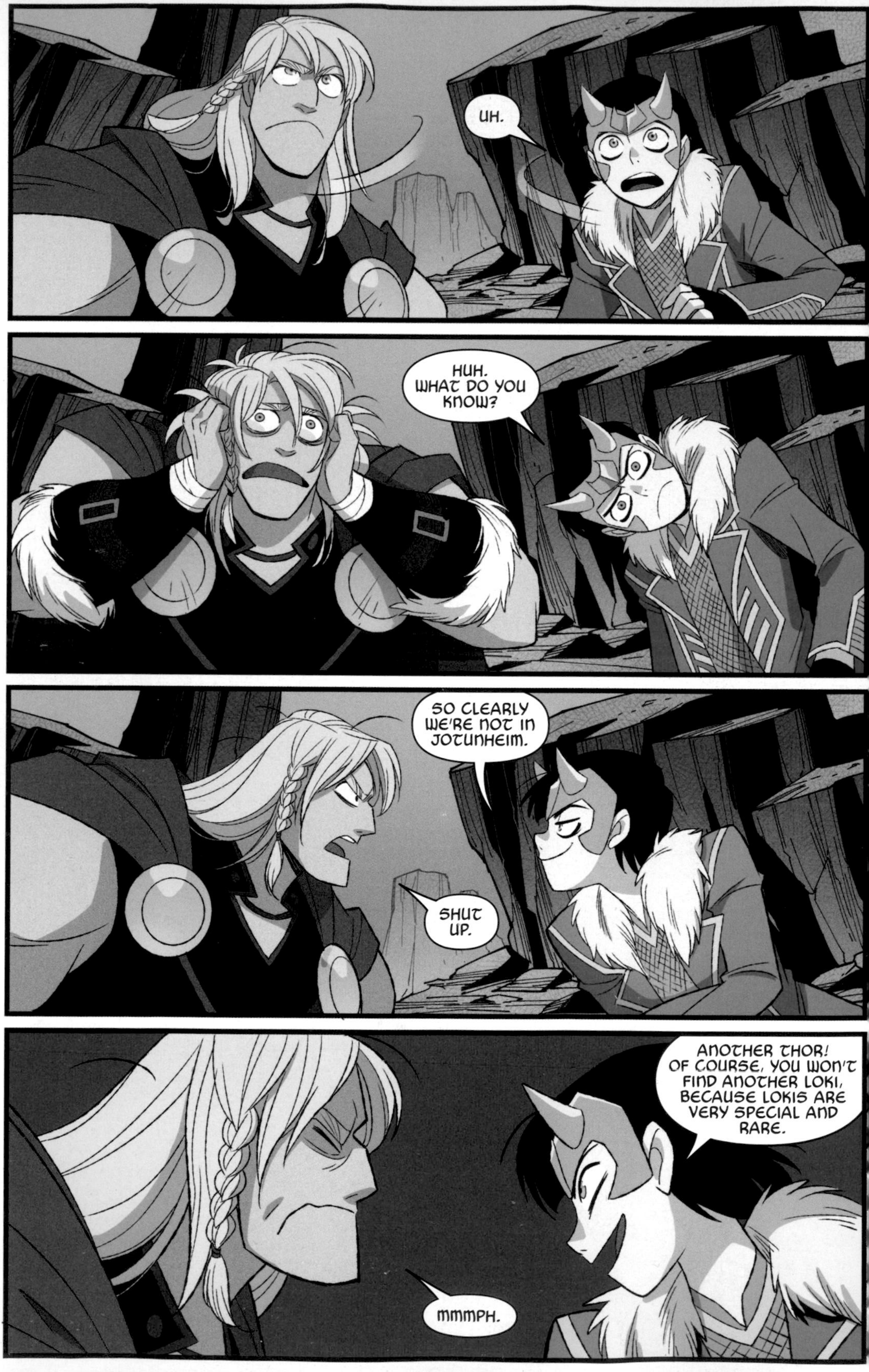
UH.
HUH. WHAT DO YOU KNOW?
SO CLEARLY WE'RE NOT IN JOTUNHEIM.
SHUT UP.
ANOTHER THOR! OF COURSE, YOU WON'T FIND ANOTHER LOKI, BECAUSE LOKIS ARE VERY SPECIAL AND RARE.
MMMPH.

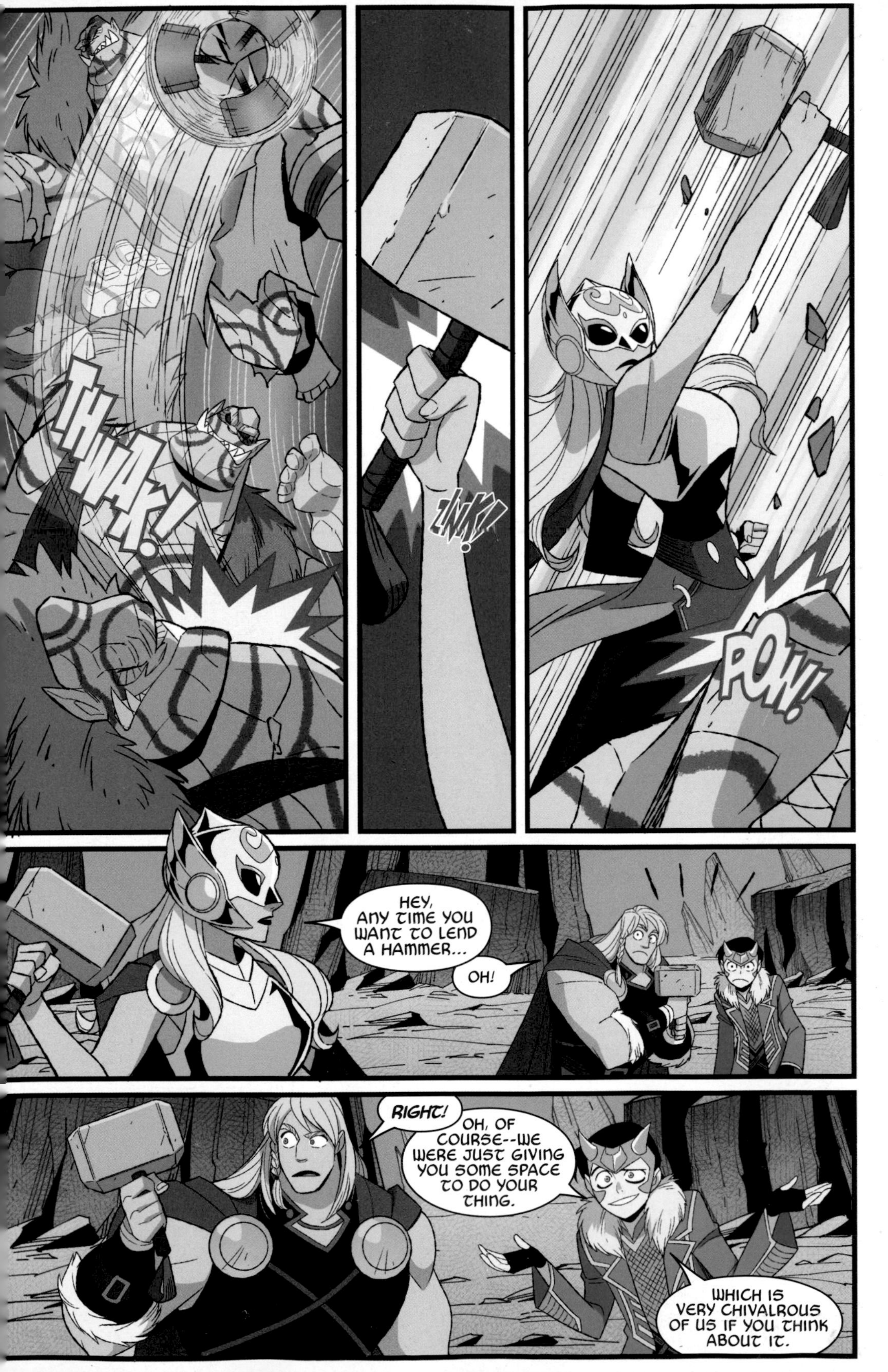
THWAK!!
ZNAK!!
POW!
HEY, ANY TIME YOU WANT TO LEND A HAMMER...
OH!
RIGHT!
OH, OF COURSE--WE WERE JUST GIVING YOU SOME SPACE TO DO YOUR THING.
WHICH IS VERY CHIVALROUS OF US IF YOU THINK ABOUT IT.

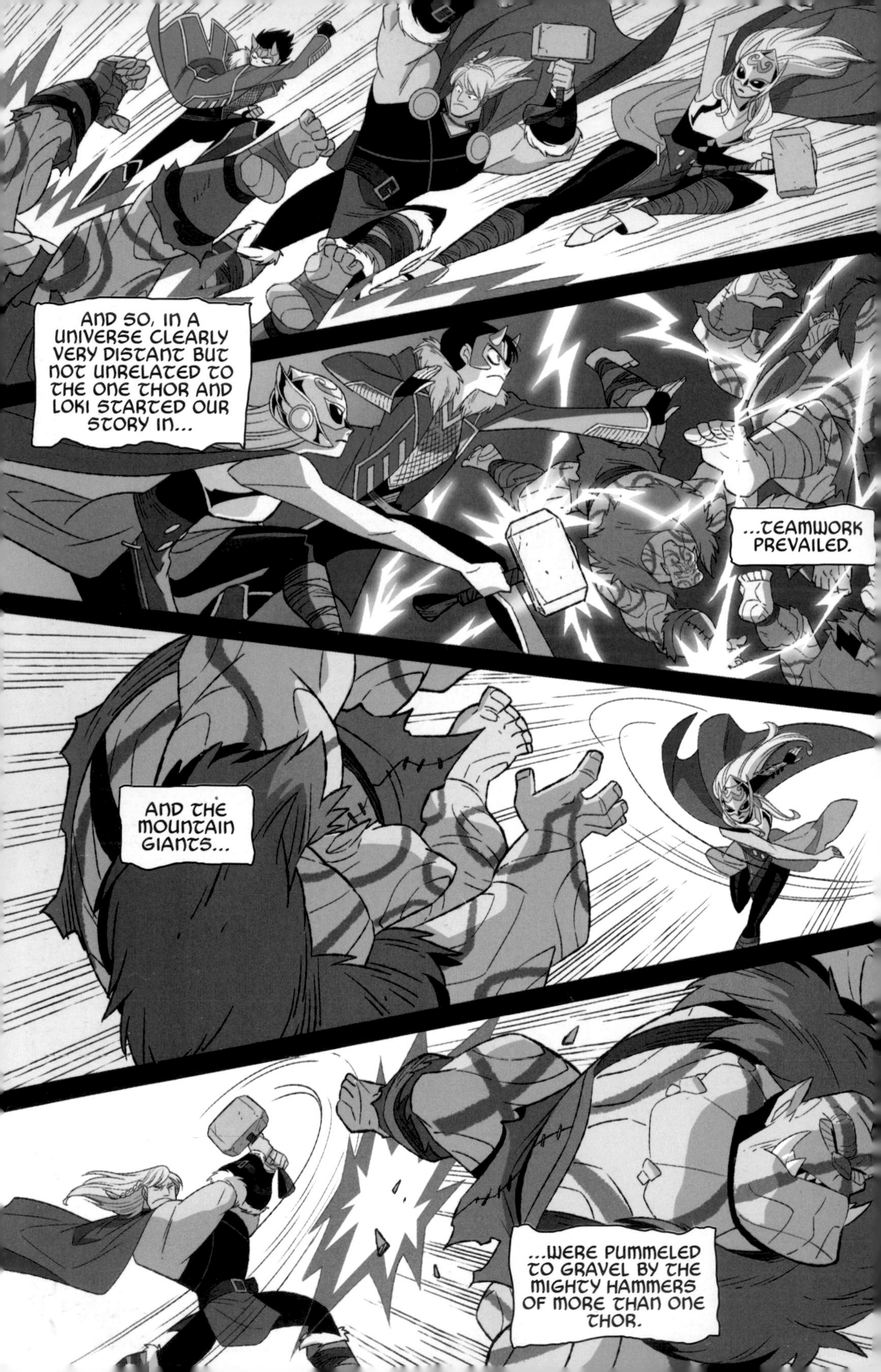
AND SO, IN A UNIVERSE CLEARLY VERY DISTANT BUT NOT UNRELATED TO THE ONE THOR AND LOKI STARTED OUR STORY IN...
...TEAMWORK PREVAILED.
AND THE MOUNTAIN GIANTS...
...WERE PUMMELED TO GRAVEL BY THE MIGHTY HAMMERS OF MORE THAN ONE THOR.

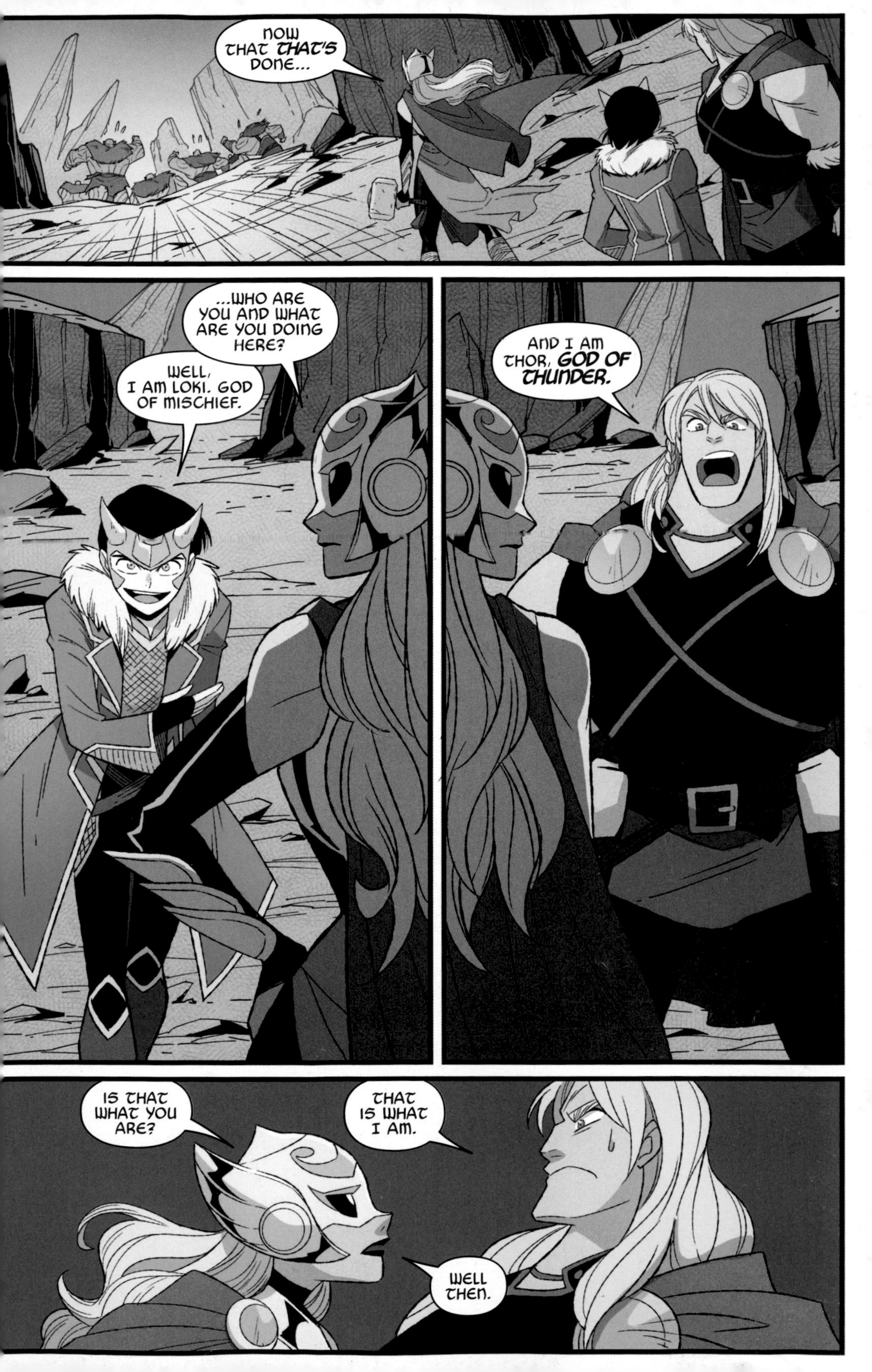
NOW THAT THAT'S DONE...
...WHO ARE YOU AND WHAT ARE YOU DOING HERE?
WELL, I AM LOKI. GOD OF MISCHIEF.
AND I AM THOR, GOD OF THUNDER.
IS THAT WHAT YOU ARE?
THAT IS WHAT I AM.
WELL THEN.

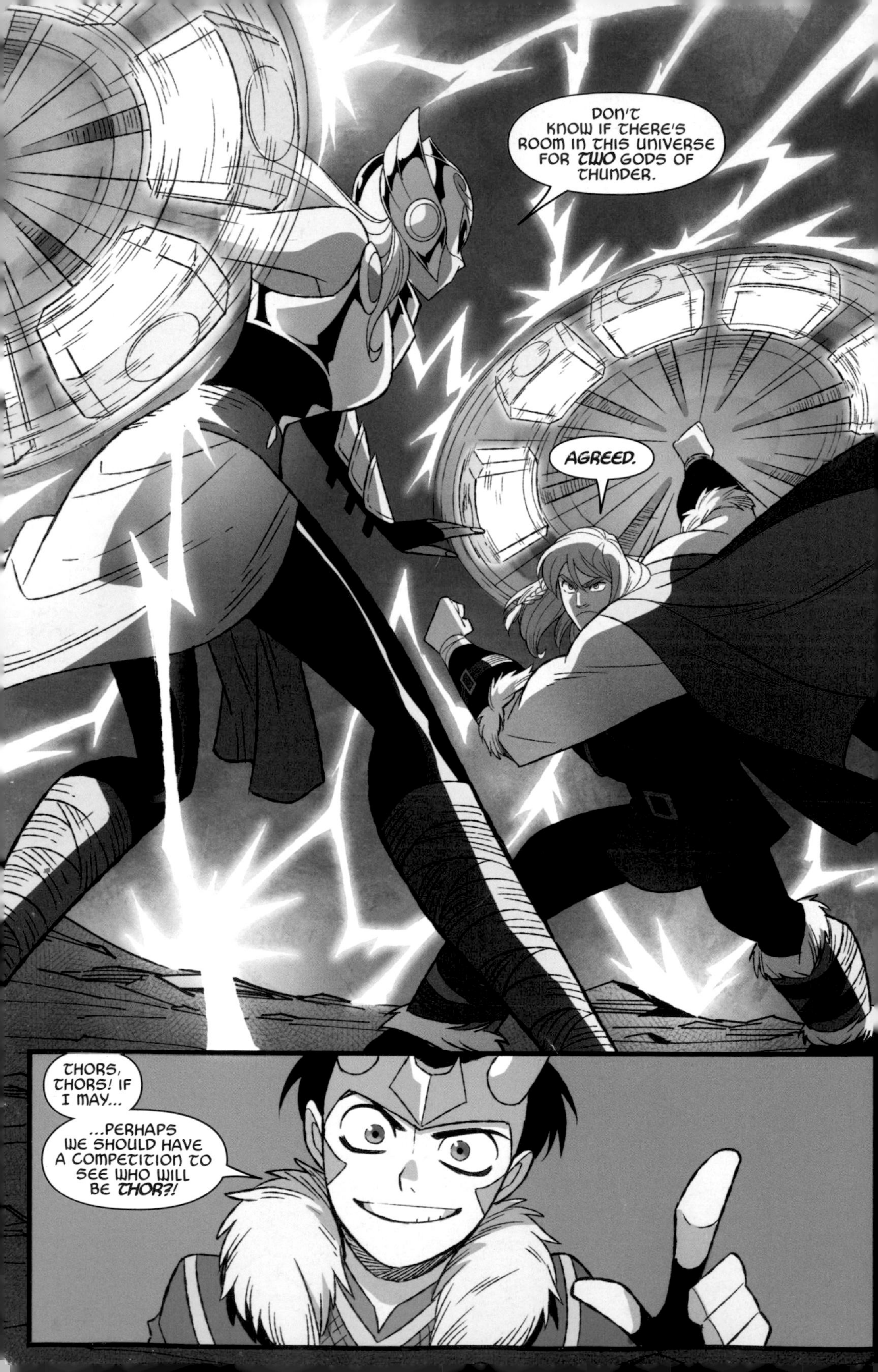
DON'T KNOW IF THERE'S ROOM IN THIS UNIVERSE FOR *TWO* GODS OF THUNDER.
AGREED.
THORS, THORS! IF I MAY...
...PERHAPS WE SHOULD HAVE A COMPETITION TO SEE WHO WILL BE *THOR?!*

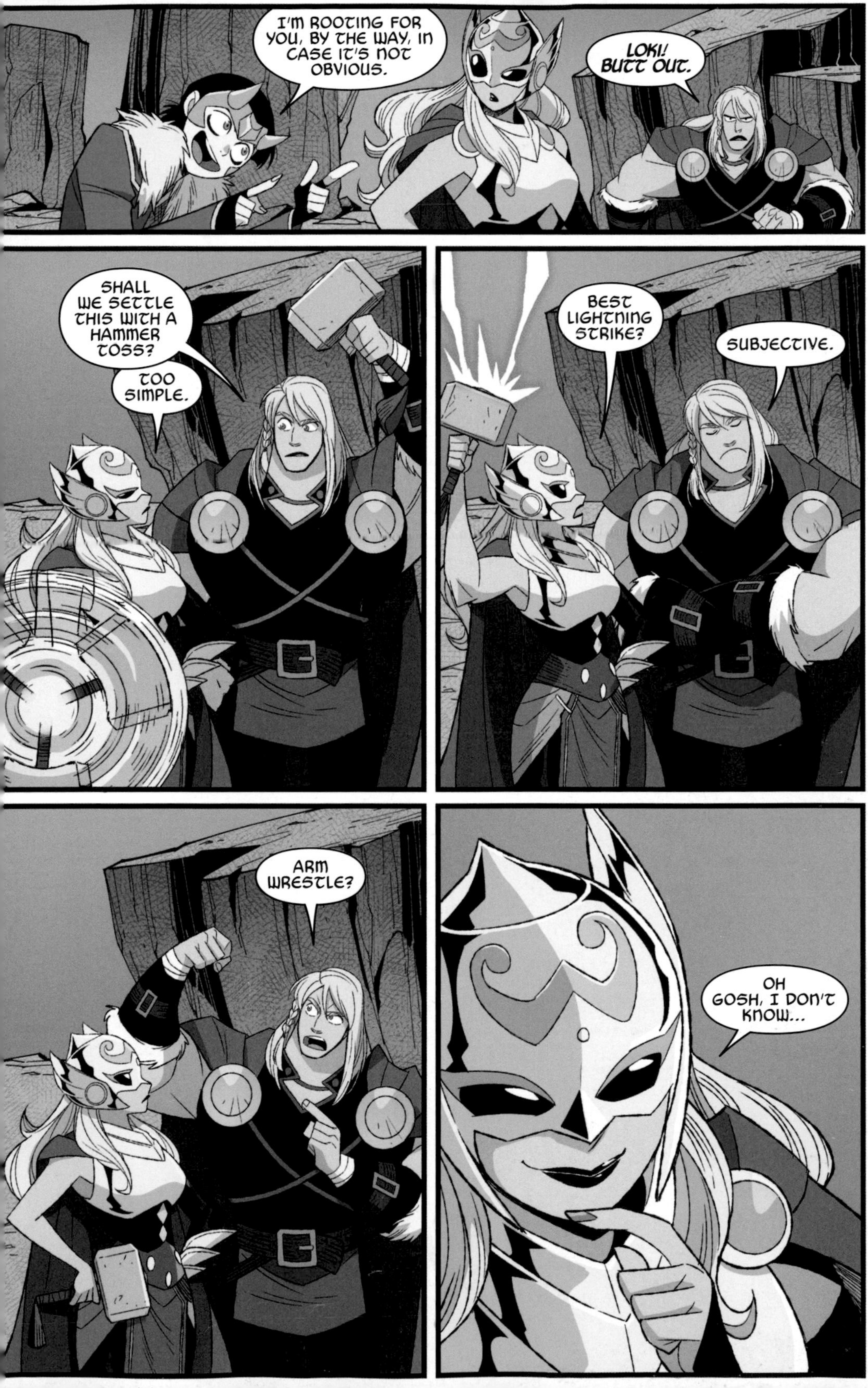

I'M ROOTING FOR YOU, BY THE WAY, IN CASE IT'S NOT OBVIOUS.
LOKI! BUTT OUT.
SHALL WE SETTLE THIS WITH A HAMMER TOSS?
TOO SIMPLE.
BEST LIGHTNING STRIKE?
SUBJECTIVE.
ARM WRESTLE?
OH GOSH, I DON'T KNOW...

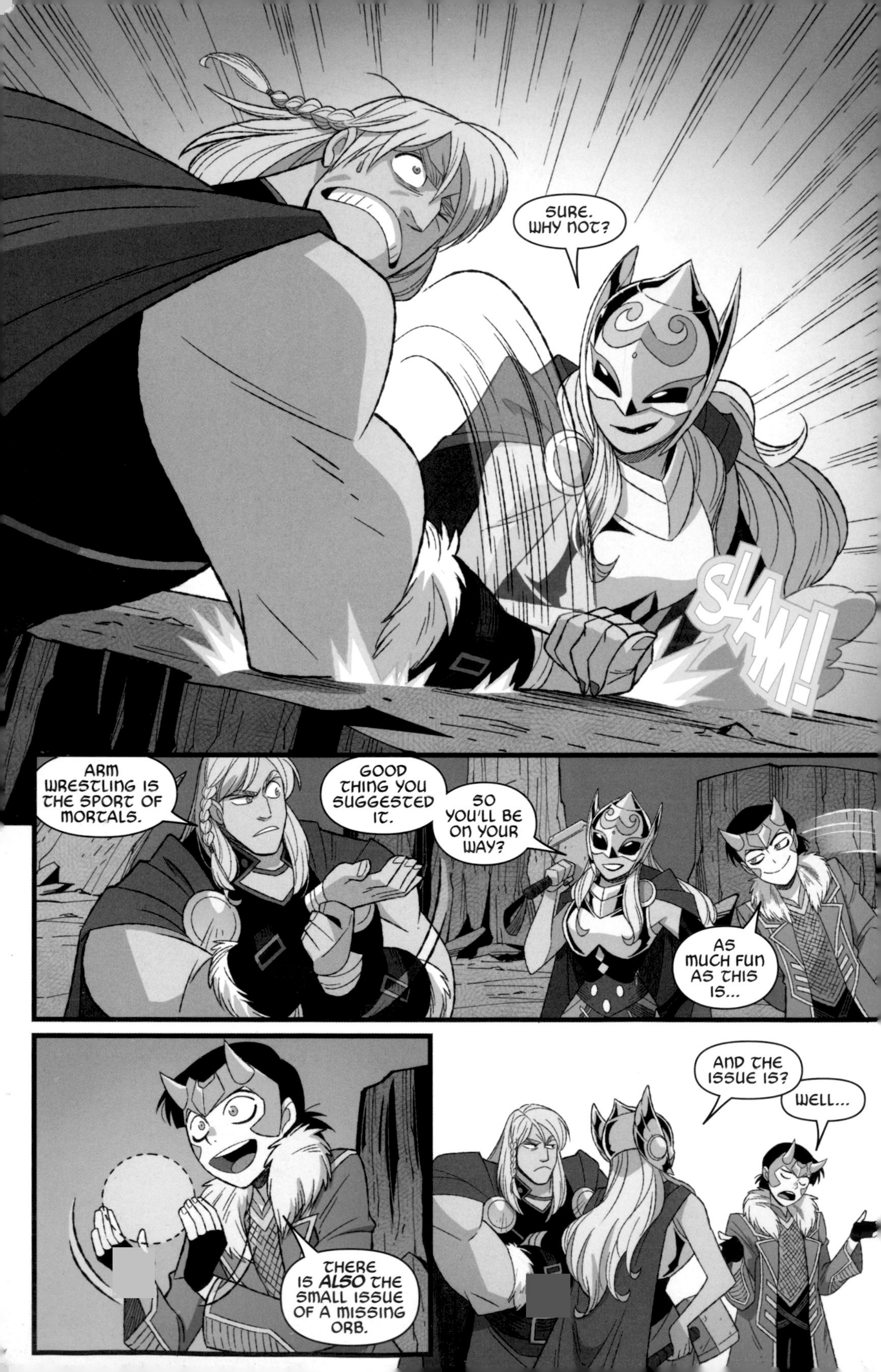
SURE. WHY NOT?
SLAM!
ARM WRESTLING IS THE SPORT OF MORTALS.
GOOD THING YOU SUGGESTED IT.
SO YOU'LL BE ON YOUR WAY?
AS MUCH FUN AS THIS IS...
THERE IS *ALSO* THE SMALL ISSUE OF A MISSING ORB.
AND THE ISSUE IS?
WELL...

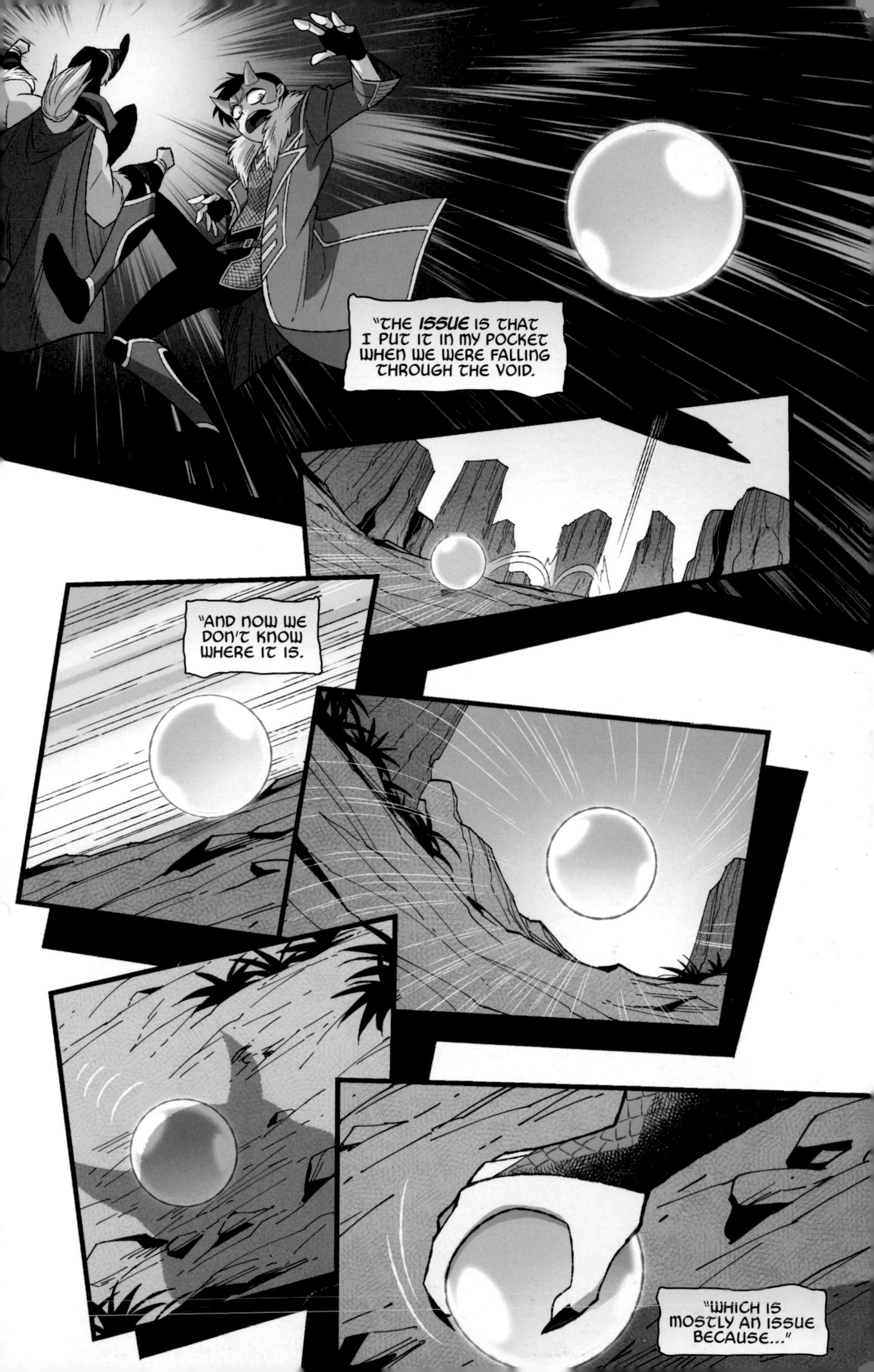
"THE ISSUE IS THAT I PUT IT IN MY POCKET WHEN WE WERE FALLING THROUGH THE VOID.
"AND NOW WE DON'T KNOW WHERE IT IS.
"WHICH IS MOSTLY AN ISSUE BECAUSE..."

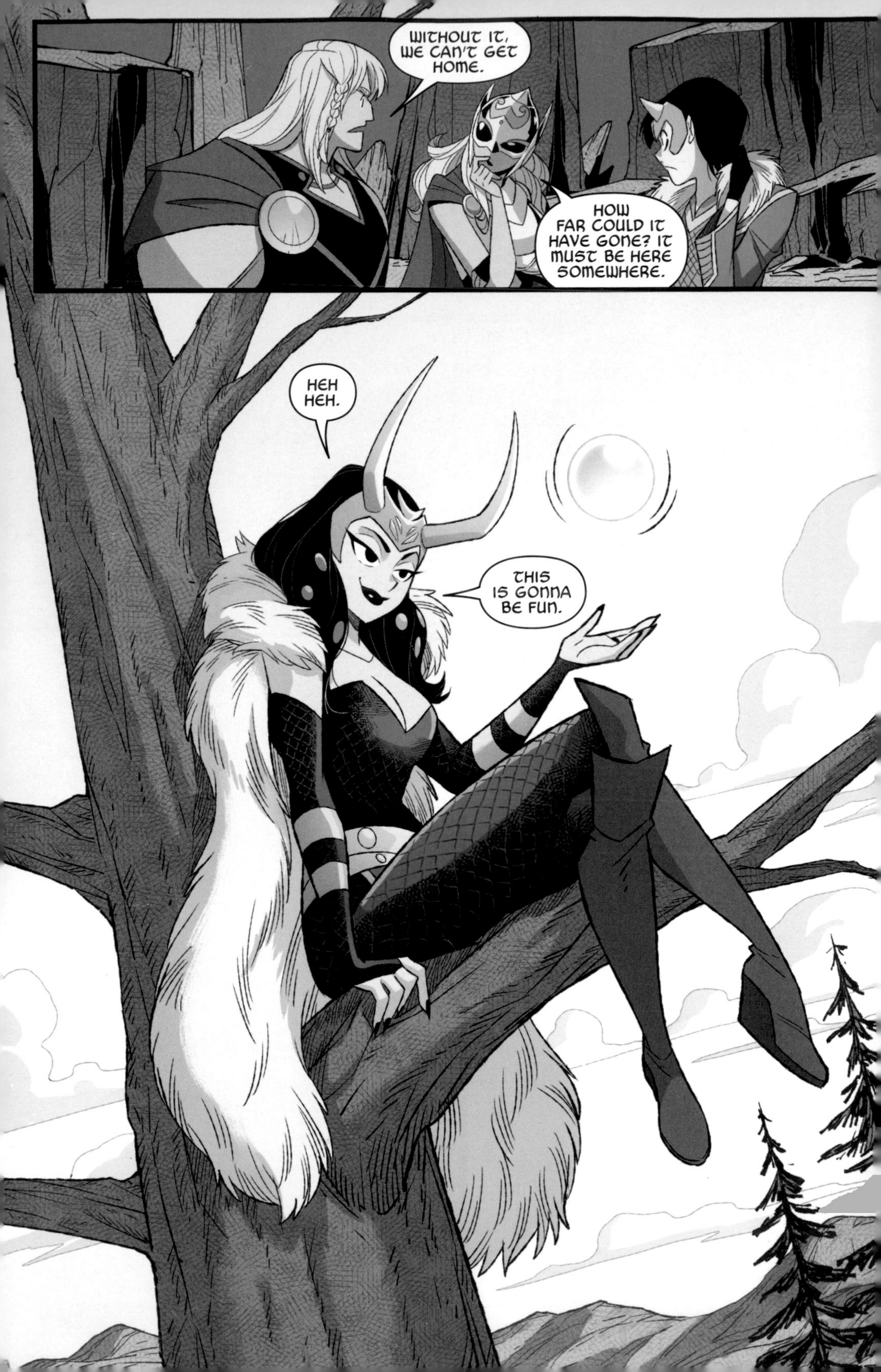
WITHOUT IT, WE CAN'T GET HOME.
HOW FAR COULD IT HAVE GONE? IT MUST BE HERE SOMEWHERE.
HEH HEH.
THIS IS GONNA BE FUN.

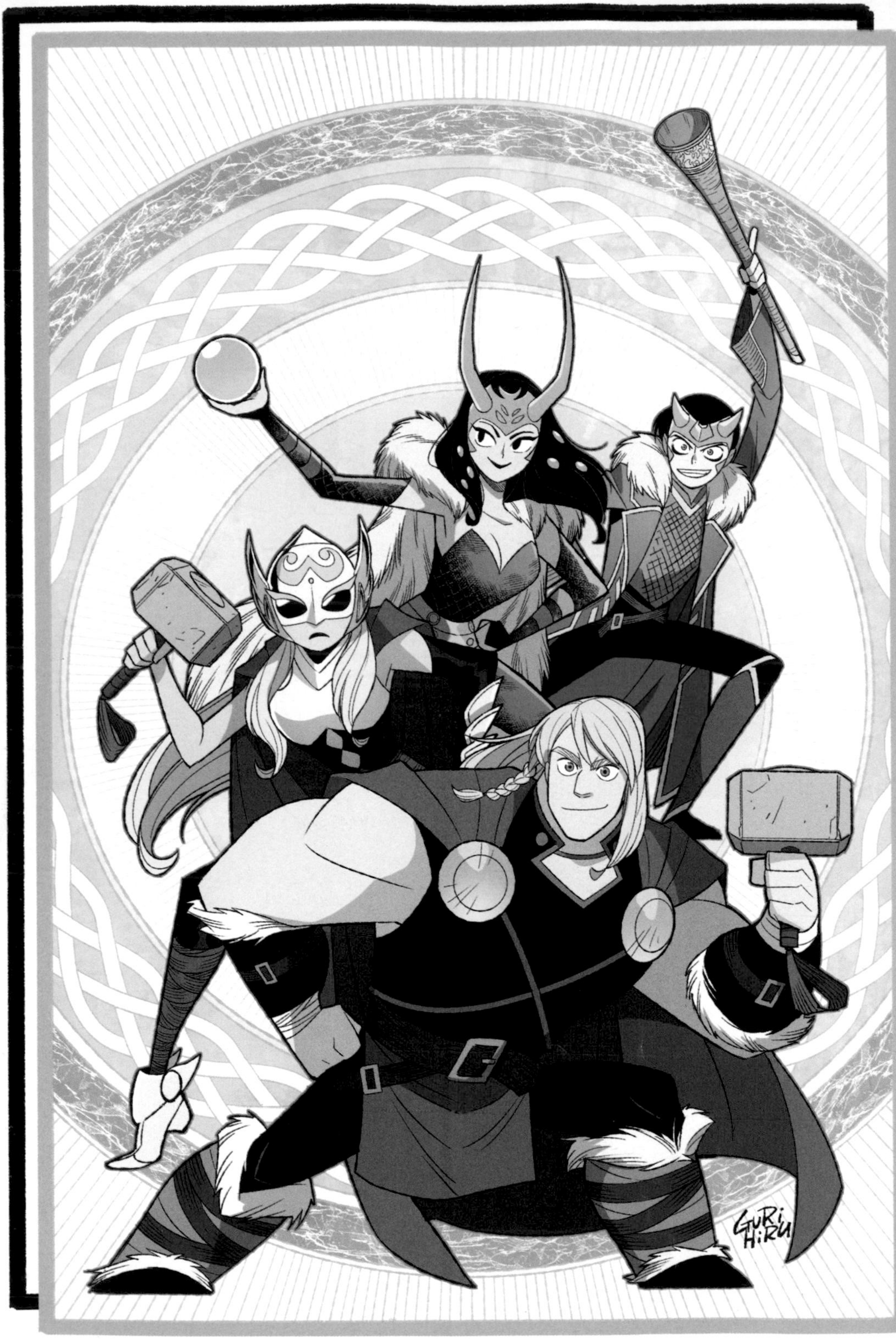
GURI HIRU

4

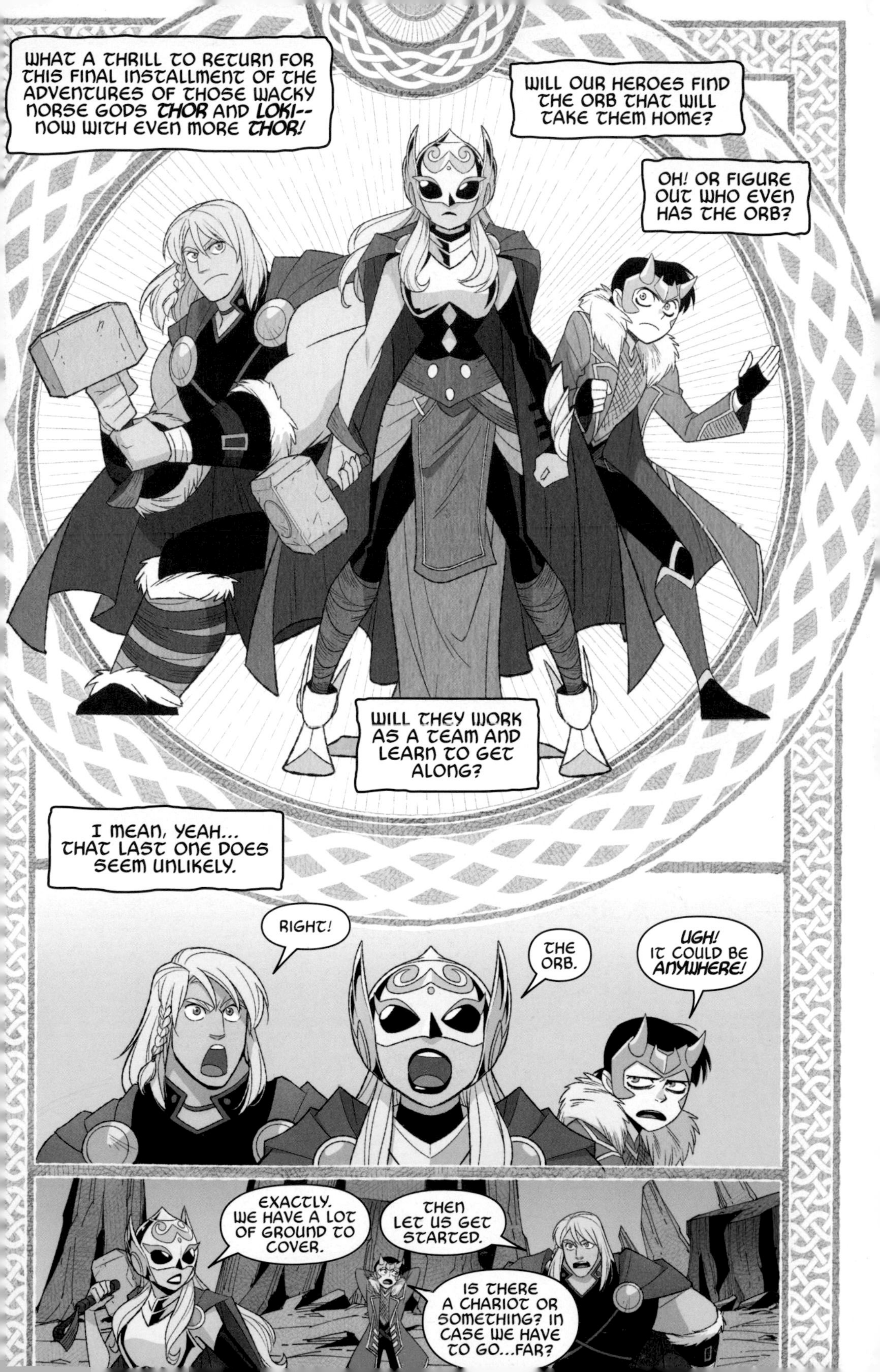

WHAT A THRILL TO RETURN FOR THIS FINAL INSTALLMENT OF THE ADVENTURES OF THOSE WACKY NORSE GODS THOR AND LOKI-- NOW WITH EVEN MORE THOR!
WILL OUR HEROES FIND THE ORB THAT WILL TAKE THEM HOME?
OH! OR FIGURE OUT WHO EVEN HAS THE ORB?
WILL THEY WORK AS A TEAM AND LEARN TO GET ALONG?
I MEAN, YEAH... THAT LAST ONE DOES SEEM UNLIKELY.
RIGHT!
THE ORB.
UGH! IT COULD BE ANYWHERE!
EXACTLY. WE HAVE A LOT OF GROUND TO COVER.
THEN LET US GET STARTED.
IS THERE A CHARIOT OR SOMETHING? IN CASE WE HAVE TO GO...FAR?

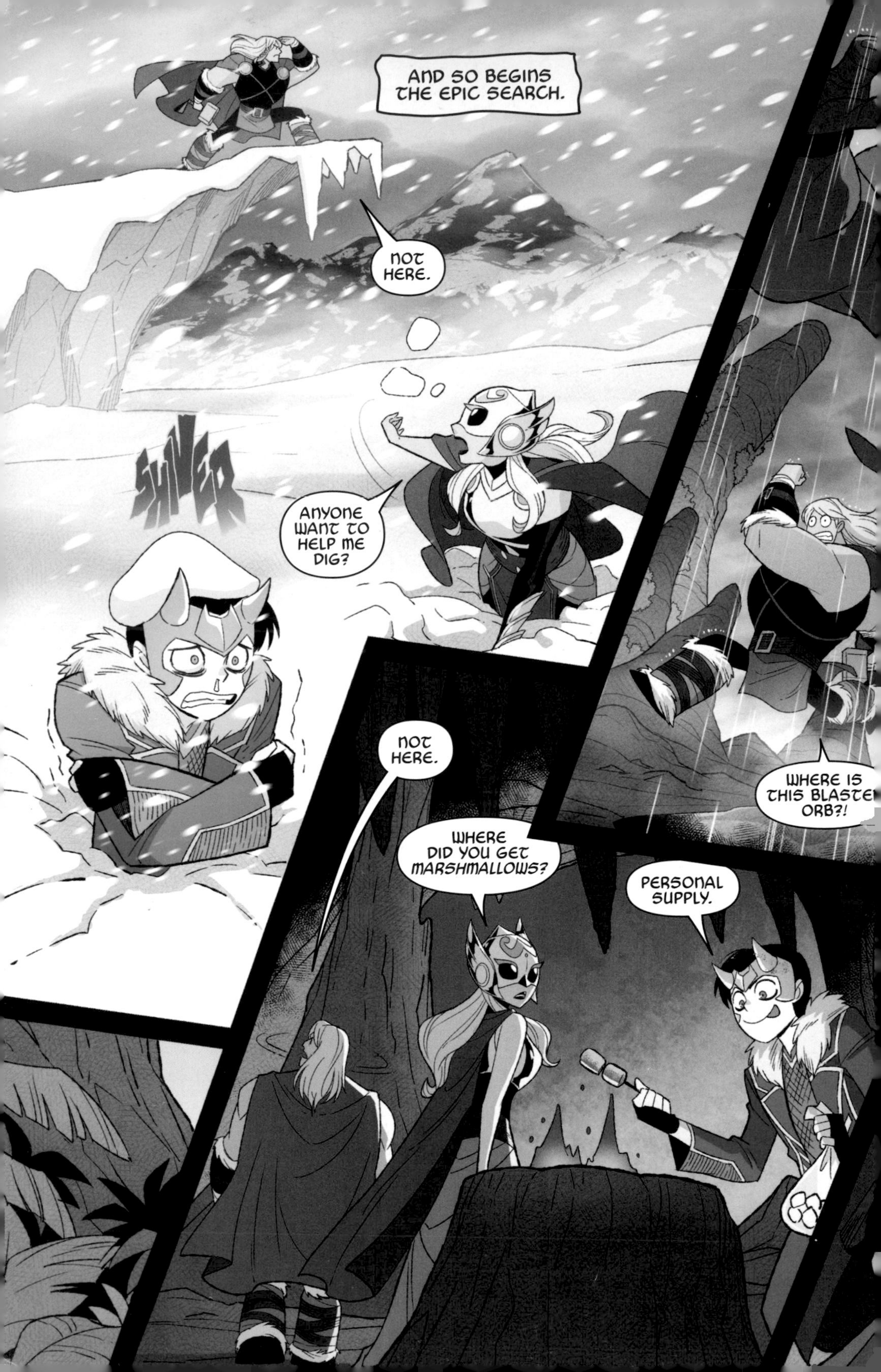
AND SO BEGINS THE EPIC SEARCH.
NOT HERE.
SHIVER
ANYONE WANT TO HELP ME DIG?
WHERE IS THIS BLASTE ORB?!
NOT HERE.
WHERE DID YOU GET MARSHMALLOWS?
PERSONAL SUPPLY.

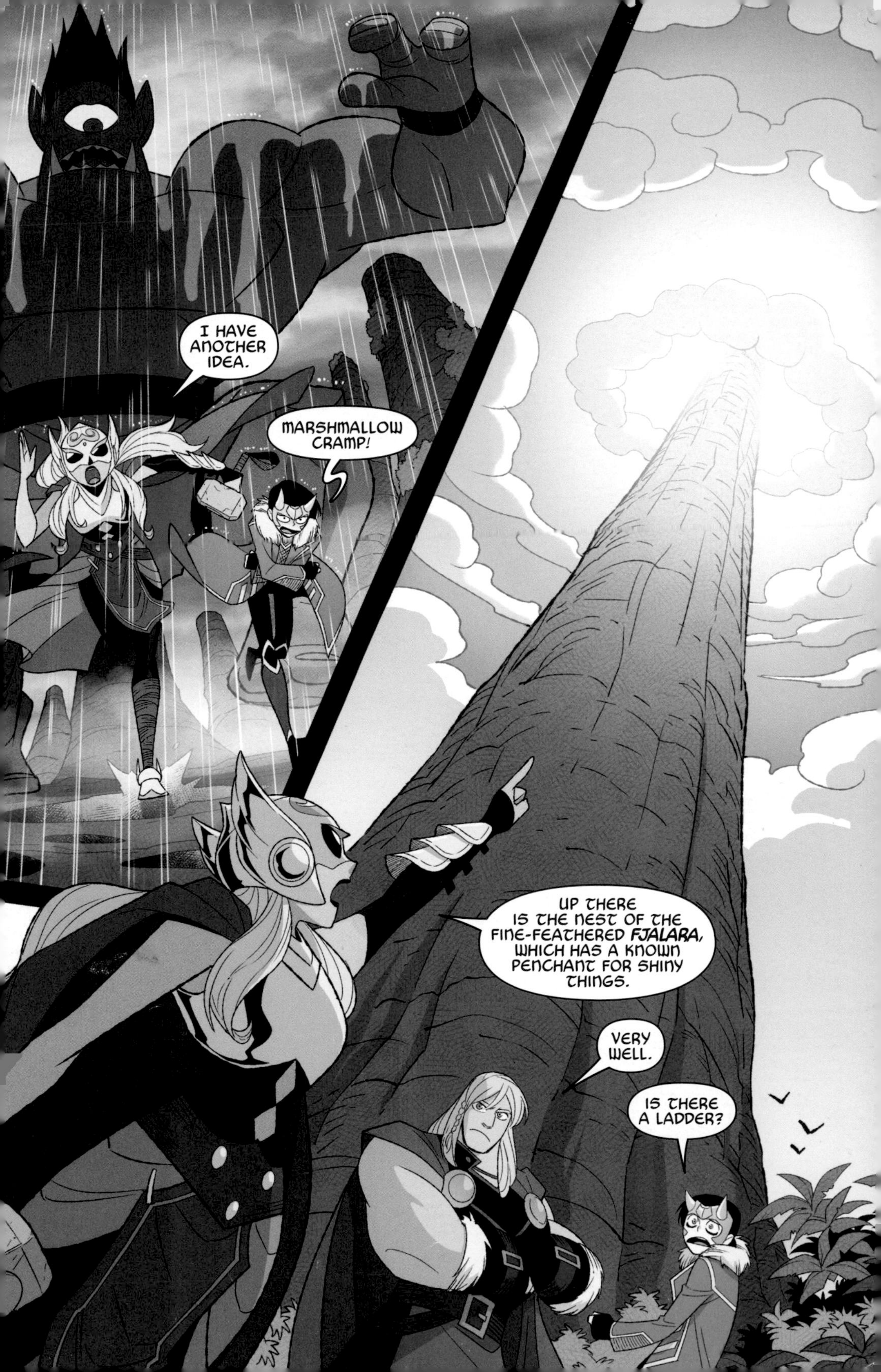
I HAVE ANOTHER IDEA.
MARSHMALLOW CRAMP!
UP THERE IS THE NEST OF THE FINE-FEATHERED FJALARA, WHICH HAS A KNOWN PENCHANT FOR SHINY THINGS.
VERY WELL.
IS THERE A LADDER?

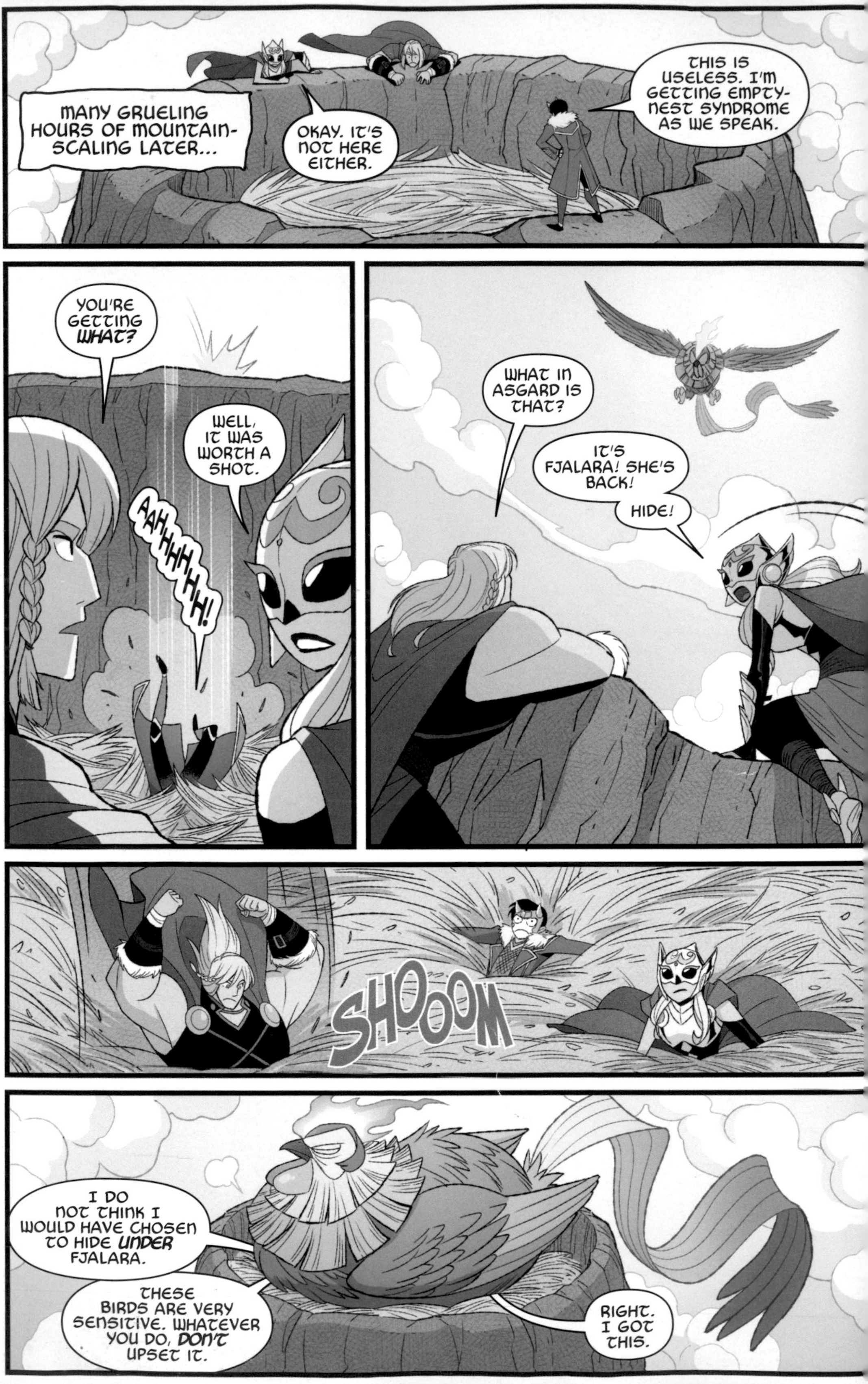

MANY GRUELING HOURS OF MOUNTAIN-SCALING LATER...
OKAY. IT'S NOT HERE EITHER.
THIS IS USELESS. I'M GETTING EMPTY-NEST SYNDROME AS WE SPEAK.
YOU'RE GETTING WHAT?
WELL, IT WAS WORTH A SHOT.
AAHHHHHHH!
WHAT IN ASGARD IS THAT?
IT'S FJALARA! SHE'S BACK!
HIDE!
SHOOOM
I DO NOT THINK I WOULD HAVE CHOSEN TO HIDE UNDER FJALARA.
THESE BIRDS ARE VERY SENSITIVE. WHATEVER YOU DO, DON'T UPSET IT.
RIGHT. I GOT THIS.

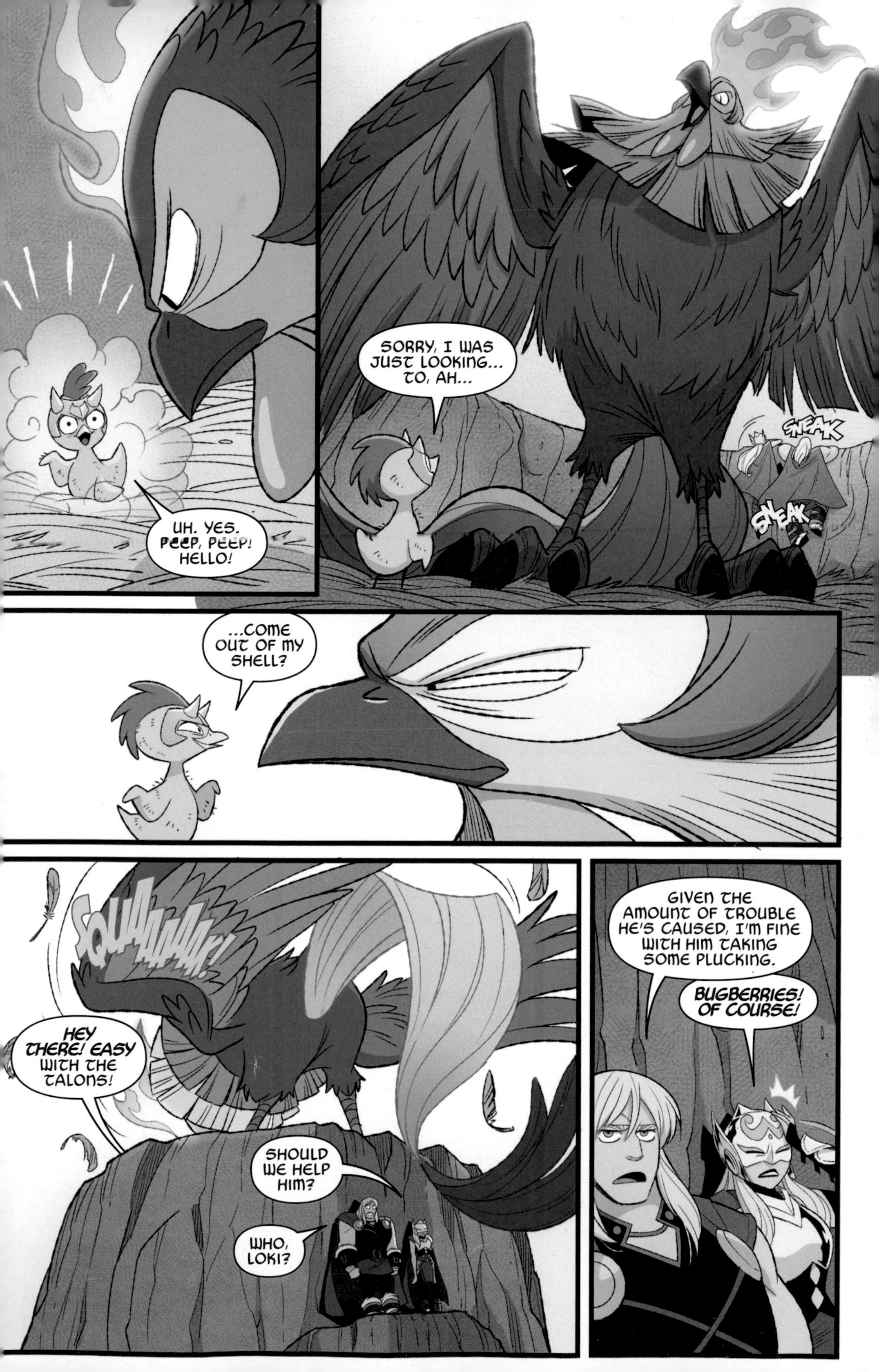
UH. YES. PEEP, PEEP! HELLO!
SORRY, I WAS JUST LOOKING... TO, AH...
SNEAK
SNEAK
...COME OUT OF MY SHELL?
SQUAAAAAK!
HEY THERE! EASY WITH THE TALONS!
SHOULD WE HELP HIM?
WHO, LOKI?
GIVEN THE AMOUNT OF TROUBLE HE'S CAUSED, I'M FINE WITH HIM TAKING SOME PLUCKING.
BUGBERRIES! OF COURSE!

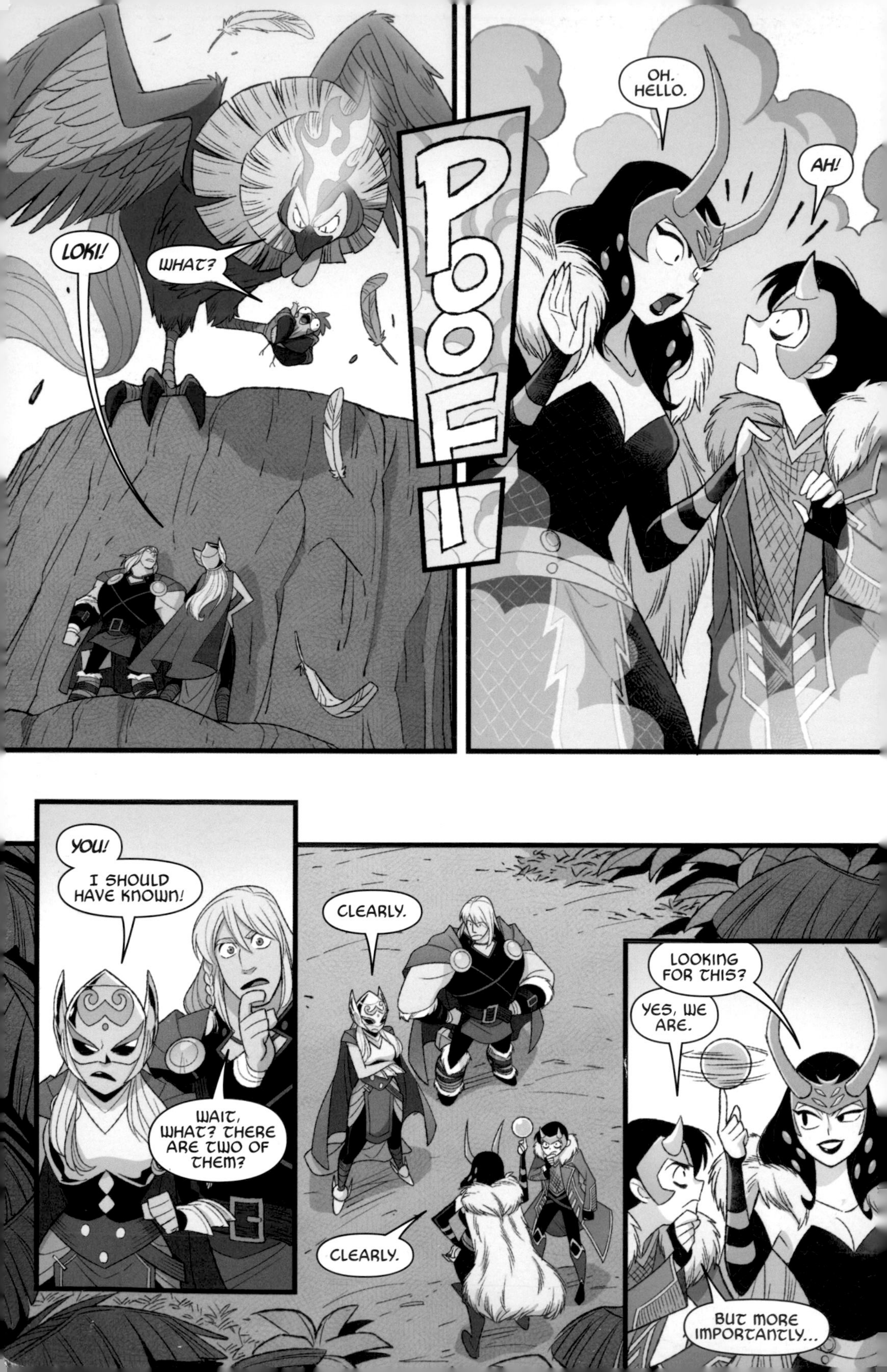
LOKI!
WHAT?
POOF!
OH. HELLO.
AH!
YOU!
I SHOULD HAVE KNOWN!
WAIT, WHAT? THERE ARE TWO OF THEM?
CLEARLY.
CLEARLY.
LOOKING FOR THIS?
YES, WE ARE.
BUT MORE IMPORTANTLY...

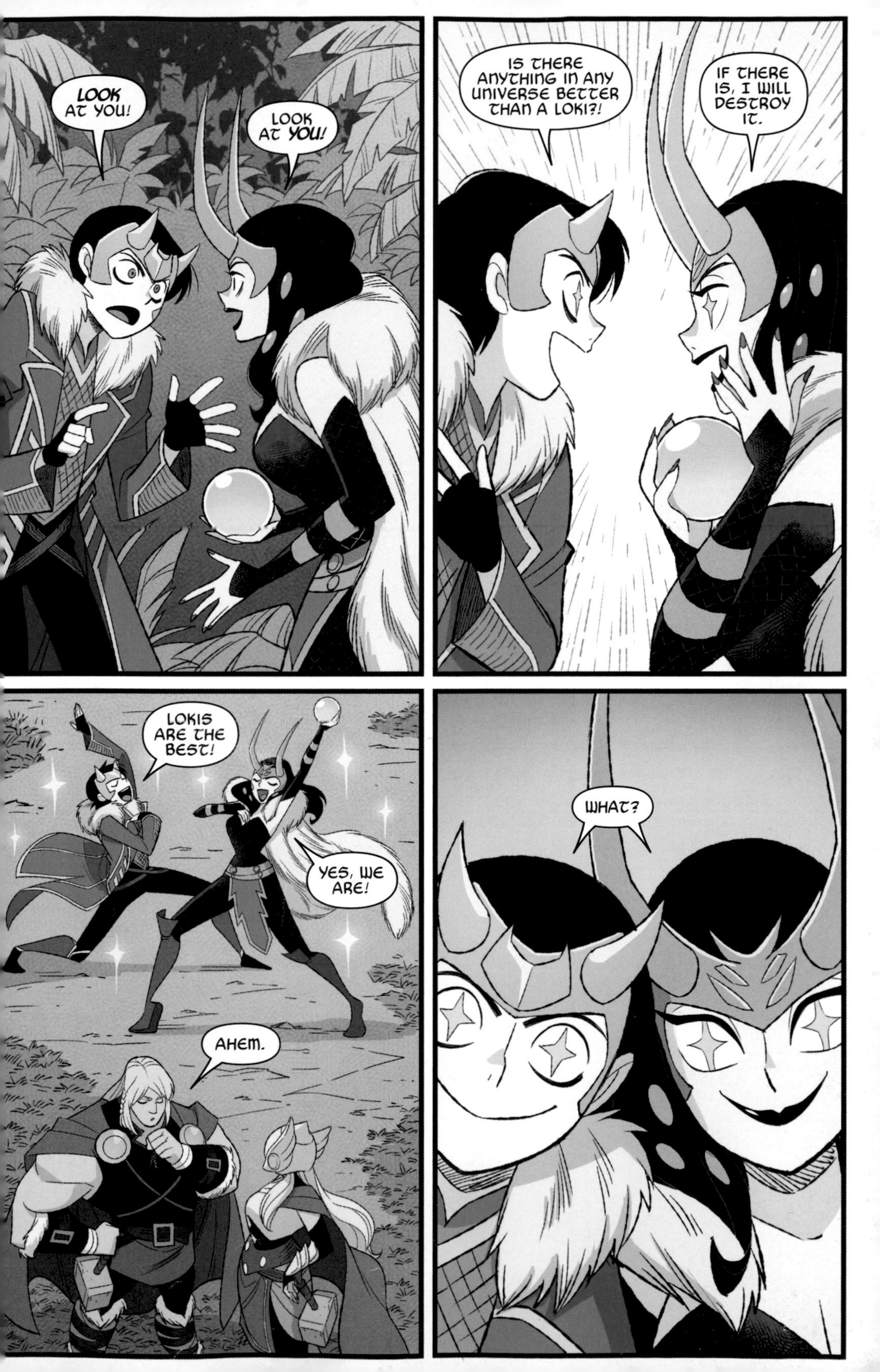
LOOK AT YOU!
LOOK AT YOU!
IS THERE ANYTHING IN ANY UNIVERSE BETTER THAN A LOKI?!
IF THERE IS, I WILL DESTROY IT.
LOKIS ARE THE BEST!
YES, WE ARE!
AHEM.
WHAT?

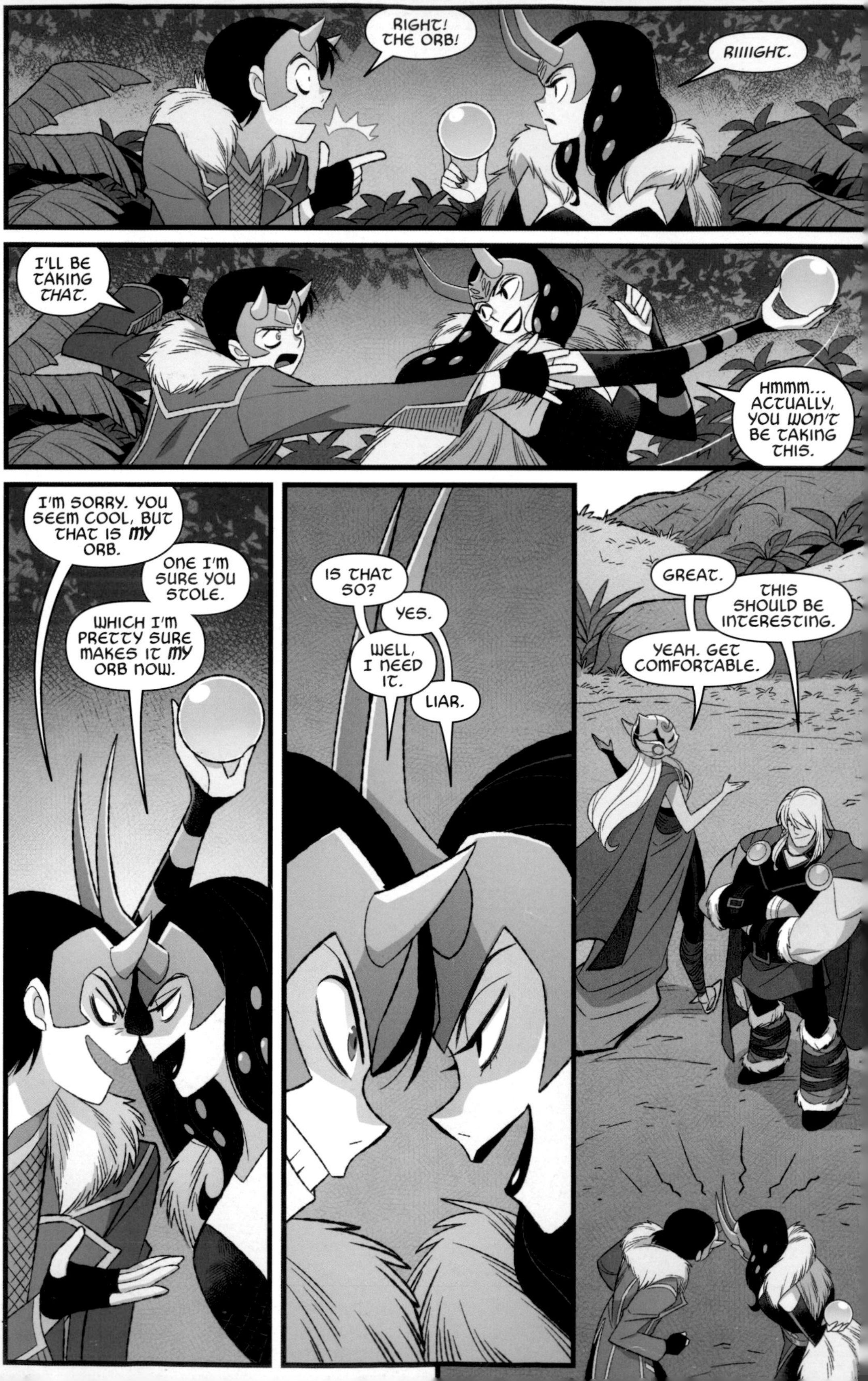
RIGHT! THE ORB!
RIIIIGHT.
I'LL BE TAKING THAT.
HMMM... ACTUALLY, YOU WON'T BE TAKING THIS.
I'M SORRY. YOU SEEM COOL, BUT THAT IS MY ORB.
ONE I'M SURE YOU STOLE.
WHICH I'M PRETTY SURE MAKES IT MY ORB NOW.
IS THAT SO?
YES.
WELL, I NEED IT.
LIAR.
GREAT.
THIS SHOULD BE INTERESTING.
YEAH. GET COMFORTABLE.

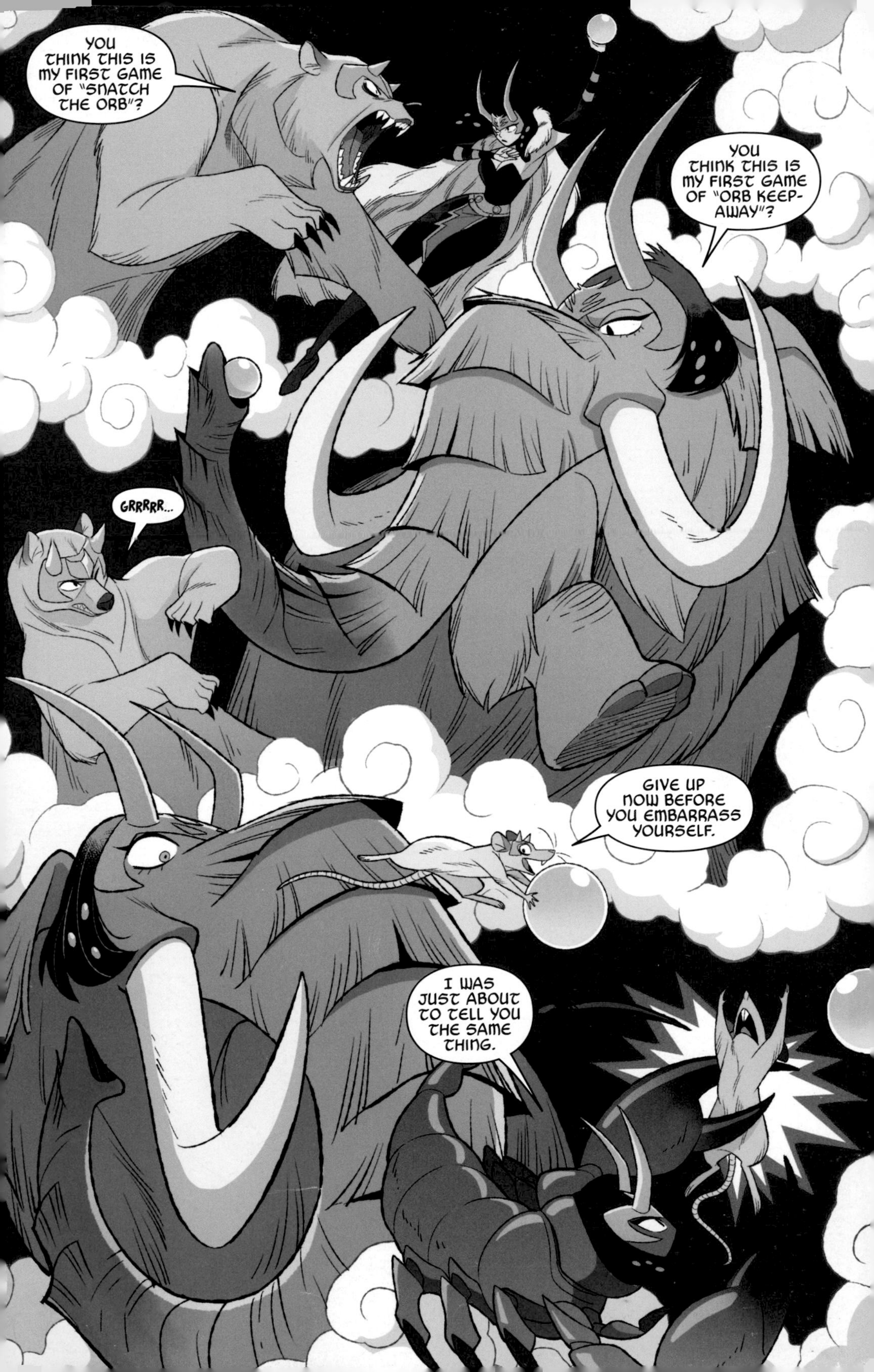

YOU THINK THIS IS MY FIRST GAME OF "SNATCH THE ORB"?
YOU THINK THIS IS MY FIRST GAME OF "ORB KEEP-AWAY"?
GRRRRR...
GIVE UP NOW BEFORE YOU EMBARRASS YOURSELF.
I WAS JUST ABOUT TO TELL YOU THE SAME THING.

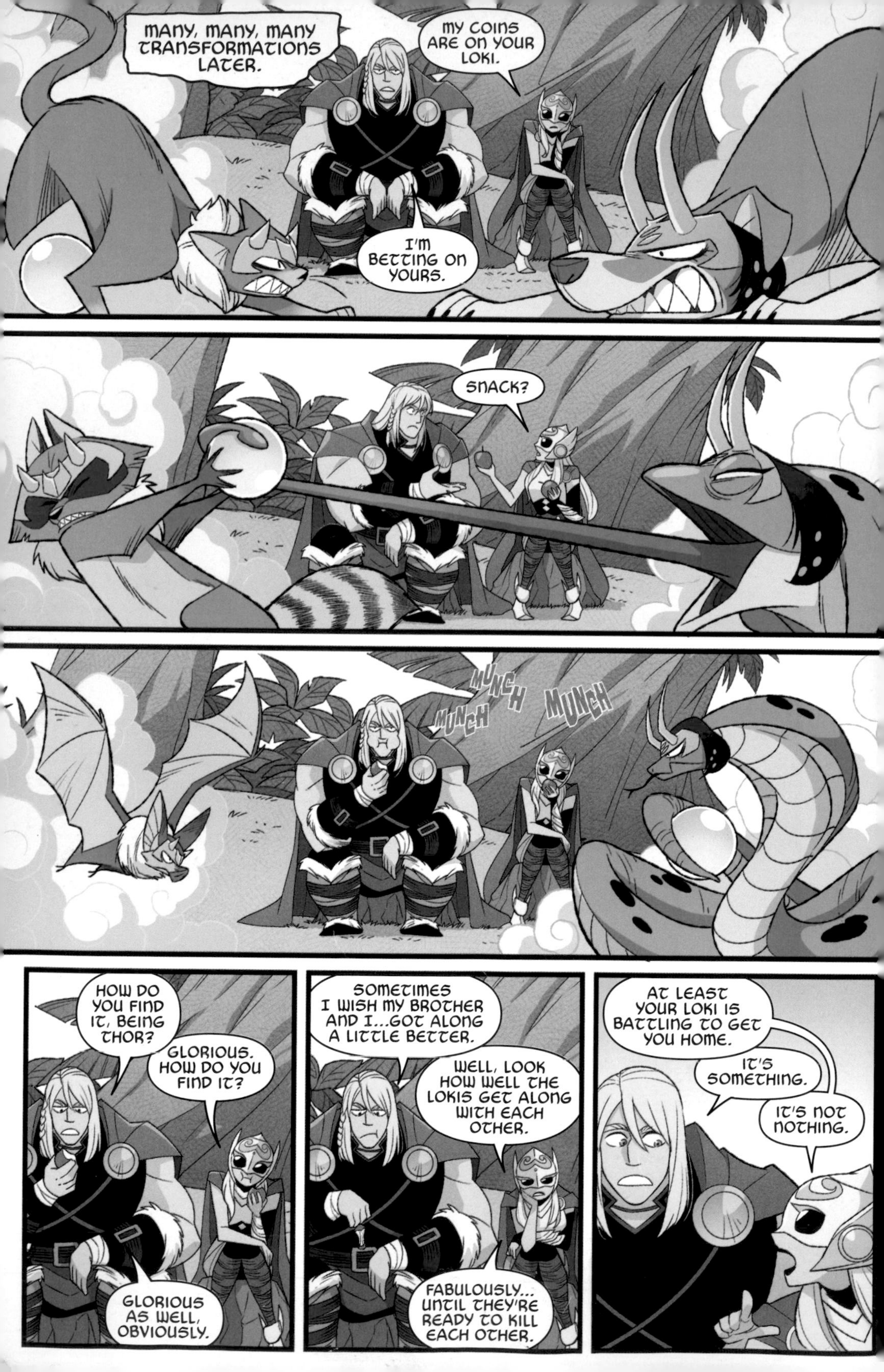
MANY, MANY, MANY TRANSFORMATIONS LATER.
MY COINS ARE ON YOUR LOKI.
I'M BETTING ON YOURS.
SNACK?
MUNCH MUNCH
MUNCH
HOW DO YOU FIND IT, BEING THOR?
GLORIOUS. HOW DO YOU FIND IT?
GLORIOUS AS WELL, OBVIOUSLY.
SOMETIMES I WISH MY BROTHER AND I...GOT ALONG A LITTLE BETTER.
WELL, LOOK HOW WELL THE LOKIS GET ALONG WITH EACH OTHER.
FABULOUSLY... UNTIL THEY'RE READY TO KILL EACH OTHER.
AT LEAST YOUR LOKI IS BATTLING TO GET YOU HOME.
IT'S SOMETHING.
IT'S NOT NOTHING.

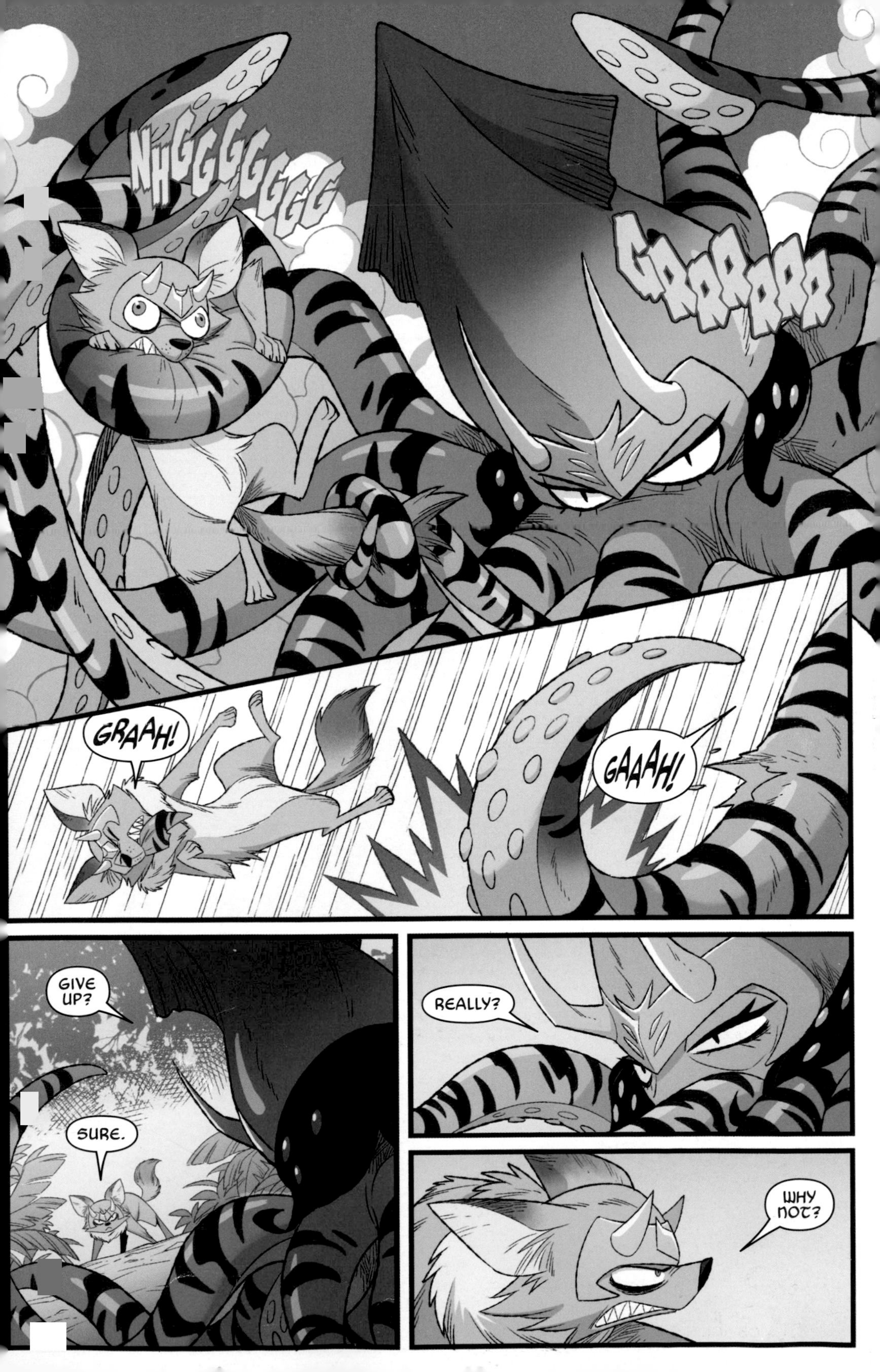
NHGGGGGGG
GRRRRRR
GRAAH!
GAAAH!
GIVE UP?
SURE.
REALLY?
WHY NOT?

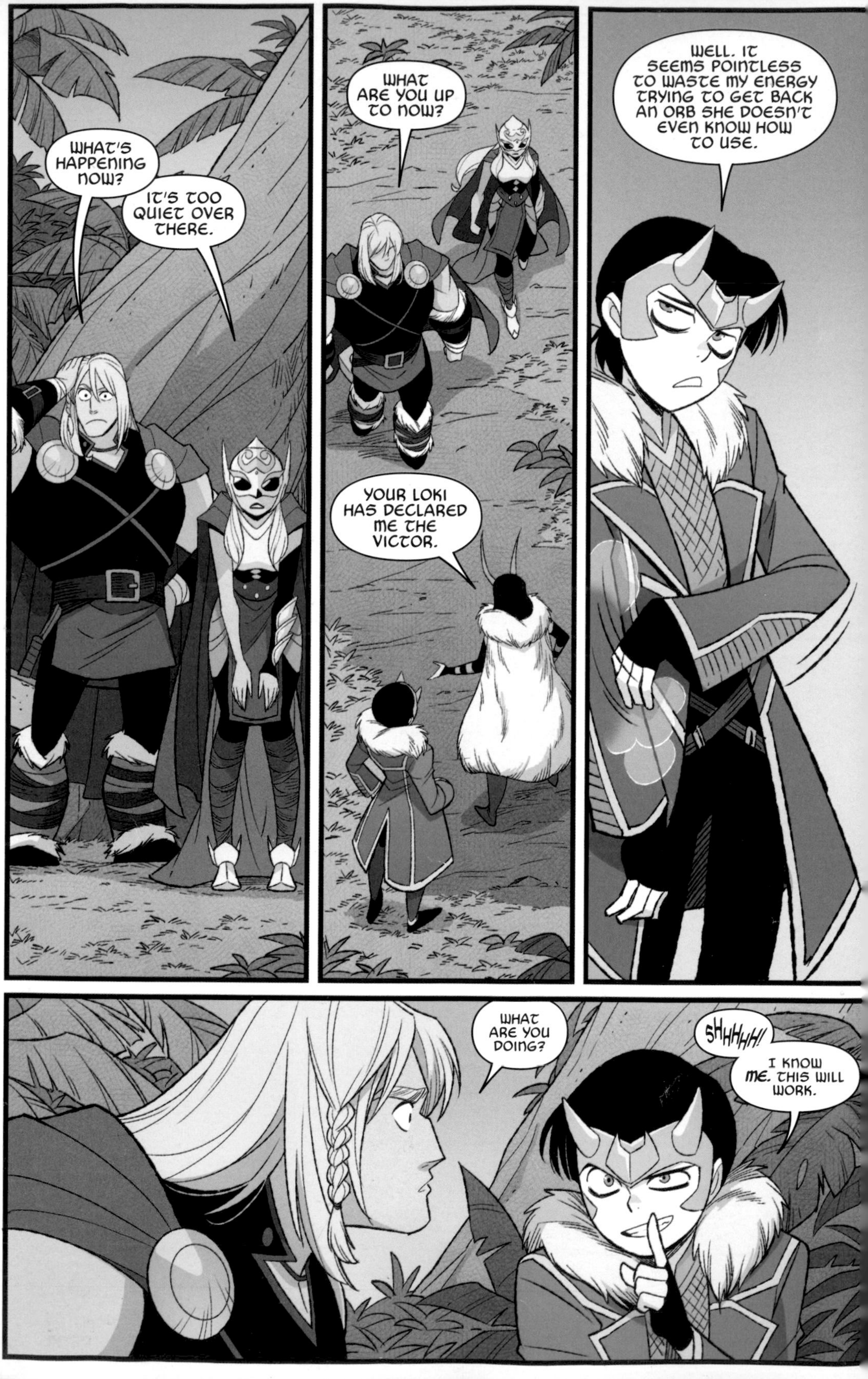
WHAT'S HAPPENING NOW?
IT'S TOO QUIET OVER THERE.
WHAT ARE YOU UP TO NOW?
YOUR LOKI HAS DECLARED ME THE VICTOR.
WELL. IT SEEMS POINTLESS TO WASTE MY ENERGY TRYING TO GET BACK AN ORB SHE DOESN'T EVEN KNOW HOW TO USE.
WHAT ARE YOU DOING?
SHHHHH!
I KNOW ME. THIS WILL WORK.

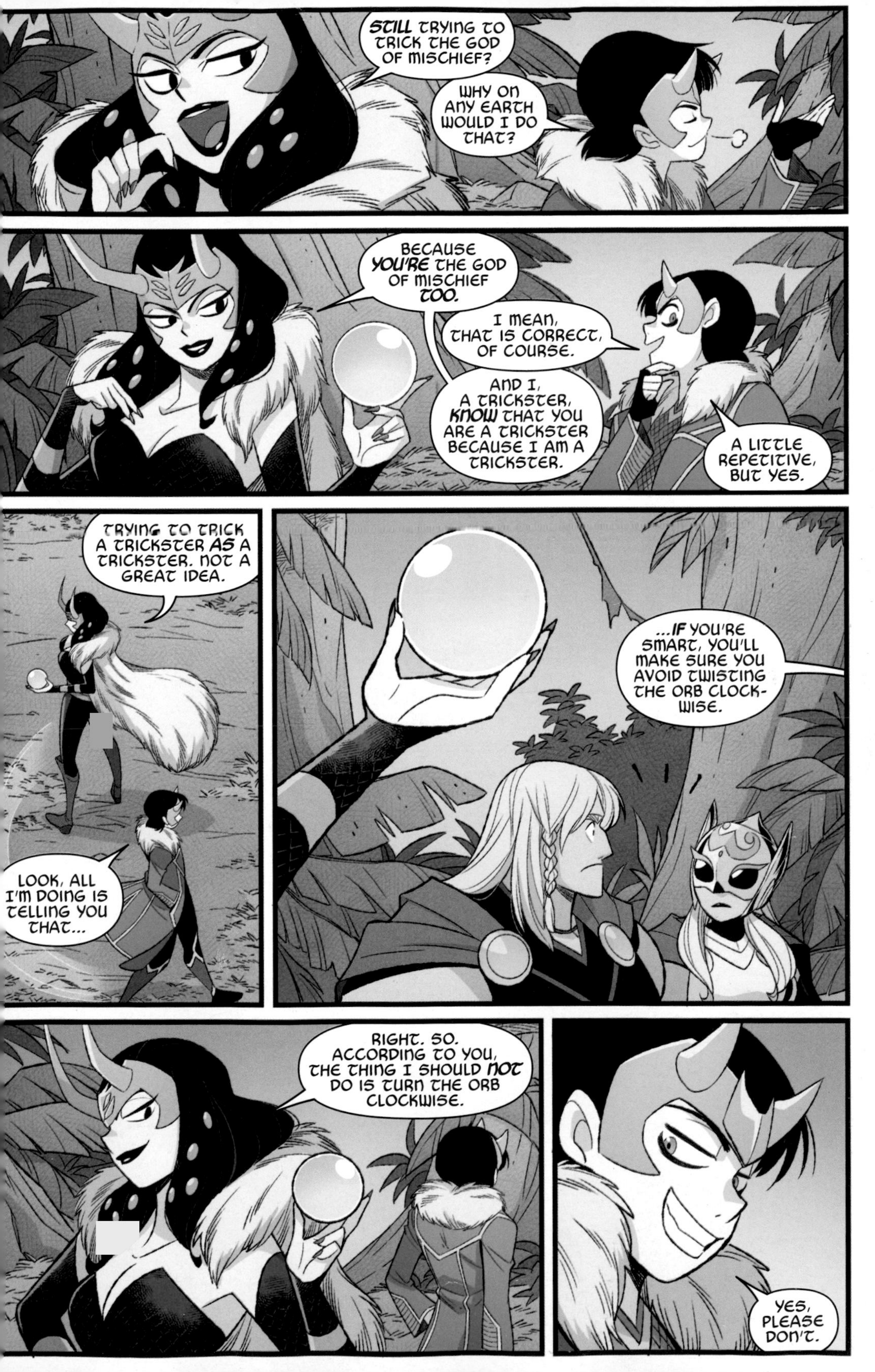
STILL TRYING TO TRICK THE GOD OF MISCHIEF?
WHY ON ANY EARTH WOULD I DO THAT?
BECAUSE YOU'RE THE GOD OF MISCHIEF TOO.
I MEAN, THAT IS CORRECT, OF COURSE.
AND I, A TRICKSTER, KNOW THAT YOU ARE A TRICKSTER BECAUSE I AM A TRICKSTER.
A LITTLE REPETITIVE, BUT YES.
TRYING TO TRICK A TRICKSTER AS A TRICKSTER. NOT A GREAT IDEA.
LOOK, ALL I'M DOING IS TELLING YOU THAT...
...IF YOU'RE SMART, YOU'LL MAKE SURE YOU AVOID TWISTING THE ORB CLOCK-WISE.
RIGHT. SO. ACCORDING TO YOU, THE THING I SHOULD NOT DO IS TURN THE ORB CLOCKWISE.
YES, PLEASE DON'T.

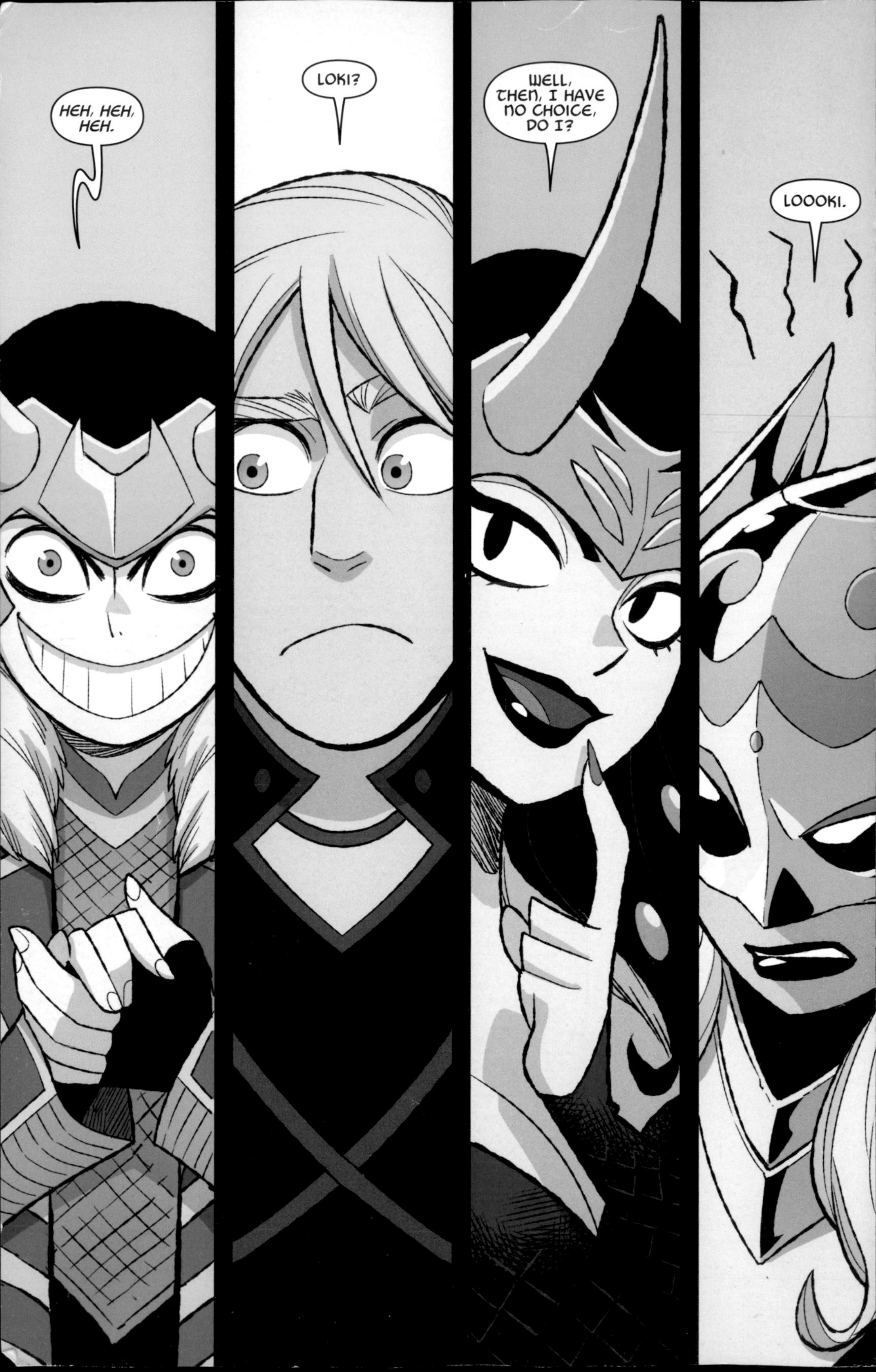
HEH, HEH, HEH.
LOKI?
WELL, THEN, I HAVE NO CHOICE, DO I?
LOOOKI.

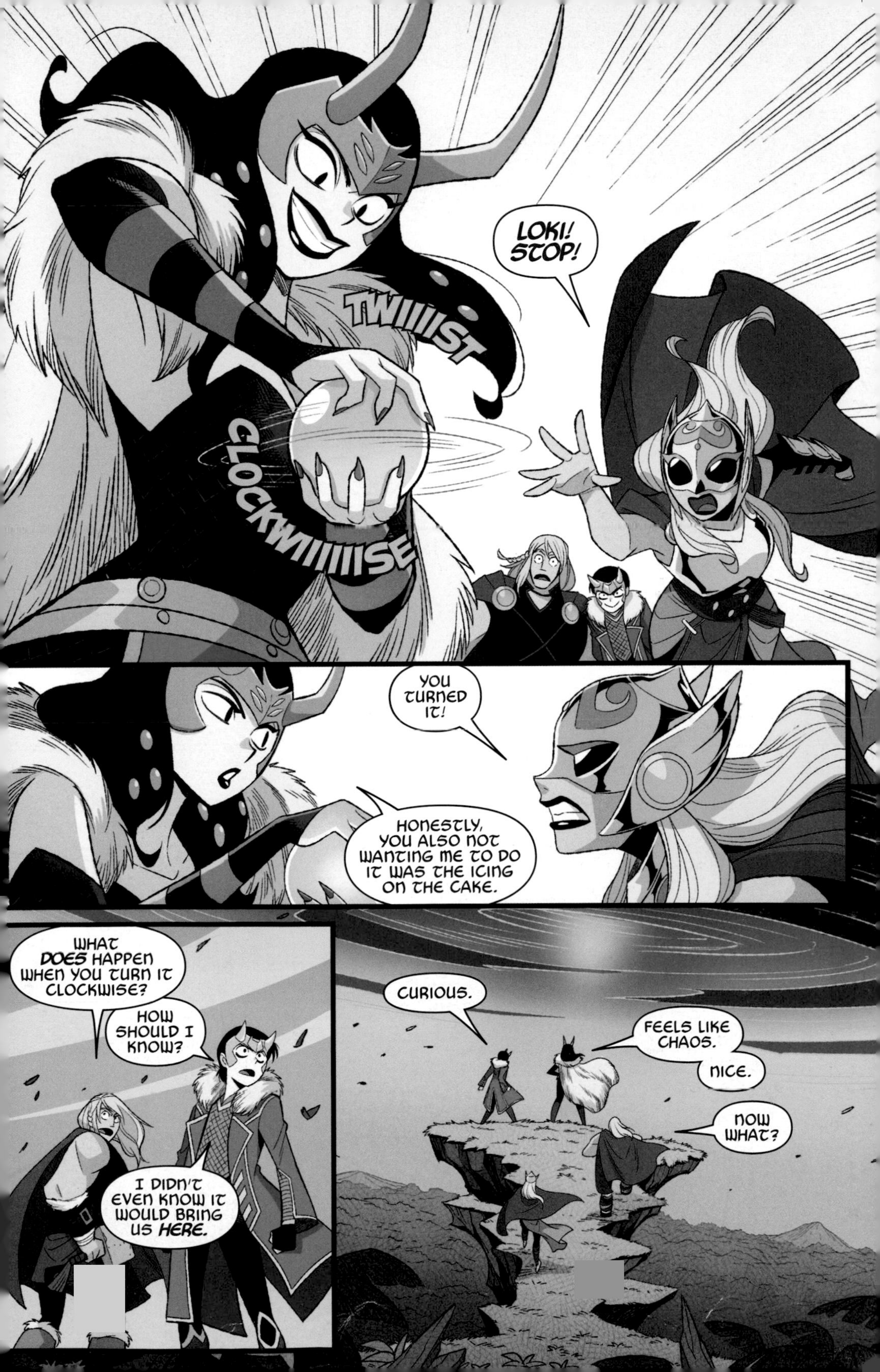
LOKI! STOP!
TWIIIIST
CLOCKWIIIIISE
YOU TURNED IT!
HONESTLY, YOU ALSO NOT WANTING ME TO DO IT WAS THE ICING ON THE CAKE.
WHAT DOES HAPPEN WHEN YOU TURN IT CLOCKWISE?
HOW SHOULD I KNOW?
I DIDN'T EVEN KNOW IT WOULD BRING US HERE.
CURIOUS.
FEELS LIKE CHAOS.
NICE.
NOW WHAT?

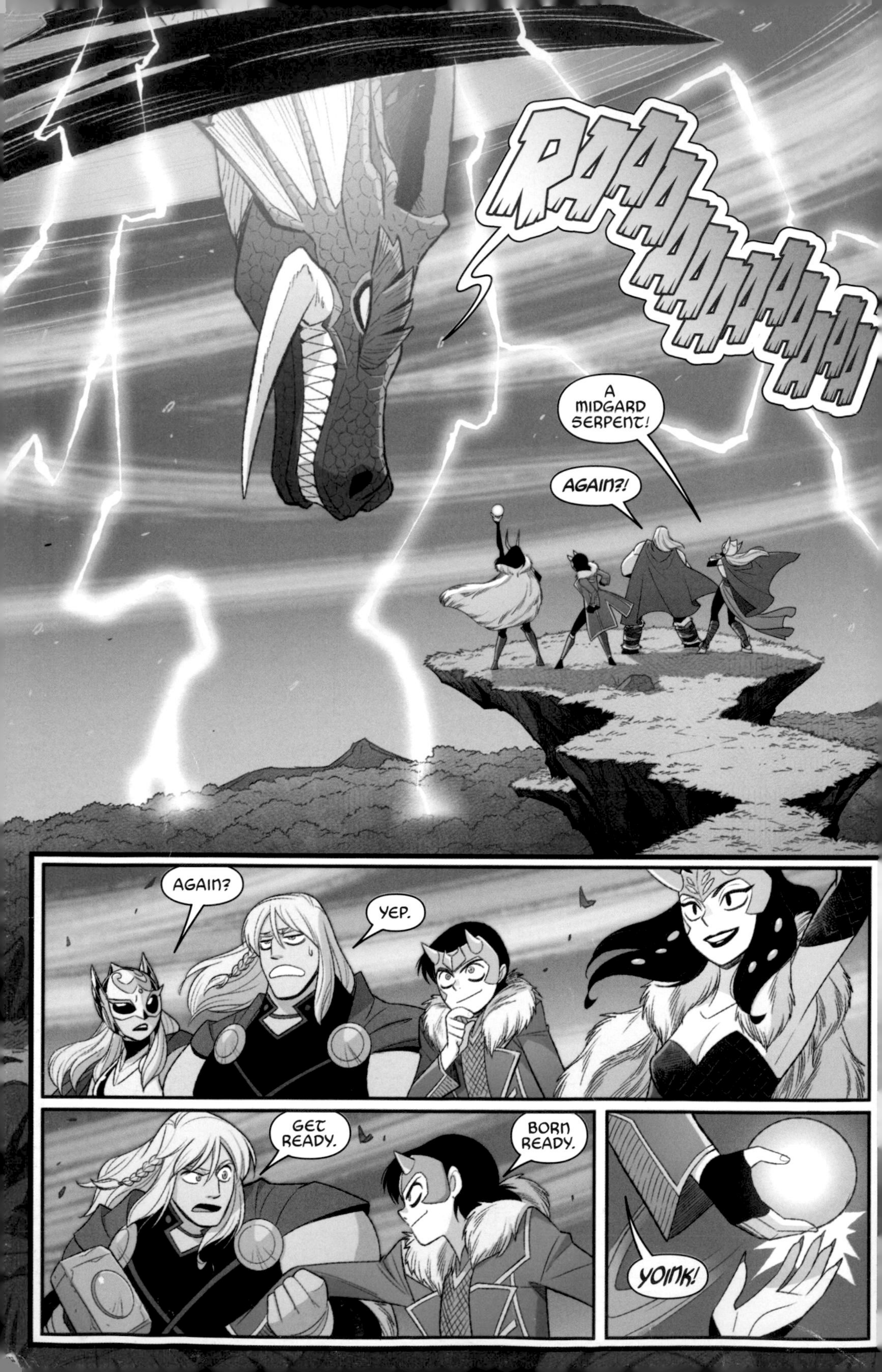
RAAAAAAAAAAAAAAAAAA
A MIDGARD SERPENT!
AGAIN?!
AGAIN?
YEP.
GET READY.
BORN READY.
YOINK!

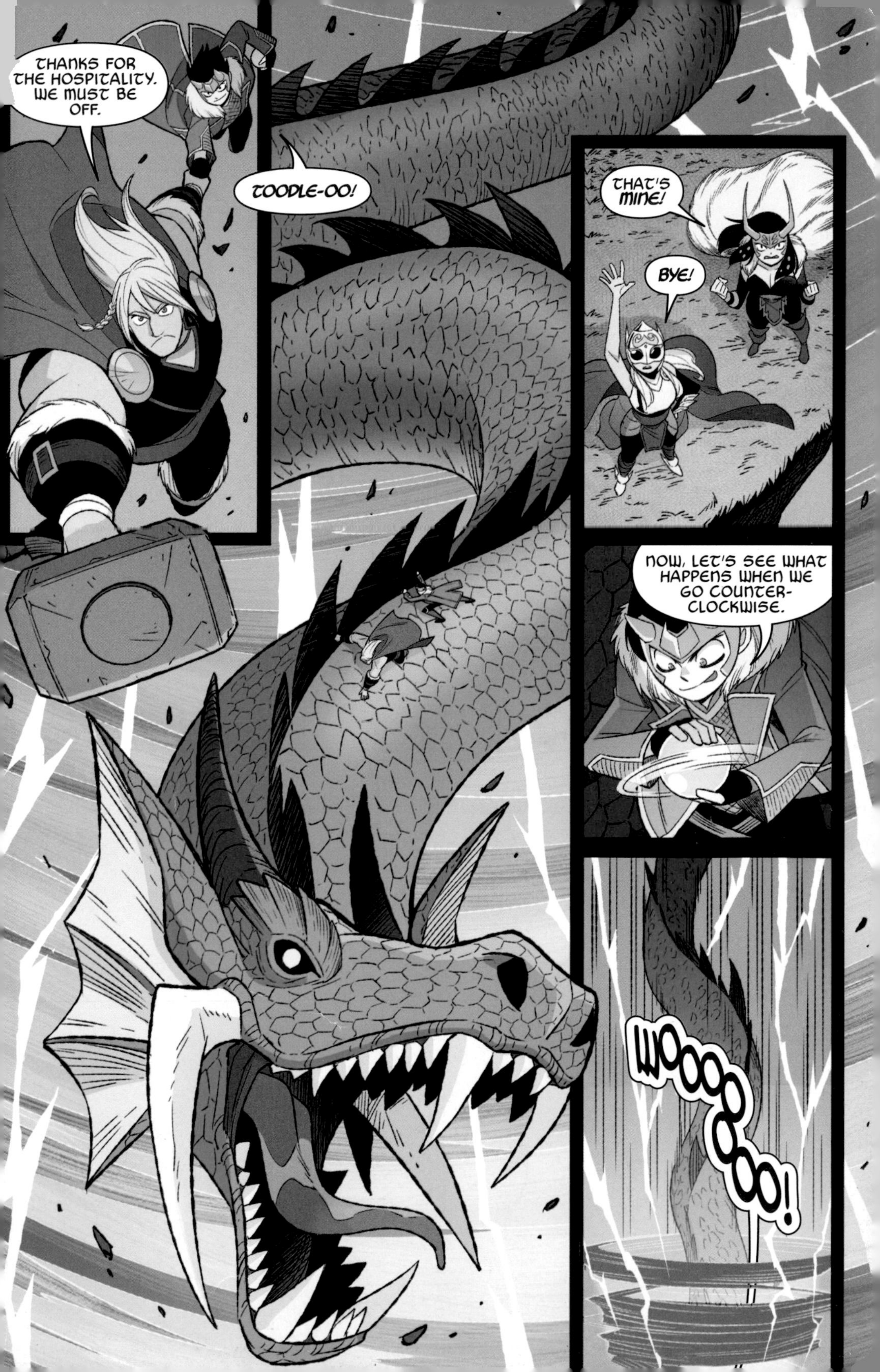
THANKS FOR THE HOSPITALITY. WE MUST BE OFF.
TOODLE-OO!
THAT'S MINE!
BYE!
NOW, LET'S SEE WHAT HAPPENS WHEN WE GO COUNTER-CLOCKWISE.
WOOOOOOO!

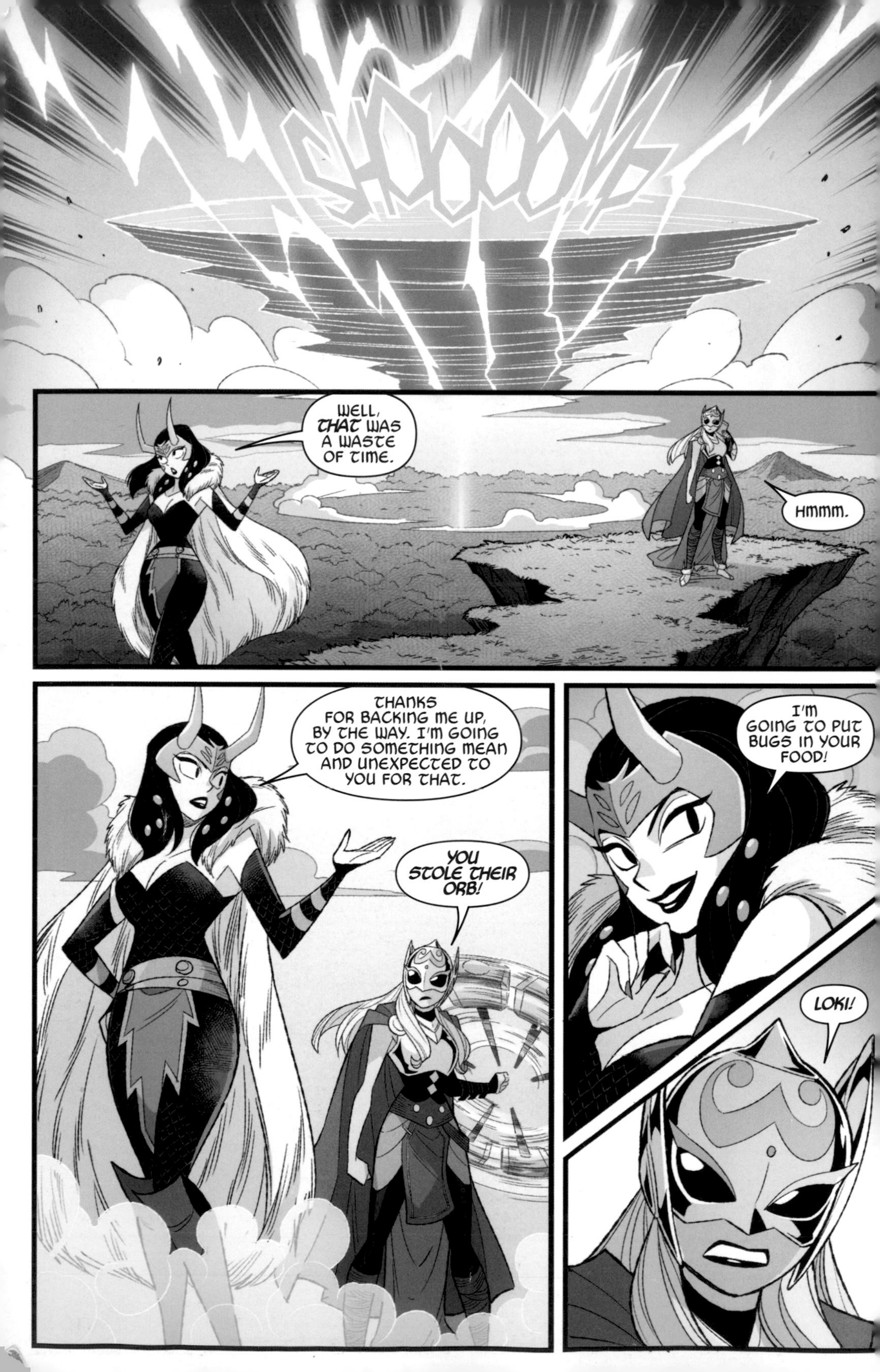
SHOOOM
WELL, *THAT* WAS A WASTE OF TIME.
HMMM.
THANKS FOR BACKING ME UP, BY THE WAY. I'M GOING TO DO SOMETHING MEAN AND UNEXPECTED TO YOU FOR THAT.
YOU STOLE THEIR ORB!
I'M GOING TO PUT BUGS IN YOUR FOOD!
LOKI!

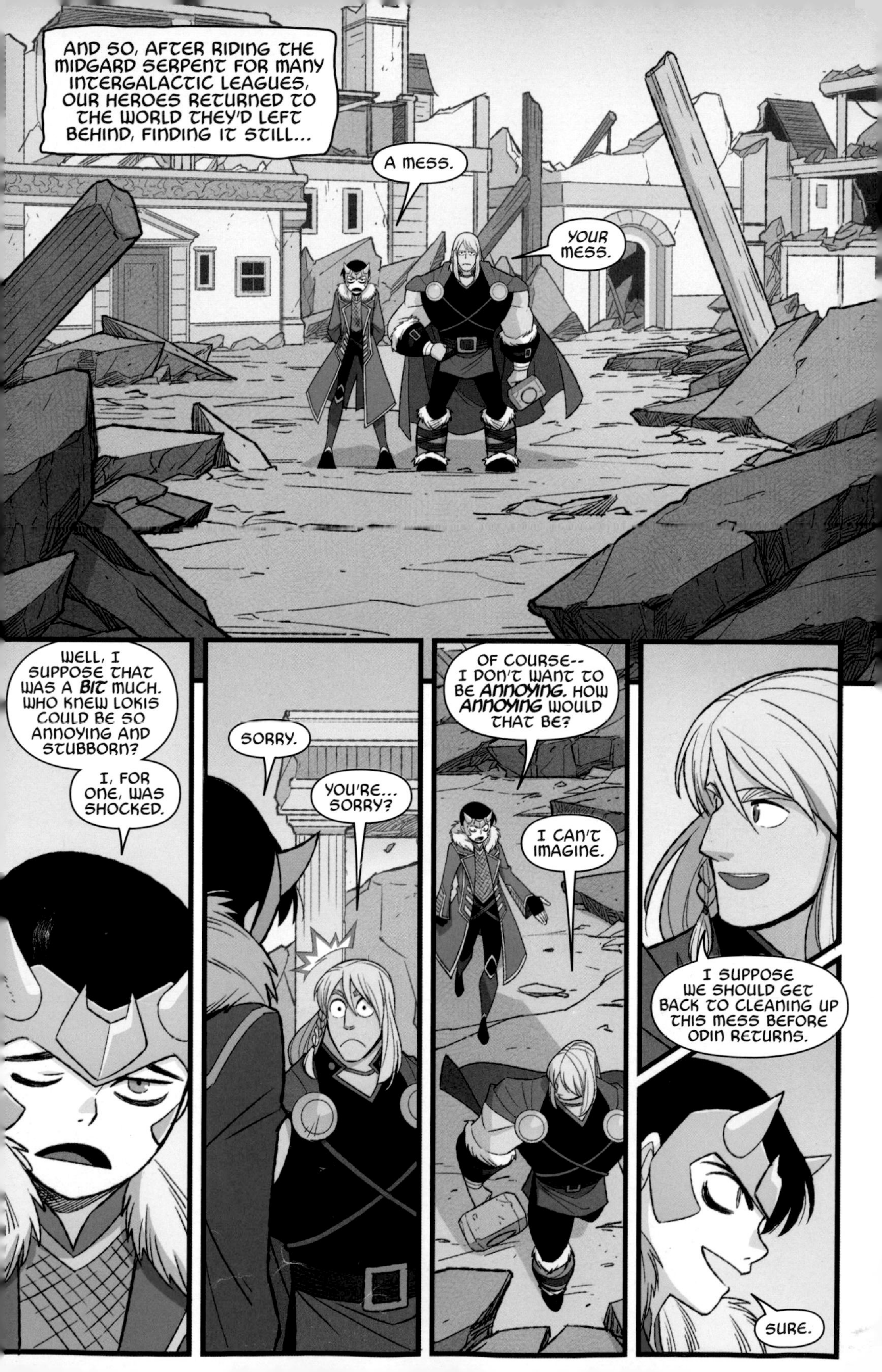
AND SO, AFTER RIDING THE MIDGARD SERPENT FOR MANY INTERGALACTIC LEAGUES, OUR HEROES RETURNED TO THE WORLD THEY'D LEFT BEHIND, FINDING IT STILL...
A MESS.
YOUR MESS.
WELL, I SUPPOSE THAT WAS A BIT MUCH. WHO KNEW LOKIS COULD BE SO ANNOYING AND STUBBORN?
I, FOR ONE, WAS SHOCKED.
SORRY.
YOU'RE... SORRY?
OF COURSE-- I DON'T WANT TO BE ANNOYING. HOW ANNOYING WOULD THAT BE?
I CAN'T IMAGINE.
I SUPPOSE WE SHOULD GET BACK TO CLEANING UP THIS MESS BEFORE ODIN RETURNS.
SURE.

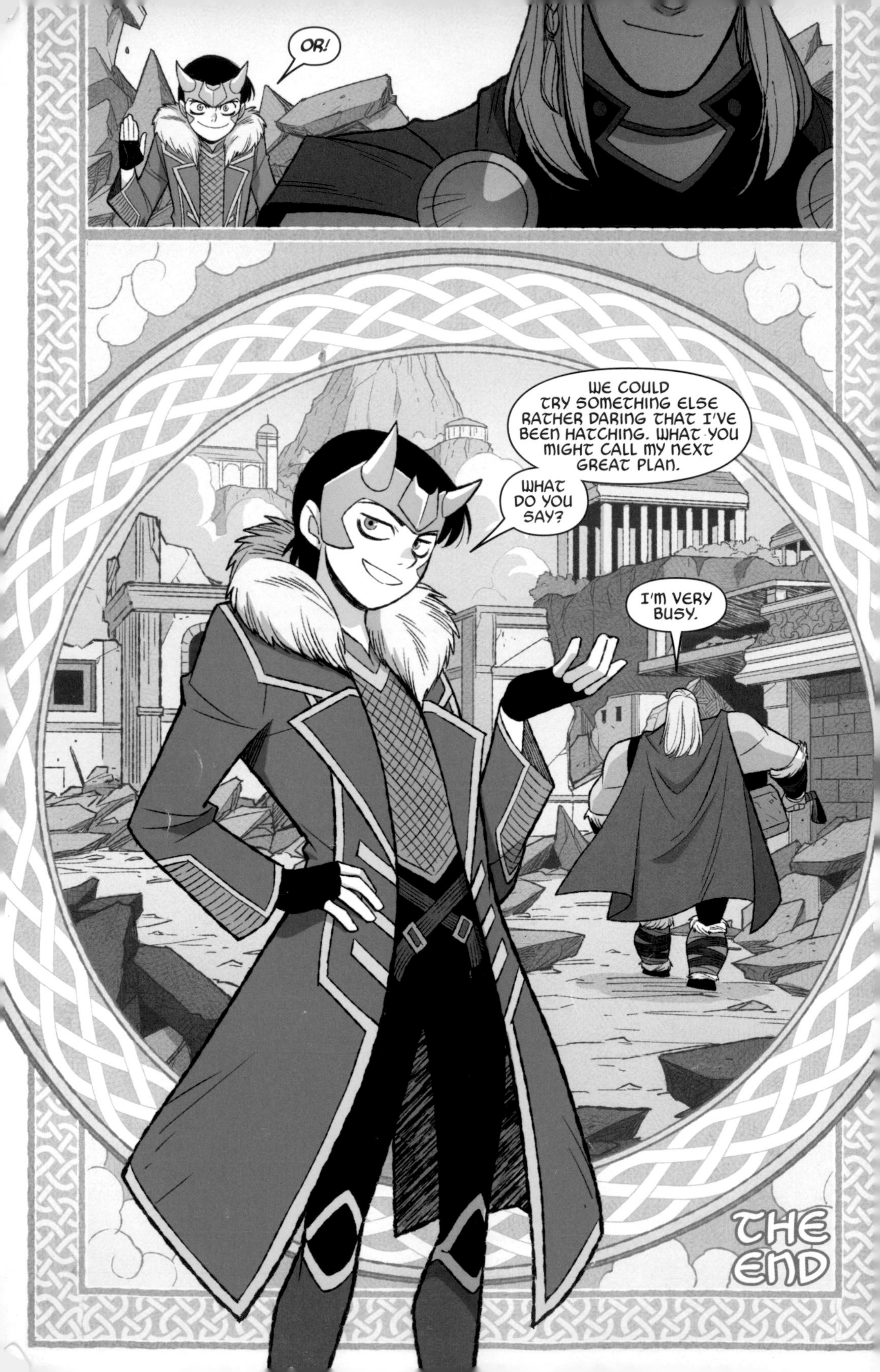
OR!
WE COULD TRY SOMETHING ELSE RATHER DARING THAT I'VE BEEN HATCHING. WHAT YOU MIGHT CALL MY NEXT GREAT PLAN.
WHAT DO YOU SAY?
I'M VERY BUSY.
THE END

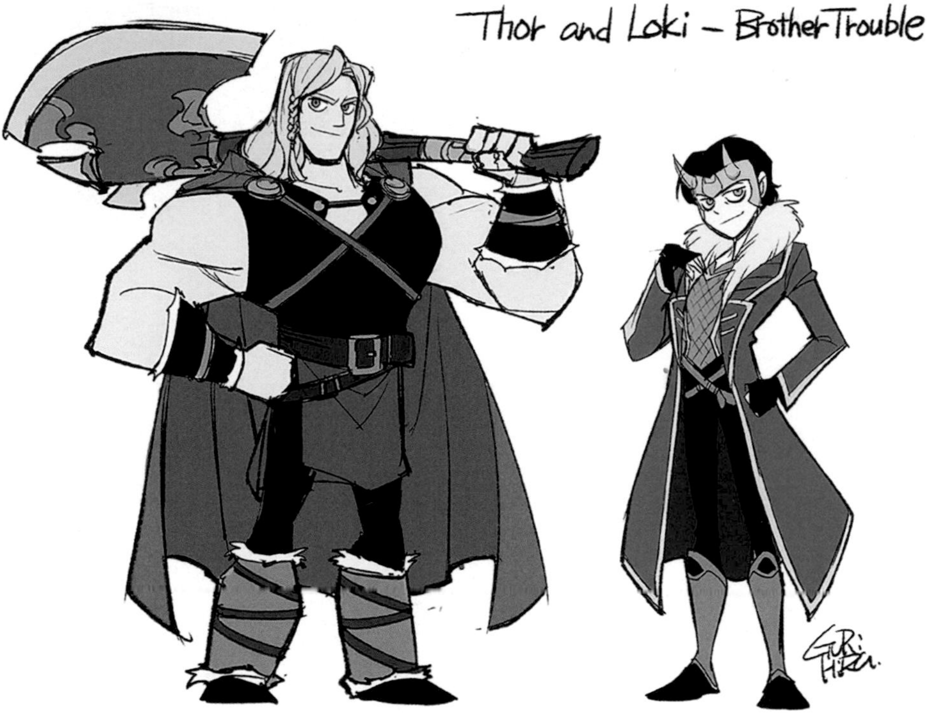
Thor and Loki – Brother Trouble
GURi HiRu.

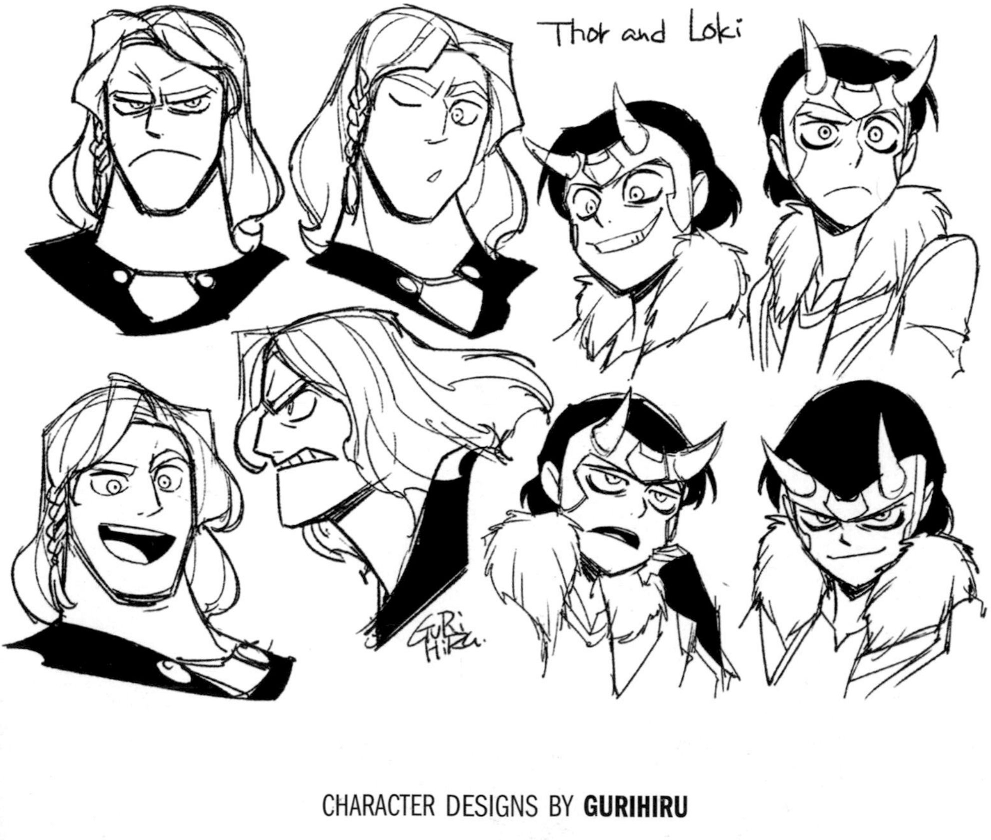
Thor and Loki
GURi HiRu.

CHARACTER DESIGNS BY **GURIHIRU**

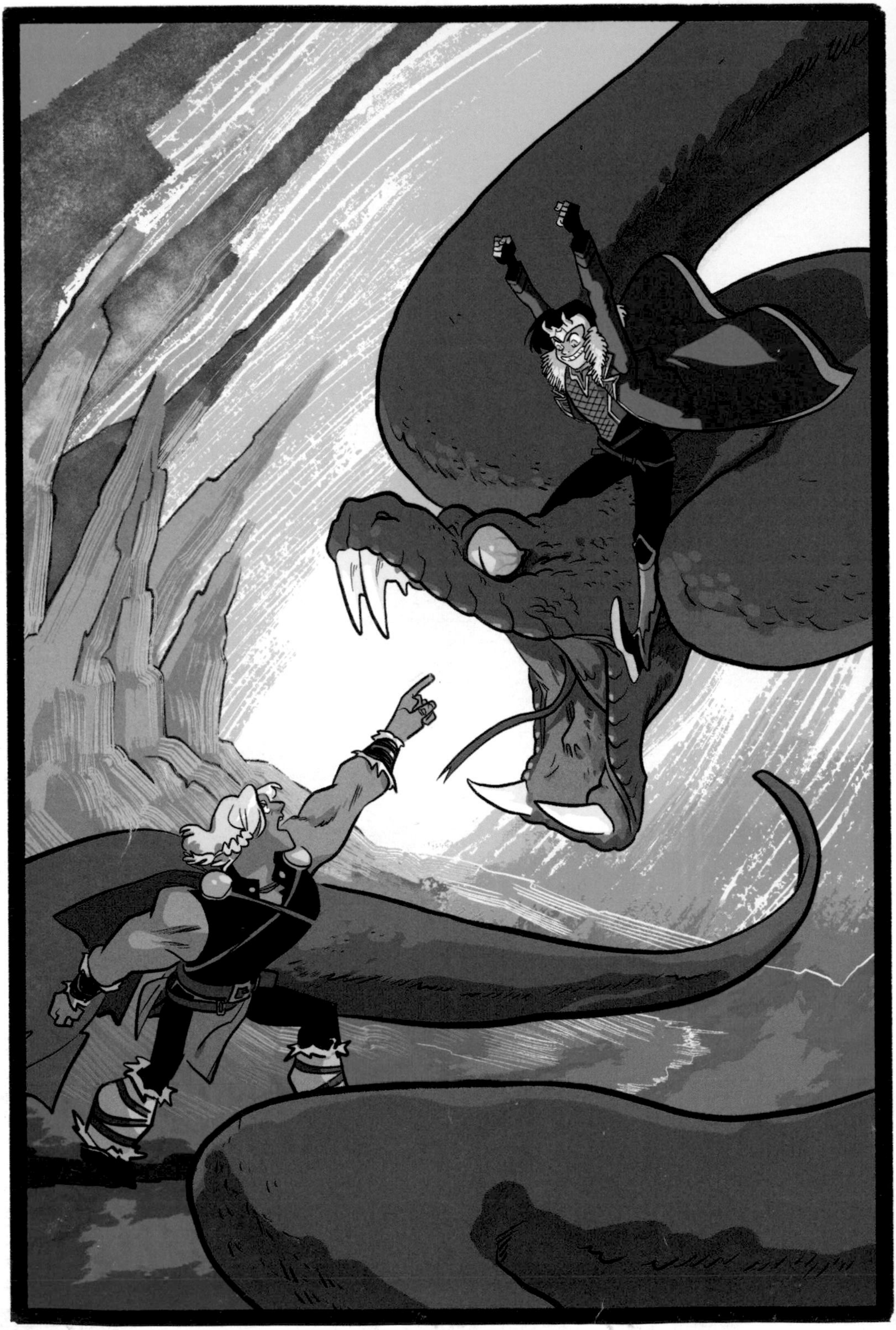

#1 VARIANT BY **ERICA HENDERSON**

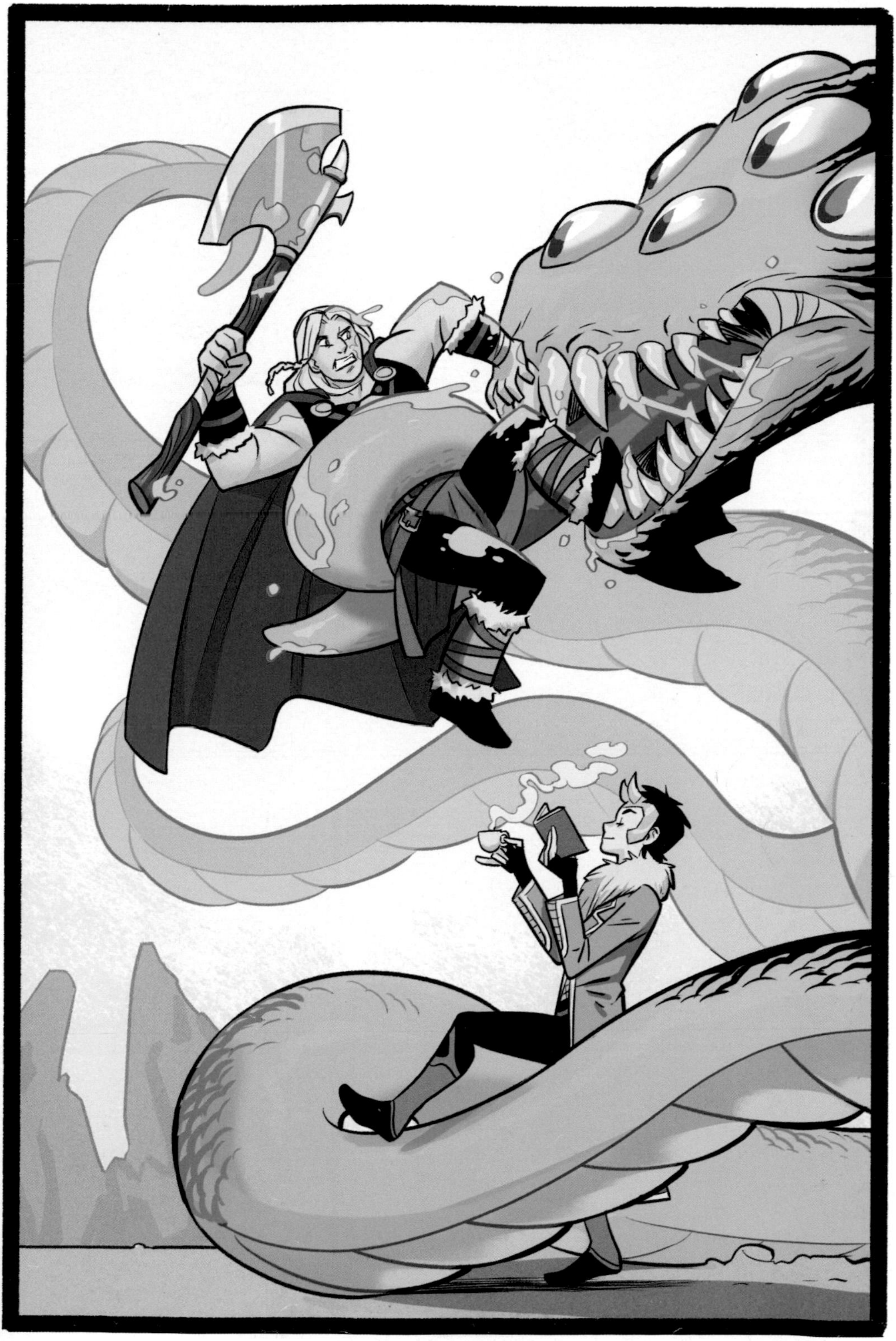

#1 VARIANT BY **NATACHA BUSTOS**

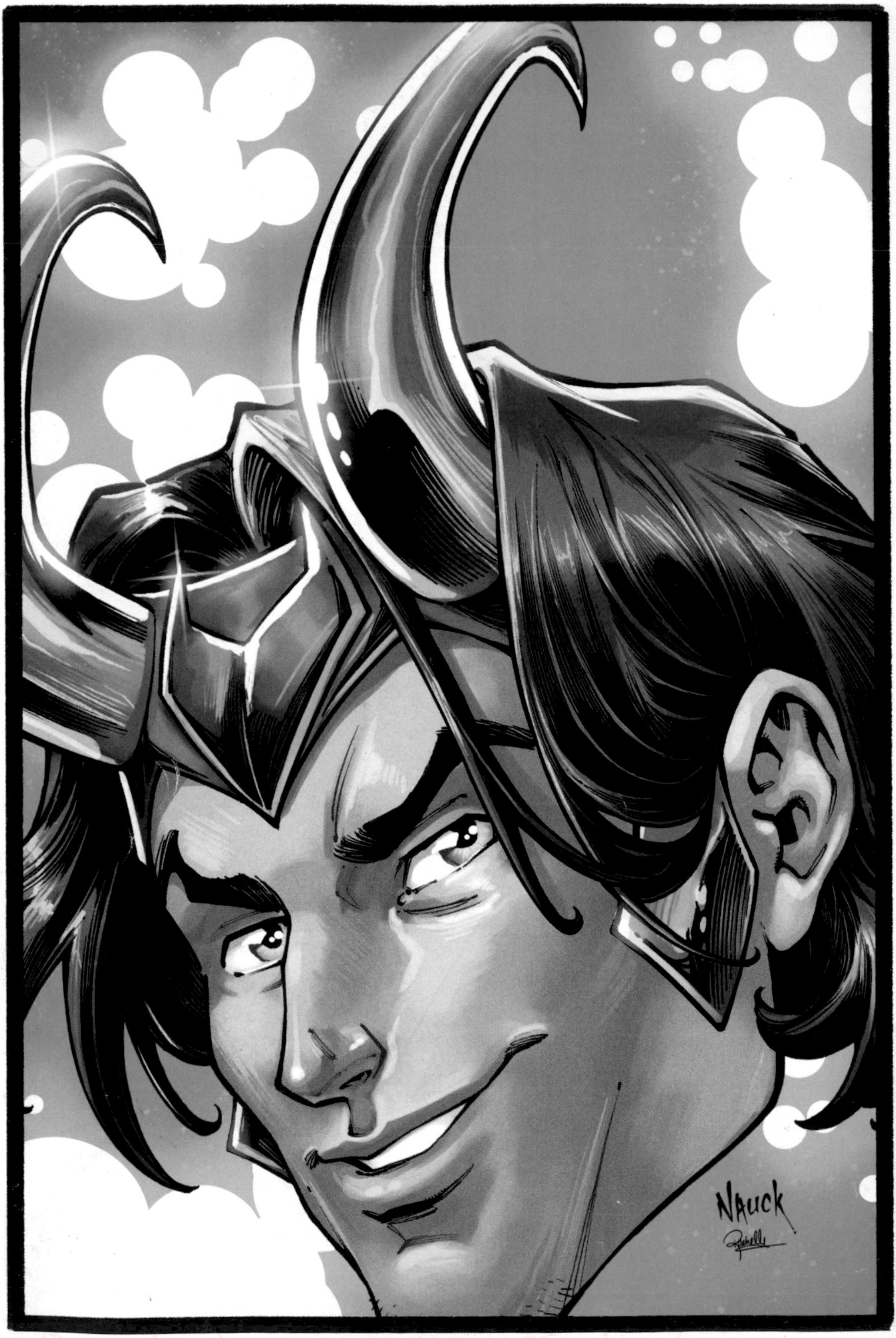
NAUCK

#1 HEADSHOT VARIANT BY **TODD NAUCK** & **RACHELLE ROSENBERG**

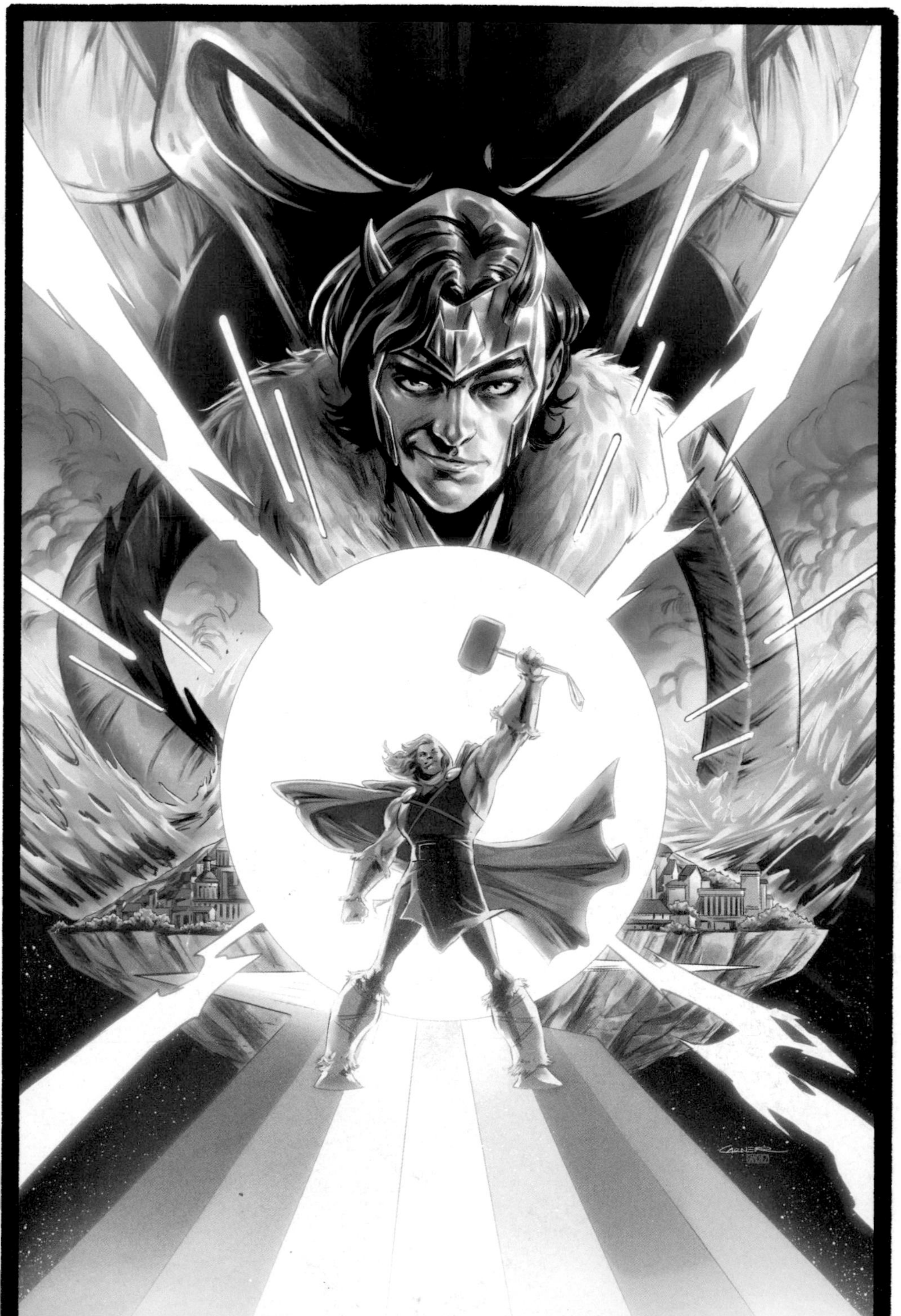

#1 STORMBREAKERS VARIANT BY **CARMEN CARNERO** & **ALEJANDRO SANCHEZ**

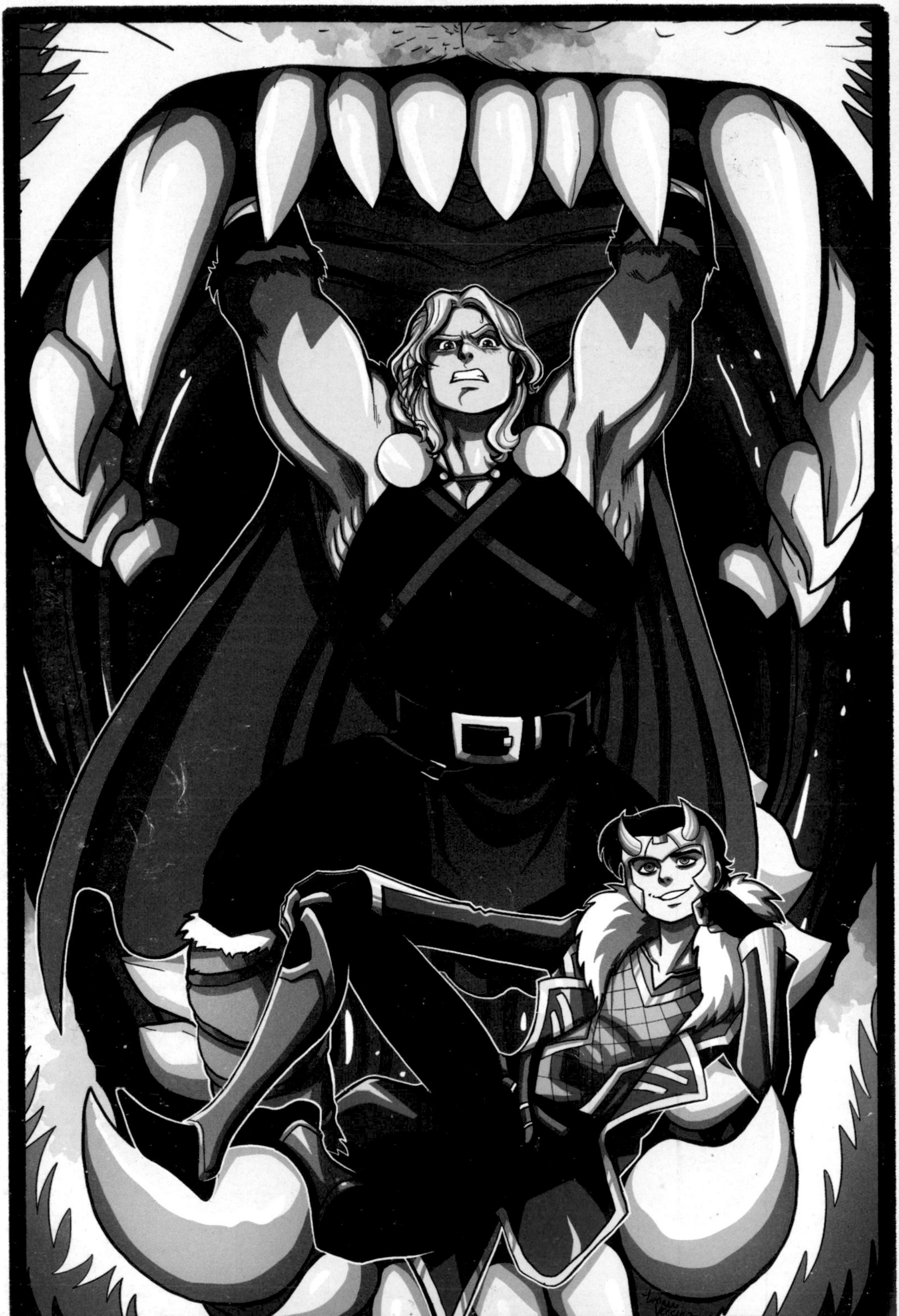

#2 VARIANT BY **LUCIANO VECCHIO**